STEPHANIE'S DOMAIN

STEPHANIE'S DOMAIN

Susanna Hughes

First published in Great Britain in 1993 by
Nexus
332 Ladbroke Grove
London W10 5AH

Reprinted 1994

Typeset by Phoenix Photosetting, Chatham, Kent.
Printed and bound in Great Britain by
Cox & Wyman Ltd, Reading, Berkshire

ISBN 0 352 32864 9

A catalogue record for this title is available from the
British Library.

This book is a work of fiction.
In real life, make sure you practise safe sex.

ONE

Stephanie lay on her stomach on the sun lounger. She was naked. The Italian sun was hot on her back, shining down from a cloudless blue sky on to the terrace of the castle bedroom. Below, and surrounding the island castle, Lake Trasimeno reflected its light. There wasn't a hint of a breeze, the waters of the lake as flat and untroubled as the surface of a mirror, and the canopy of vegetation, dripping from the walls of the castle, was still too, though the heady perfume of jasmine and bougainvillea filled the air. The only sound was the gentle lapping of water against the pillars of the jetty below and at the front of the castle, and the soft squelch of flesh on flesh as the man's strong hands massaged the thick sunscreen into her back.

He knelt at her side, naked too but for the hard leather-covered metal pouch that was chained tightly over his genitals.

He worked conscientiously, smoothing the glutinous white cream into her shoulder blades, down over her slim hour-glass waist and rich fuller hips. From the small of her back her tight neat buttocks rose precipitously. His hands followed the tantalising curves, feeling her plump flesh rippling as he spread the cream out with his fingers. As he worked down from the round summit to the lower slopes, where the buttocks joined her long shapely thighs, he could see the deep channel between her legs, fringed by stray pubic hairs as dark and black as the long hair she had pinned up off her shoulders. He massaged the cream into her thighs.

He tried not to look, he tried not to think, he tried not to

1

feel. There was no room for an erection in the metal pouch.

She opened her legs. Now he could see it all, the whole slit of her sex from the puckered corona of her arse to the long thick labia folded over her cunt like the petals of some exotic flower protecting the stamen. The matted abundance of her pubic hair was plastered down with sweat and did not hide the details of her sex. He tried to concentrate on his task. He squirted more cream from the spout of the bottle on to her thigh. Using both hands he massaged it into the perfectly smooth, already tanned flesh. He worked conscientiously, spreading the white cream evenly across her thighs and down between her legs. He worked it right up until he could feel pubic hair brushing the sides of his fingers. She had complained before when he hadn't dared go that high. Then, with relief, he moved his hands away, down to her slim calves and pinched ankles.

His relief would be short-lived, he knew. As soon as he'd finished her legs she would turn over. Then it would be useless to try and prevent himself getting an erection as he made him massage her breasts, her belly, and the top of her thighs. The hard metal pouch was unyielding. There was no room for expansion. It would be agony. It had been last time.

Stephanie turned on to her back and sat up to reach for her Cartier sunglasses. Her firm breasts trembled, the nipples flattened into the flesh by the pressure of her weight. Through the sunglasses she looked at the slave. He was hot, his face red, sweat beading on his forehead from his exertions.

'Hot work Paul,' she said. It was not a question. A round metal disc hung on a light chain around his neck. It was enscribed with his Christian name.

'Yes, madam.'

Stephanie lay back on the lounger, immediately feeling the heat of the sun warming her body. She stretched, her arms above her head, her back arched off the padded mattress.

Paul knew better than to start before she had ordered it. He tried not to look at her. If only she hadn't been such a beautiful woman . . .

'Get on with it then,' Stephanie ordered.

He squirted the cream from the little nozzle of the bottle on to her upper arm. He did her arms first, right down to her fingers. For her right arm he had to lean over her body. No matter how he tried to avoid it, her breasts grazed his stomach and his side. The nipples, given their freedom, had erected. He could feel them. He wished he couldn't.

Stephanie knew what he was going through, knew his cock would be pushing against the unforgiving metal chained around it so tightly. It was, after all, part of the punishment. Paul had been at the castle for two months. He had been caught embezzling from one of Devlin's companies. It was a simple choice, like all the other slaves at the castle: the police and, inevitably, prison – or the castle. Paul had chosen the castle. At this minute it was a decision he was probably regretting.

He massaged her shoulders. Her shoulders were wide, finely-boned, the hollows of her collar-bone in contrast to the fleshy richness of her breasts.

'More oil,' she said.

He squirted the cream in great gobs on to her chest between the firm mounds of her tits, then worked it into the flesh, feeling the corrugated nipples under his palms, feeling the rubbery, spongy mass respond as he kneaded it. He tried to forget the other times in his life he'd kneaded breasts like this. Other times he'd worked his hands from breasts to navel, as he did now, until the tips of his fingers touched the perfect triangle of pubic hair. He tried to think of anything, cars, cold water, computer programs, anything but what he was doing. It was impossible.

He was on to the top of her thighs now. She parted her legs slightly. He could see the folds of her labia again. He really wished he could take his eyes away but he couldn't. Her labia seemed to be smiling at him. A cruel, knowing smile.

The worst was when she had the slaves wank her. Every morning a different slave – men and women – brought her breakfast on a strict rota. Sometimes she wanted nothing more. They set the tray down and fled gratefully. Sometimes, like now, they were made to oil her in the sun (the males slaves prayed for an early winter). Sometimes she lay naked on her bed and had them lick every inch of her body, then use their mouths and fingers to wank her. That was the worst for the men.

Sometimes, rarely, she had them fuck her. She would free them from the pouch. That was the best and better not thought of.

'That's enough,' Stephanie said as Paul reached her ankles. Paul stopped instantly and with relief. Not that stopping relieved the pressure of his cock as it pushed hopelessly against the hard metal shell. Not that, despite himself, he could stop looking at the beautiful naked body, oiled and shiny, that was stretched out before him, so close he could feel its heat.

What he wouldn't have given to be able to free his cock from its constriction, strip off the pouch, plunge into the depths of her sex, which was so close at hand. He knew how it would feel, wet and tight and hot.

'You may go,' she said breaking into his painful reverie.

'Oh thank you, madam.' He scrambled to his feet as quickly as he could.

'Does it hurt, Paul?'

'Yes, madam.'

'Perhaps you made the wrong choice.'

'No, madam,' he said firmly. Whatever the discomfort the alternative would have been worse.

Stephanie watched him hobble away. She closed her eyes and relaxed, the hot sun creating a feeling of wellbeing that perfectly matched her mood. The last weeks had been among the most contented in her life. Now that she had been able to enjoy the pleasures of her new life at the castle, now her revenge on Gianni was complete – made more complete every day by the accounts of his divorce in the courts, his failed attempt to get his hands on even the smallest asset, and his wife's recent instigation of a case against him for criminal fraud in the running of their company – Stephanie had been able to concentrate on what to do with the responsibilities and power she had been vested over the castle.

4

It seemed like years ago – though in fact it was only months – since Devlin had first brought her to the island castle in the middle of Lake Trasimeno in Italy, since he'd first shown her the cellars and the slaves, since she had, literally, enslaved him as well, and he'd asked her to stay and run the castle for him. She had never thought of herself as having any particular sexual bent. In fact, she rarely used to think of sex. It was something she did because it was expected of her; she enjoyed it, she got pleasure from it, but like breathing it was not something she had paid much attention to.

But that had changed. Something had made her change – suddenly. She had no idea what. She had developed an urge to find out, to explore the undiscovered country. She had bought books and read them avidly. And when she had studied the theory she progressed to the practise. She found a man – or did he find her – to take her to new territory. And then there was no turning back. She had crossed an invisible line, a Chinese wall. There was so much to learn. So much to discover about herself, about her sexuality: she had discovered pleasures, and feelings, and sensations unlike anything she had even dreamt of, so different from the sex she had experienced previously. But more than the discovery of her own pleasures, she had found she had a talent, an ability to read the sexuality of others, to reach into their sexual psyche and extract its deepest secrets, secrets that were perhaps even unknown to them.

That is what had happened with Devlin. His sexuality had always been complex, his excitement and arousal dependent on factors he had only half understood. Stephanie had changed that. She had discovered the key to Devlin's libido. The master of the castle, the master of a multi-million-pound business empire, the master of all he surveyed had actually wanted to be a slave – her slave.

But Devlin's enslavement had been intricately bound to her own sexual development. At the castle Stephanie had found that power – the power to dominate, to control, to command – was in itself an aphrodisiac. Slowly at first, she

5

had come to realise that the sustained and heightened pleasures she was so readily experiencing came from her position of power.

Like now. She was sexually excited, as she lay in the sun her body glistening with sun oil, because she had played the role with Paul, had teased him, played with him, made him her slave. She knew it had made her wet. She didn't need to dip her fingers between her nether lips to know what she would find there. An oozing wetness. It was the power. Power over her slave. Power to tell him to go away or stay. Power to have him do whatever she wanted him to do – to her, for her. Lick her, suck her, fuck her. Anything and everything. There were no taboos, no inhibitions. It excited her. The thought and the reality thrilled her.

She squirmed slightly, thigh against thigh, exerting a faint pressure on her clitoris. She took one of her tits in her hand and squeezed it. A pang of pleasure shot through her.

There she stopped herself abruptly, stayed her hand from roaming down to her clitoris. She looked at her watch. The Phillipe Patek that Devlin had given her, its case as thin as an after dinner mint, lay on the little white cast-iron table by the lounger. It was ten o'clock. At eleven Devlin would be coming up to say goodbye. She should save herself for him.

At quarter to eleven Stephanie hauled herself to her feet and went inside. In the Carrera marble bathroom she showered the oil off her body and dried herself briskly. The sexual tension in her body had not abated: her self-control had made it more piquant. She was very much in the mood for Devlin.

Devlin was off to New York on business for at least five days. It was a big deal, something he'd been working on for months, he'd told her. But Stephanie had decided his schedule would have to be delayed: her priorities came first. The plane would have to wait for him. Wasn't that one of the advantages of having a private jet?

Stephanie felt wickedly capricious. She walked, still naked, to the wardrobes that lined one of the walls of her palatial bedroom. What should she tease him with today?

6

Something smooth and silky, feminine and soft; or something hard and cruel, in tight black leather?

She searched the drawers built into the wardrobes, looking for something to take her fancy. Something did. She pulled out a garment she had brought in Rome at the very special lingerie shop she had discovered in the back streets. Made of a sheer black material woven with Lycra, it fitted her body tightly. The full bra moulded itself to her breasts, the material stretching down over her waist to end, at the front and side, in four spikes of suspender. At the front it barely covered her navel, at the back it finished abruptly in the hollow of her spine leaving her arse exposed.

Stephanie pulled the elasticated material down over her body. As soon as the material was stretched it became almost entirely transparent. Though her breasts were completely covered they were, at the same time, visible; every curve and detail, including the nipples and the circles of her areolas, were apparent under the shiny veil of tight black nylon and Lycra.

Sitting on the bed Stephanie opened a packet of the sheerest black stockings. Like the tight girdle – corset, basque, she didn't know how to describe the garment – the stockings were woven with Lycra too giving them a wet slippery look. She rolled them up over her legs until the black welt at the top of each bisected her thigh. She clipped them into the suspenders, the tautness of the elastication pulling them tight.

She slipped into a pair of black high heels and admired the effect. The heels shaped her calves, pinched her ankles more, tipped her arse into the air so it seemed to be pouting. She stood in front of one of the many full-length mirrors. The areas of her body that were exposed looked, by contrast to the flesh covered by the tight nylon, somehow more naked, creamy, soft. Her arse, the tops of her thighs above the stocking, her shoulders, so available, so rich.

She took a pair of black lace panties from a drawer full of panties of every type and colour, stepped into them and pulled them up over her hips and on to the wide curve of her pubic bone and the long slit of her sex. She ironed them into place with her hand, making them comfortable, fitting them between her legs, smoothing them over the mounds of her buttocks.

Devlin knocked twice, tentatively. Right on time. Eleven o'clock precisely.

'Come . . .' Stephanie said, letting the tone of her voice reflect her mood, and smiling at herself in the mirror. She looked like she felt, excited and hot. She wiped the smile away and replaced it with a scowl as she turned to watch Devlin shuffle in.

Devlin was an incredibly ugly man. His body was short and misshapen, his trunk too long for his height, and his face scarred with pockmarks. It was dominated by a huge bulbous nose, which was veined and hairy. Thick, wiry white hair grew in profusion from every inch of his body, from his nostrils, from his ears, even from his back.

'Stephanie – my God you look wonderful,' he said as his eyes devoured every detail.

It wasn't what she wanted to hear.

'Did I tell you to look at me?' she said sternly.

'No.'

'No what?' Her pretended anger thrilled her. The game had begun. Devlin's head went down, his eyes staring at the carpet.

'No, mistress.'

'That's better. Get your clothes off, and quickly, Devlin,' she snapped.

'Yes, mistress.'

He hadn't expected this. He felt his erection growing, his excitement instantaneous. Not for one second did he think of not complying. She was in control. When she was in this mood, there was no telling what she would do. His heart was beating faster at the thought. Quickly he stripped off his shirt and tie. By the time he unzipped the fly of his trousers his penis was eager to be free, as hard as a rod of steel.

He pulled his boxer shorts off and shifted from foot to foot to pull off his socks while his penis bobbed about in

8

front of him. Stephanie had seen it many times but could never quite get used to its monstrous proportions. Nor its ugliness. It was gnarled and twisted and veined, like a rotten tree trunk curled with ivy.

She would never forget the first time he had thrust it inside her. Never.

He stood naked, uneasy, not sure what to expect, his penis standing out from his matted wiry pubic hair, a tear of Cowper's fluid already formed at its tip. All thoughts of the world outside, his business, his schedule, his trip to New York, had disappeared. His world had shrunk, encompassed now entirely by the extent of Stephanie's commands.

'Well, Devlin, what am I going to do with you? You come in here as though you've forgotten everything I've taught you. What am I going to do with you, Devlin?'

'I don't know.' His voice was breathless with excitement.

'I'll have to think of something, won't I?'

'Yes, mistress.'

She took his cock in her hand, circling it with her fist. With the tip of her other hand's forefinger she massaged the tear of fluid that had formed into the dappled smoothness at the end of his circumcised cock. He could not help but moan. It felt so sensitive.

With most men a hand wrapped around their cock would cover more than half of it: with Devlin at least two thirds remained visible. Stephanie felt a frisson of excitement sing through her body as she felt its heat and hardness.

Power was an aphrodisiac. So many possibilities, so many things she could do, so many things she could ask for and get by right.

She let go of his cock and bent to adjust her stocking on her left leg. She unhooked both suspenders and pulled the stocking up tighter before reattaching it. She saw Devlin's eyes following every movement while he tried to pretend he was staring at the floor.

'You didn't answer my question,' she said.

'I didn't think . . .' he stammered.

'You didn't think what? I don't ask questions for fun, do I?'

9

'No, mistress.'

'So what am I going to do with you?'

'I don't know, mistress,' he replied quickly.

'Well I'll tell you then. You're going to give me some pleasure. That's what I'm going to do with you. I'm in the mood to take some pleasure. You're going to please me. You're going to keep the plane waiting until you've given me some pleasure. Is that understood, Devlin?'

'Yes, mistress.'

'Good.' She circled him, her stockings rasping against each other as she moved. Coming around behind him she pressed herself into his back, letting him feel the slippery silky material between their flesh, rubbing her body very slightly up and down against his. She reached round to his cock and took it in both her hands, wanking it not at all gently. He gasped with pleasure.

She released his cock and stood back, legs apart, arms akimbo. 'Take my knickers off,' she ordered.

He turned to reach for the elastic.

'Not like that,' she said slapping his nearest hand hard.

'How then, mistress?'

'With your teeth,' she smiled having only just thought of the idea. What a good idea, she thought. 'Come on, I haven't got all day and neither have you.'

She could seeing him trying to work out what to do. He dropped to his knees in front of her. Slowly he moved his head towards the triangle of material at the junction of her thighs, puffed up by the thick pubic hair it contained.

'Come on, Devlin.' She could tell he was trying to work out what to do.

He leaned forward against her navel and grasped the top of her panties in his teeth. He tried to pull them down. They were very reluctant to leave her waist. He pulled again, sawing his head from side to side. Slowly the panties begun to slide down over her iron-flat belly but snagged when they reached her pubic hair. Devlin moved his head to the elastic at the sides and used his teeth to pull them down. By alternating his head from one side of the panties to the other, pulling first one side down an inch and then the

10

other, he gradually worked the black lace over her hips and down her thighs. One side caught on a suspender. He managed to unhook it with his tongue, knowing better than to try and use his hands.

The crotch of the panties still clung to her sex, the triangular shape of the panties now inverted. He moved his head so he could gather the material in his teeth. He could smell the delicious aroma of her perfume combined with the musky scent of raw sex. As his teeth pulled the lace away he felt his desire surge as the pouting lips of her body were unveiled. The panties fell to the floor.

'Since you're so good with your mouth . . .' Stephanie stepped out of the twin circles of lace around her feet. Still wearing the black high heels she lay back on the bed. She opened her legs and bent her knees, the heels of the shoes digging into the counterpane. She arched her back off the bed, angling her cunt to point at Devlin. 'Come on, Devlin, you know what to do.'

Her cunt seemed to be alive, like an animal, like a cat. It purred and throbbed like a domestic cat, it hunted hungrily like a lion, and devoured like a tiger. It was independent of her, a wild creature needing to be fed.

Devlin was about to stand up. 'On your knees,' Stephanie snapped. Obediently he crawled forward until he reached the edge of the bed. Stephanie slid forward, wrapped her thighs over his shoulders, her heels digging into his back, and levered her cunt on to his face.

He ignored the pain in his back as the sharp metal heels gouged into it like spurs, to gain purchase. Eagerly he lapped at her sex, teasing out her clitoris from the forest of pubic hair, tasting her salty wetness as he dipped down to push between her swollen labia, poking his tongue as deep as it would go into the black wet depths of her cunt.

Almost from the first moment that his hot mouth had clamped itself to her, Stephanie felt a sequence begin, the first stirrings, as her body changed gear, began to prepare itself for what would be, now, inevitable. She looked down at herself, Devlin's wiry grey hair framed between her open legs, her thighs bisected by the black welts of the stockings, the suspenders loose at the front of her thigh as her legs were bent but tight and stretched at the side.

What she said next would thrill her more, and continue the sequence, the words themselves as exciting as their consequence.

'Use your fingers.'

Devlin's other physical attribute, besides the size of his cock, was the size of his fingers. His fingers were huge, fat, thick and long, his hand like a hand of bananas. She had noticed it the first time they had met, when he'd taken her hand. Compared with his, her hand looked like that of a tiny child. She would never forget the first time he had thrust a finger inside her either. It opened her, filled her, swamped her. It was an experience she wanted again and again. She wanted it now.

She felt his hand move up to her thigh. She felt her body tense, the sequence accelerating rapidly, slipping out of her control. His mouth went back to her clitoris as he nosed the tip of his finger between her labia. She was in no mood for gentleness though.

'Do it, Devlin,' she moaned.

Immediately she felt him push forward, her cunt filled as comprehensively as if he was using his cock. But his finger didn't feel like a cock. It felt more like a dildo except it was warm and alive. She could not help but squeal with pleasure.

She spurred her heels into his back again, as if riding a horse, urging him on, levering herself down on to his mouth as his tongue lapped at her hardened clitoris and his massive finger reamed back and forth along the wet channel of her cunt. She had wanted to wait, to delay, to tease herself, hold her orgasm at bay, but her body wouldn't let her. The sensations were overwhelming, his finger and tongue in combination, wringing feelings out of her, feelings she could not ignore, feelings that started the last sequence, making her squirm and moan and cry out as she felt her orgasm peak, crunching her nerves, and she let herself fall into a black abyss.

It was a long time before she recovered, before she

relaxed completely, before her body decided there were no more delicious sensations to extract from the embers of her climax.

Devlin had not moved, his mouth still at her sex, his finger still inside her.

'Now it's your turn, isn't it?' Stephanie said in a tone of authority. She sat up and pulled his head back, kissing him hard on the mouth, licking at his lips and tasting her own juices. His finger slid from her cunt. He was going to New York. She wanted to give him something to remember her by. She knew what thrilled Devlin, she knew the source of the secret rivers of passion that ran through this strange ugly man. He would do whatever she commanded him to do and his submission would be excitement enough. But there was more. The rivers ran deep.

Stephanie's swung her leg over his head and got off the bed. Her mood had not changed. She felt energised and alive. She felt wonderfully open and wanton; prepared to do anything. It was Devlin's lucky day.

'Stay where you are,' she ordered, crossing the bedroom to a large chest of drawers. The top drawer held what she was looking for.

'I have decided, Devlin,' she said returning to the bed and dropping the items from the drawer on to the now heavily rucked counterpane, 'to punish you.'

'No,' he said. But his voice betrayed him. It was breathless with excitement as he looked at what lay on the bed.

She picked up the silk blindfold and slipped it over his eyes. She saw his cock pulse as she smoothed it into place.

'Hands behind your back, Devlin. I shouldn't have to tell you, should I?'

He obeyed instantly.

She strapped a leather cuff tightly around each of his wrists. The cuffs were joined by a strong metal ring. She took a plain leather strap, wide and black, and used it to cinch his arms together just above the elbow. He winced. The black leather cut into his soft white flesh. Another tear of fluid wept from his cock. His body betrayed his excitement again.

13

'Stand up,' she ordered. With difficulty he struggled to his feet not having his arms available for balance.

She stood behind him, pressing herself into his imprisoned arms, letting him feel her tits under the tight Lycra.

Two more plain leather straps. She knelt and bound his ankles together with one strap and his knees, just above the knee joint, with the other. She pulled both straps tight, as tight as they would go. She had made a neat little package.

She stood up. There was no hurry. She went to the fridge, which was set into the silk panelling of the bedroom walls and took out a bottle of champagne and a chilled crystal flute. Expertly, she eased the cork out of the bottle; she had drunk more champagne in her months at the castle than in the whole of the rest of her life, and poured the bubbling wine into the glass. Sitting on the oatmeal sofa opposite the bed, she crossed her stockinged legs and sipped at the chilled champagne.

'Turn around,' she ordered wanting to see Devlin's cock. With diminutive steps he managed to shuffle around. His erection was massive and wet from his own fluid. She had never seen it bigger, more engorged, and veined and ugly. A frisson of excitement leapt from her body, reminding her of the orgasm she had just enjoyed.

Putting the glass down she unclipped the suspenders on one of her black stockings. When it was free she rolled it off her leg. She could see Devlin listening to the sounds, wondering what she was doing. She got up. She trailed the stocking over Devlin's chest. It was still warm. She let the nylon brush against his cock. It soaked up the wetness, absorbing a tear of moisture and forming a dark patch on the sheer black. Dropping to her knees in front of him Stephanie pulled the stocking under his balls and around the stem of his cock before knotting it into a neat bow. She pulled the bow tight. Devlin's cock pulsed.

Devlin's body was trembling with excitement. He made little involuntary noises that sounded a little like the word 'please' repeated over and over again.

'I think we'll use the clips today. To please me.'

14

'No,' he said in a tone that meant exactly the opposite.

The clips lay ready on the bed. Two bright chrome clips, like little bulldog clips but with edges serrated with tiny metal teeth. She picked them up. Opening the jaws, she positioned the tiny teeth over her own veiled nipple. Slowly she allowed the spring of the clip to close. She felt the metal biting into her soft puckered flesh. She felt pain but pleasure too, sharp hard pleasure. Another wave of feeling came as she pulled the clip away.

Devlin's nipples were as hard as her own. She positioned the clip over each nipple and watched as the tiny teeth sunk deep into the tender flesh. Devlin moaned, a sound of pure passion. She flicked the clips with the tip of her finger. He moaned again, the same sound, the same feeling.

Stephanie's body had started to churn again, change gear again, moving from objective to subjective. She could still feel the little metal teeth biting into her nipple. She could feel her heart beating faster.

'I'm going to whip you now,' she said. The words echoed in her mind, feeding her passion. This was no longer a performance. Her body was alive with pangs of arousal, the first harbinger of its needs.

The riding crop lay on the bed too. She picked it up and in almost the same movement slashed it across Devlin's buttocks. He gasped. His cock pulsed.

'More?' she said not caring what he said.

'Yes.' He couldn't lie this time and say no. His whole body ached for more.

She slashed the whip down on his buttocks again, feeling her own passion, her pulse racing.

Three more cuts. She had never seen Devlin's cock harder, bigger, its monstrous grid of veins engorged and angry, swollen by the nylon stocking tied at its base. A network of red marks crisscrossed his buttocks.

Despite her feelings Stephanie was in more control this time. There was no hurry she told herself dropping the whip and picking up the champagne flute. This time she could tease herself, pretend she wasn't going to use that massive cock. She sipped the wine then pressed the cold glass against the tip of Devlin's cock. A little of the moisture there attached itself to the side of the glass. She licked it off. Slowly she put the glass down.

'Well, Devlin. You are in a state, aren't you.' With the flat of her hand she pushed him hard in the chest. Unable to use his hands or feet to balance he fell back on to the bed, like a roll of carpet, bouncing slightly on the springs of the mattress.

If she had cared to think about it Stephanie probably came before she threw herself on to Devlin's prostrate body and impaled herself on his cock. As it penetrated into the silky wetness of her cunt her orgasm was already quivering through the nerves of her body. But the arrival of his cock, its size, filling her, choking her, engulfing her, drove her body further, higher – made her come again. Or perhaps not. She couldn't tell and didn't care. Perhaps it was the same orgasm elongated, expanded, intensified. There was no need to analyse. All that mattered was the feeling.

As the mists of her passion cleared she opened her eyes. Devlin lay beneath her open thighs, bound and blindfolded the nipple clips like little jewels decorating his chest. She eased herself off his cock. It stood straight up at right angles to his body. As he felt the wetness slide away he moaned what sounded like 'no'.

Kneeling at his side, she picked up the whip again from where she had dropped it on the bed.

'Count,' she said. She aimed the little leather loop fixed to end of the crop at the base of his cock where her black nylon stocking bound it tightly. It was a delicate flick, no more, but she knew that was enough.

'One,' said Devlin, his voice hoarse with pleasure.

She aimed again, this time higher up the huge stem.

'Two,' he entoned obediently. His cock was taut, stretched to the absolute limit, like every nerve in his body, straining for release. In the blackness behind the blindfold his fantasy had become reality. It was what Stephanie did for him. No other woman had ever understood. The blackness was full of images, her body, the tight black

16

girdle, her labia, the feel of her panties in his teeth . . .

'Three . . .' He couldn't complete the word. His spunk jetted into the air like a firework, splashing down on to his hairy body in great white gobs. His cock spasmed uncontrollably, spitting out its load. Then, as the tension lessened, the spunk oozed out, white pearls slipping over the wet glans.

When there was no more, when Devlin's body went limp, Stephanie pulled the bow she had made with her stocking and released his cock from its constriction. Using her hand she squeezed the cock to milk the last drops of spunk out of it, as Devlin lay, wallowing in the final tremors of his volcanic eruption, rocking himself slightly from side to side, the only movement his bondage would allow.

Stephanie smiled to herself. This was definitely not an experience Devlin would forget.

TWO

'So I'll be back in a week. Not more than a week,' Devlin said. He was dressed again, his silk Sulka tie neatly knotted, his Huntsman suit perfectly tailored for his oddly shaped body, his hair as tidily brushed as its wiry stubborness would allow, the air of business and money wrapped around him again like a heavy cloak. There was a bruise, to remind him of the encounter when he undressed for bed in New York, on his upper arm were the leather strap had bitten into his flesh as he'd fallen back on to the bed. It was hidden under the suit. It hurt slightly when he moved his arm. His buttocks hurt too. They felt tender, abused.

Stephanie had pulled on a black one-piece swimsuit and a light chiffon wrap and was walking him down the wide marble staircase, her arm in his, intending to swim as soon as she'd seen him off.

'And the Clarkes are arriving when?' she asked.

'This afternoon. The car's driving them up from Rome. They should be here about three. I've told them I've got to be away . . .'

'Don't worry. I'll look after them.'

'I don't know what they like.'

'Don't worry.'

'It would be very good if . . .'

'If?' Stephanie prompted.

'If they had a . . .' he searched for the right word, 'satisfying weekend.'

'They've never been here before then?'

'No. I've asked them before. This is the first time they've accepted.'

'Are they happily married?'

'As far as I know. I've done business with them for years. They're efficient, reliable. If I'm going to expand my textile business they'd be ideal partners.'

'And?'

'Well so far they've resisted all my approaches. They want to remain independent, or so they say.'

'And you can't buy them out?'

'No. Not unless they agree. They're a private company. If they were public it would be a different matter.'

They walked out through the thick wooden doors of the main castle entrance past the cobbled courtyard, littered with huge terracotta pots containing orange and lemon trees, and down the stone steps, worn by four centuries of use, to the sturdy wooden jetty that projected out into the still waters of the lake. The powerboat waited, its varnished wood and polished brass glittering in the sun.

Looking down into the clear water, Stephanie watched the shoals of tiny fish, blue and yellow and deep red, swimming between the wooden piles, darting energetically from one direction to another for no apparent reason.

'So you want to show them the advantages of being associated with you,' Stephanie said.

'The less obvious advantages. Of course, they may not regard them as advantages at all.'

'I'm sure I can find something to tempt their fancy,' she replied smiling almost to herself. It was an interesting thought. A challenge.

'I don't want to scare them off.'

'Perhaps all they want is a quiet weekend in the sun.'

'Perhaps . . .'

'Then that's what they'll get. On the other hand I might be able to interest them in something more . . . energetic.'

'I hope you can.'

'I'll give you a progress report tomorrow.'

Devlin's luggage had been loaded into the powerboat. Stephanie kissed him on both cheeks.

'Did I give you something to remember me by, Devlin?' she whispered.

19

'How could I forget?'

He climbed aboard the boat and sat on the padded seat in the transom. The boatman released the forward and aft lines and let the boat drift away from the rubber types hanging down from the wooden piles before gunning the big inboard motor.

'Don't forget Mrs Bloom,' Devlin shouted over the noise of the engine.

'I won't,' Stephanie shouted back. She waved as the boat cut a huge swaith through the clear water.

As soon as the boat had cleared the jetty and was heading out into the lake, Stephanie stripped off her wrap and dived into the water, made choppy by the boat's propellers. She swam out into deep water, stretching her muscles and feeling the silky soft water streaming around her slim body. In the distance she could see the powerboat heading across the lake, a diminishing dot on the horizon.

The fish, disturbed by the churning water, soon returned. They swam alongside her, not worried by the strange monster that had invaded their territory.

After thirty minutes she swam back to the jetty where a servant was waiting with a large white bath towel. In the downstairs cloakroom she stripped off the swimsuit and dried herself with the towel. She had taken to keeping a few clothes down here in the cloakroom to save herself the trek back upstairs to her bedroom. She changed into a creamy one-piece trouser suit, not bothering with underwear; its tailored plunging neckline revealed her naked cleavage.

On the terrace outside the main reception room of the castle, where guests were entertained al fresco, she ordered a light lunch of salad and fruit, all grown on the island. She allowed herself one glass of champagne. Though she had only sipped at the champagne while she was dealing with Devlin this morning, one glass was enough. She wanted to have all her wits about her when the Clarkes arrived.

By the time she had drunk a foamy cappuccino and nibbled a pair of Amaretti biscuits it was two o'clock. She had just time to check the gardens before she went to her room to change.

She walked through the long winding corridors that lead to the castle's back entrance and its extensive gardens that formed the rest of the island. There was no other habitation. The paid servants either lived in or went back to the mainland at night by boat.

It was a tortuous route and at first she had always got a servant to escort her. Eventually she'd learnt the way through the maze of poorly lit windowless halls and finally out, through a small wooden door at the top of the stone staircase on the outside of one of the thick round walls. From the top of the steps she could see most of the island beyond; a huge orchard neatly laid out, and, nearer to the castle, a red brick walled garden enclosing extensive green-houses, plots for every sort of vegetable and flower, and a small vineyard planted on the north side of the enclosure.

It was in this acreage which most of the slaves spent their daylight hours. There were exceptions, of course. Some were employed in the castle, some cleaned the cellars, but generally speaking the castle and the castle kitchens were served by paid staff and the slaves were used for more menial duties out here in the gardens. There was a great deal of work to be done to keep the horticulture in order. It was hard work too.

Stephanie walked through the wrought-iron gate into the walled garden. There were three male overseers who supervised and instructed the slaves in what had to be done, and saw to it that they did what they were told to do. They were all Italian. Stephanie knew them all now and had learnt enough Italian to ask them if they had any problems whenever she roamed the gardens.

The regimen at the castle was strict. Occasionally one of the slaves would forget the reason for his enslavement and rebel, refusing whatever task he or she had been allotted. Generally the rebellions did not last long. It was pointed out to the individual concerned that if they did not wish to continue at the castle then they would be taken to the mainland and hence to their country of origin, and the evidence of their early wrong-doings – which had landed them at the castle in the first place – presented to the police. It was, and

21

always would be, their free choice to go back whenever they wished.

The first reminder usually – in fact to date, always – seemed to bring compliance. Prison was not an acceptable alternative. However the initial rebellion could not go unpunished and there were various means to see that the slave would think twice before having to be delivered of another lecture on freedom of choice. It was now a rule, one that Stephanie had introduced, to require the slave to ask for the punishment of any transgression, in fact to beg to be punished. This served as a simple reminder that they had a choice, though a choice they had chosen not to take.

But despite the logic of these rules, Stephanie had noticed that among the constantly changing population of slaves at the castle there were always troublemakers, those willing to take the punishment and still, by further insolence or disobedience, come back for more. She supposed it was not surprising. In any group there were always those who wanted to challenge the system. Or perhaps the rebels had a different motivation; perhaps they actually liked the punishment. After her experience with Devlin that was not, after all, too far-fetched.

As she passed through the rows of the vegetable garden she saw one of the 'rebels' now hoeing weeds between long lines of courgette plants. Three times in the last weeks Amanda had refused allotted tasks and three times had been lectured and punished. It would not be the last time either. Stephanie was sure of that.

Amanda looked up as Stephanie walked by. She was a short-haired brunette with very light brown eyes. Though not tall her figure was well proportioned. She had high breasts, a slim waist and full round hips, though all well hidden under the baggy working clothes all the slaves wore in the gardens.

'Bitch,' she whispered when she thought Stephanie was out of earshot.

'What did you say?' Stephanie barked turning back.

'Nothing,' Amanda replied not bothering to look up from the blade of the hoe.

Stephanie thought of letting it go, but she didn't want to give Amanda the satisfaction of thinking she'd got away with anything.

'What is it, Amanda?' she said solicitously, walking up the row of courgettes to stand besides her. Amanda was sweating. The band of cloth that held her hair out of her eyes was wet; her forehead was beaded with sweat. 'Are you homesick perhaps? Would you like to go home? That can be arranged. I've told you that, haven't I? You only have to say the word.'

'No,' Amanda said adding 'madam' grudgingly.

'Then you want to be punished for insolence?'

'No, madam.'

'It must be one or the other, Amanda. I don't understand you. Why do you make life so difficult for yourself?'

One of the punishments was to be given to one of the garden overseers. The female slaves hated this most of all. The overseers were hard and crude. They had little finesse but an apparently boundless appetite for sex. Amanda had been given to one last week. The experience seemed to have done nothing to quieten her dissidence.

Amanda looked up into Stephanie's eyes. Her expression was defiant.

'You didn't answer my question,' Stephanie said.

'Yes,' she replied. 'Punish me, you bitch.' She said it firmly, her eyes not wavering. 'I like it,' she hissed.

Stephanie raised her hand and touched Amanda's cheek. It was flushed with effort and hot. Amanda did not flinch as the back of Stephanie's hand moved up her cheek gathering beads of perspiration from her ruddy complexion. Their eyes remained locked together. Stephanie licked the sweat from her hand. It tasted salty. Her desired flared.

'Tonight then,' Stephanie said walking away, managing to control the strong reaction Amanda had provoked.

If she had had time she would have liked to punish her there and then, and had her stretched out against a tree, her working clothes pulled down, her buttocks exposed. She would have had all the other slaves watch while one of the

23

overseers delivered the punishment, which the girl would be made to ask for again.

But there was no time. It would have to wait. The Clarkes were the first priority.

Back in her bedroom Stephanie thought about what she should wear to meet the Clarkes. As they knew nothing of the more exotic recreations available at the castle – not yet at least – she didn't want to appear too obvious or outrageous. As Devlin had said she didn't want to scare them off. On the other hand a suggestion of the delights that lay ahead if they chose, would not be a bad idea. It might set the agenda and that would do no harm.

She chose a white suit and decided not to wear a bra or a blouse. With the suit jacket buttoned there was more than a suggestion of rich cleavage and, if someone cared to worm themselves into the right position at the right time, no doubt the jacket would reveal a great deal more, but not without effort.

Under the skirt she wore a white suspender belt, white stockings and lacy white French knickers, split at the sides almost to the waist. In the spirit of modesty the skirt of the suit was well over the knee in length. If the Clarkes ever got to see the expensive trappings under the skirt, by that time, they would have taken the bait.

Stephanie was equally careful with her make-up, wanting it to make an impression but not, at the same time, be over dramatic. As she applied the last strokes of the eyeliner and pinned her long black hair into a chignon at the back of her head, she heard the engines of the powerboat approaching from across the lake. By the time she had slipped on her high heels – the shoes she had decided should be another hint, they were much higher than normal day wear, with wicked spiked heels – and walked through the castle and down the stone steps to the jetty, the boat was already nosing its way into the rubber tyres and one of the white-linen coated servants was tying off the forward line.

Mr and Mrs Clarke were sitting in the seats on the transom both wearing hats and sunglasses against the glare of the sun, which was reflected off the waters of the lake.

'Welcome,' Stephanie said as the aft line was secured. She held out her hand to help Mrs Clarke ashore and, once she was safely on the jetty, did the same for her husband. 'Stephanie Curtis . . . I hope you had a good journey.'

'Lovely. Such beautiful countryside,' Mrs Clarke replied, pulling off her hat and raking through her hair with her fingers. She was a golden blonde, her hair the colour of ripe wheat on a sunny day. She was slightly taller than Stephanie even in the lower heels she was wearing. Perhaps it was the radiant hair or her flawless peachy complexion but Mrs Clarke gave the impression of rude health.

Her husband, on the other hand, was rather pallid and unhealthy looking; too many days spent inside in an office. He was shorter than his wife and Stephanie and almost completely bald, his only hair growing in a greying horseshoe around his shining pate. He was not fat but could not accurately be described as thin either. A slight paunch was beginning to droop over the waistband of his trousers.

'It's very nice of Devlin to invite us,' Mr Clarke said.

'Everything he said about this place is true so far,' his wife added. 'It's like a fairy-tale castle. Is there a sleeping beauty inside?'

'You'll have to discover that for yourself.' Stephanie said. 'If you follow me. The servants will bring your luggage.'

Stephanie led the way up the stone steps, across the cobbled courtyard and into the castle. The two guests 'ohhed' and 'arghed' over the various features like the view, the potted orange trees, the huge modern tapestry that hang in the main hall, and the long sweeping marble staircase up to the galleried first floor.

'Would you like to see your rooms first or have a drink. Tea, coffee, champagne?'

'Oh champagne definitely,' Mrs Clark said. 'That would be wonderful.'

They walked up to the main terrace. Mrs Clarke headed for a table in the shade of a large lime tree. Her husband joined her while Stephanie arranged for the champagne.

'The lake is marvellous for swimming,' she said coming to sit at the table. Mrs Clarke had taken off her sunglasses. Her eyes were bright and quite dark shade of blue. She was a startlingly beautiful woman, the long flaxen hair framing the perfect complexion, high cheek bones, a straight nose and a firm angular chin held proudly by a long elegant neck. In fact everything about Mrs Clarke was a picture of elegance, the practical but well-fitted shirt-waister she was wearing, the way she moved, the way she sat, the way she held her hand, with one finger touching her throat and the others spread, as she talked.

'I think we must be in heaven,' she said, her fingers caressing the arch of her collarbone.

Stephanie was leaning forward, her jacket hanging loosely. She saw Mrs Clarke's eyes flick down: they were not quick to leave.

'I'd love to have a swim,' Mr Clarke said.

'Let's have our champagne first, darling,' his wife said seeing the waiter emerging from the castle.

The waiter set the silver tray on the table. A Georgian silver wine cooler held a bottle of Louis Roederer Crystal swaithed in ice. The waiter opened the bottle and poured the wine into three crystal flutes.

'Here's to a pleasant stay,' Stephanie said, raising her glass and clinking it against the side of both of the others.

'How rude of us,' Mrs Clarke said. 'This is Terry and I'm Jacqueline. Inevitably everyone calls me Jacqui . . . Oh, this is delicious.'

They chatted about this and that. Stephanie noticed that Terry's eyes also wandered to the V-shaped lapels of the jacket and the single button that struggled to contain her unconstricted breasts. But she, in turn, found herself watching his wife, her long cultured legs, her bare arms, the very distinct line of her bust. Behind the conviviality and small talk Stephanie felt an undertone in the conversation. Or perhaps she was just imaging it. Perhaps Jacqui's attractions were affecting her judgement.

'Well I'd like to swim now,' Terry announced. 'The water looks so good!'

'And I need a shower,' Jacqui said.

Dutifully Stephanie showed them upstairs. All the bedrooms in the castle for the guests were vast and palatial, all with *en suite* marble bathrooms and most with terraces overlooking the lake or gardens and orchards at the rear. But Stephanie had chosen a room next to Jacqui's for convenience sake. Having a south facing terrace, it would also provide the most sun.

Stephanie showed them into the pink silk panelled room with its deep olive carpet. Flowers had been freshly picked from the garden and arranged in a huge display on the occasional table in front of the large sofa that faced the bed. Jacqui walked out on to the terrace and admired the view of the lake. There were more 'ohs' and 'arghs' as the couple roamed around. Stephanie showed them the fridge hidden in the silk panelling and the telephone to order breakfast or anything else they might want.

'I'll leave you to get unpacked then,' Stephanie said. Their luggage was neatly stacked by the wardrobes. 'If there's anything you want just ask for it.' She felt like the manager of a first-class hotel.

'Thanks,' Terry said. He'd opened his suitcase and was routing around for his bathing trunks.

'There's towelling robes on the back of the bathroom door,' Stephanie said helpfully.

'Oh great . . .' he said disappearing into the bathroom and closing the door behind him.

'We'll see you at dinner then,' Jacqui said.

'And don't hesitate if there's anything you need. I'm in the room next door.'

'I won't,' Jacqui said. For a second their eyes met. Jacqui's expression was quizzical, enquiring, probing.

'Dinner's at eight if that's all right?'

'Fine.'

Stephanie let herself out of the room.

Half an hour later, from her terrace, Stephanie was watching a solitary figure swim out into the lake. Terry swam strongly and well, cutting a swaith through the calm waters until he reached one of the many tiny outcrops of rock that were dotted here and there in the great expanse of the lake. Stephanie watched as he hauled himself on to the rock and sat in the sun, giving a a good impression of Rodin's 'The Thinker'.

There was a confident knock on her bedroom door. Stephanie got up and went inside.

'Hope you don't mind.' It was Jacqui.

'Not at all, I told you. Come in.' She stood aside to let Jacqui in.

'Terry's charged off. Couldn't wait to get into the water. Surprisingly he's quite athletic. Always playing games of some sort.'

'I saw him. He's a very good swimmer.'

Jacqui was wearing the towelling robe from the bathroom. Her hair was still wet from the shower.

'I wondered what I should wear tonight. Is it very formal?'

'Let's go out on the terrace. The sun'll dry your hair.'

They walked outside and Jacqui arranged herself at the table sitting with her back to the sun so her hair got the maximum benefit.

'My husband thinks you're stunning,' Jacqui said as Stephanie sat opposite her.

'That's very flattering. But he can hardly complain. You are a very beautiful woman.'

'Thank you. I always think a compliment from another woman is a real compliment.'

'Real?'

'Well men will say anything to get into your knickers, won't they?'

'I suppose so.'

'A woman doesn't have any ulterior motive.'

'Doesn't she?' Stephanie said it firmly, wanting Jacqui to understand what she was saying. 'Do you mind if I take my jacket off, it's too hot out here for clothes.'

'Of course not.'

'I was just going to change . . .'

Stephanie slipped the jacket off to reveal her firm up-tilted breasts. She watched Jacqui's reaction. Outwardly there was none. Her eyes weighed Stephanie's breasts as if trying to guess her bra size.

'I'll go and get a bikini,' Stephanie said.

'Not on my account, please,' Jacqui said flatly.

'As you can see I don't usually wear anything out here.' Stephanie's breasts were as tanned as the rest of her.

'It must be marvellous.'

Stephanie unzipped her skirt and stepped out of it.

'Stockings!' Jacqui exclaimed. 'My God, I can't remember the last time I wore stockings.'

Stephanie said nothing. She put her foot up the chair and unclipped the two suspenders on her right thigh. She rolled the white stocking off her leg. Taking her time, she repeated the process with her left leg.

'You're sure you don't mind?' she said disingenuously as she hooked her thumbs into the waistband of the French knickers.

'No . . .' Jacqui said quietly. She watched the silk and lace knickers shimmer down Stephanie's long legs.

As Stephanie reached behind her to unhook the suspender belt she saw Jacqui's eyes centred on the thick thatch of her pubic hair.

'That's better,' Stephanie said sitting down at the table again.

'No bikini lines at all.'

'None.'

'You've got a beautiful tan.'

'I should have, shouldn't I? All this sun and privacy.'

'I suppose so.'

They sat for a moment in silence. It was a pause. A pause before the next step. Both women knew it.

'It's hot,' Jacqui said breaking the silence. She stood up and pulled off the towelling robe. Her body was as sensational as its outward appearance had suggested. Her shoulders were slim and bony, her waist well defined, her long legs firm and contoured. The light hair of her pubic triangle was short, almost as though it had been trimmed, the hairs soft despite their lack of length. But it was Jacqui's

29

breasts that most attracted Stephanie's attention. They were full, heavy, thick breasts, rising from her chest precipitously with no hint of sagging. They stood proud, their nipples surrounded by a wide band of brown areola.

The two naked women faced each other. Jacqui did not sit down again. There was another pause. Now it was Stephanie's turn to do something.

'I'm going to lie in the sun,' Stephanie said getting up. She pulled the large double-sized lounger round until it was in the full sun, then adjusted it so that the padding was completely flat, just like a bed. A bed of desire. She lay down and stretched herself out on it. There was lots of room for two. Or there was another lounger Jacqui could use. It was her choice. Stephanie closed her eyes and waited.

'What did you mean?' Jacqui said, coming to stand by the foot of the lounger.

'About what?' Stephanie replied, her eyes still closed.

'About women having ulterior motives?'

'Isn't it obvious?'

'Not to me.'

'Well perhaps we'd better leave it at that then.'

Another silence. The waters of the lake lapping against the side of the jetty down below them was the only sound.

Jacqui's hand was at her throat again, her fingers spread, her hand moved slightly, unconsciously. She looked down at Stephanie's naked body. Stephanie's legs were slightly apart and she could see the crinkled rough skin of her labia. She wasn't at all sure she wanted to admit to herself what she was feeling. Without really being aware of how, she found herself sitting on the edge of the lounger, her thigh inches from Stephanie's side.

'You *are* very beautiful,' Jacqui said emphasising 'are' in her mind as well as in her speech, as though it were a justification, as though it were somehow Stephanie's body that was making her feel the way she did.

'And you say that without an ulterior motive?'

Beautiful and clever, Jacqui thought. 'I don't know.'

'Do you want to find out?'

30

It was a good question. Did she want to find out? Did she want to be honest with herself or run away?

'I suppose . . . you've made me feel . . .'

'What?'

'Feel.'

Jacqui leaned forward and, as though expecting to receive an electric shock, touched Stephanie's thigh.

'You're a very beautiful woman, Jacqui,' Stephanie said. She put her hand on top of Jacqui's hand.

'And you have an ulterior motive?'

'Definitely,' Stephanie said.

The word hung in the air. Jacqui did not remove her hand, nor did Stephanie.

'I've never done anything like this before.'

'Neither had I – until recently.'

'Recently?'

'The last months. I discovered I could get a lot of pleasure from a woman. Different pleasures.'

'Oh.'

'What?'

'I thought you were . . .'

'Jacqui, I love men. It's just different with a woman. It didn't put me off men. In fact it makes it better. It's all part of sex.'

'Is it?'

'I think so.'

There was another silence. Very slowly Jacqui's hand moved out from under Stephanie's. It inched up her long flank, over her waist to her breast. As though in slow motion the nail of her middle finger, painted a reddish shade of peach, reached the puckered nipple and gently grazed against the half-inch tip. Stephanie remained perfectly passive.

Tentatively Jacqui's hand covered the whole of Stephanie's breast and then cupped it, squeezing it gently, as though trying to judge its weight. This done it continued down over Stephanie's navel. It reached the first outcrop of thick curly black pubic hair. It pushed on, until the fingers were entwined with the hair, half veiled by it. There her hand came to rest.

31

There was a chance that Jacqui would end her experiment there, that she would pull her hand away, stand up and go back to her room. Run away.

'Lie next to me,' Stephanie said sensing her hesitation, sensing she needed to say something.

Jacqui lay down and closed her eyes. Very gently Stephanie turned on her side and kissed her on the upper arm. Jacqui's body was rigid, unyielding. Stephanie kissed her shoulder. Equally gently she moved her hand to cup one of her breasts. As Jacqui did not react, did not push her hand away, she was emboldened. She squeezed the mass of flesh. Jacqui moaned the faintest of moans.

It was as though the same thought occurred to them both at the same moment for the same reason. As Stephanie came to lean over to kiss Jacqui on the mouth, Jacqui wanted to hesitate no longer and turned her head to Stephanie to find her mouth. They kissed hungrily, their mouths meeting in midair, until Jacqui sank her head back on to the padding of the lounger allowing Stephanie's lips to feel hers. But Stephanie was cautious. She kept her tongue back, wanting to take things step by step. Neither did she move to lie on top of Jacqui, pressing herself into her side instead.

But Jacqui's tentativeness had disappeared, falling away like a veil from a statue, as a wave of acute desire swept through her body. Almost immediately Stephanie felt Jacqui's tongue probing up into her mouth, hot and wet, as her hands came to hold Stephanie's cheek in the kiss. She was kissing hard, pushing up, turning her head this way and that to move her lips, squirming them against Stephanie's mouth as her tongue exploded and her mind tried to cope with the new experience. It felt so different from kissing a man, softer, more sensual.

It was as though the kiss ignited her, as though it confirmed whatever had decided her to take the final step. Her hands ran down Stephanie's back, wrapping around it, while she turned on her side so that their bodies met, breast on breast, navel on navel. Stephanie felt Jacqui's heavy tits pressing into her own, their nipples hard as little pebbles, the flesh squashed flat, ballooning sideways in an effort to escape the crush. Jacqui's hands were on Stephanie's buttocks now, caressing and kneading them, pulling her closer until she could feel her pubic bone hard against her own.

If Stephanie had thought at all about this encounter – and truthfully she had not, other than the looks she had seen Jacqui giving her – she would have thought that she would have been the one to take the initiative. But so far, despite her inexperience, it was Jacqui who was leading. Stephanie, her pulse racing, was happy to follow.

In this spirit Jacqui rolled on top of her and broke the kiss, moving her mouth down to Stephanie's neck instead, and then down further until she gobbled up her nipple, squeezing it first with her lips and then pinching it between her teeth. She had never felt a woman's nipple before. It felt good. It made her feel excited. It made her feel wild.

As she pinched again Stephanie gasped with pleasure arching off the padded mattress of the lounger.

Jacqui had pushed one thigh between Stephanie's legs so her thigh muscle was hard against the curve of Stephanie's pubic bone. Now she let go of her nipple and moved herself so her body could press itself into the whole length of Stephanie's body, and her short soft pubic hair was pushed exactly over Stephanie's thick black curls. Triangle on triangle, their breasts once again nestled together. As soon as their bodies were matched Jacqui started to thrust forward, using her hips, exactly as if she were a man, as though she were a man with a cock, moving as though she were fucking Stephanie. But there was no cock, only the hardness of her pubic bone. At first Stephanie felt little, but then, as Jacqui's body drove forward rhythmically she found, by angling herself up off the lounger, she could increase the pressure on her clitoris. As soon as she had done this she heard Jacqui moan. The angle of their bodies had changed, their clitorises had come together, one on one, ground together by hard bone, both stretched and exposed. The more Jacqui thrust, the more Stephanie felt. Though there was no penetration it felt like Jacqui was going deeper

33

because the pressure was gradually stripping away every-thing but the tiny knot of swollen nerves. One on one.

'Don't stop,' Stephanie managed to say, as she felt her orgasm beginning.

'Yes, yes . . .' Jacqui said, then kissed Stephanie on the mouth, again taking the initiative, plunging her tongue deep between Stephanie's willing lips.

The more she drove forward, the more the contact between their two buds of feeling seemed to increase. Stephanie could feel her own wetness, or was it Jacqui's, there was no way of knowing. She had never experienced this before, a hard swollen clitoris, like a miniature cock, fucking her own so exquisitely. Such a tiny area of sensitivity producing such mammoth waves of sensation. She tried to kiss Jacqui back, push her tongue into her mouth, but suddenly she could do nothing but feel. Her orgasm was coming now like an express train roaring down the track, all noise and steam and energy, and there was nothing she could do but lie there and feel the inevitable explosion as Jacqui's clitoris hammered into her own.

She came, the feeling focused in that tiny knot of nerves like she had never felt it focused before. But almost instantaneously every nerve in her body joined in, locked into the pleasure, turned her whole body into a trembling mass of uncontained sensation.

She knew Jacqui had come too. It may have been entirely the product of her fevered imagination but she thought she could feel Jacqui's clitoris flare, like the tip of a safety match striking a light, as Jacqui could not help but stop the rhythm and surrender to the climax she, herself, had induced.

They clung to each other, breathless. Their orgasms subsided but there were little wrinkles and notches of feel-ing in the aftermath that caught them by surprise in the ebb tide, like big rocks in the sand holding back the water. Their grip on each other was mutual, as though letting go would be the final admission that their orgasm was over. It was a long time before their bodies were completely stilled.

'My God . . .' Jacqui was the first to speak. 'I never thought I'd do it.'

'What? Have sex with a woman?' The words didn't sound as if they matched what they had just experienced.

'Yes.'

'Have you ever thought about it before?'

'Yes. I've thought about it a lot. A hell of a lot if I'm truthful. I thought about it when I first saw you on the jetty too. And at the table. I could see your breasts.'

'And?'

'And?'

'Is it better than you imagined?'

'Oh yes, yes,' Jacqui said definitely. 'I don't know how it would be with someone else though. There's something about you. I wanted *you*. I've thought about it before in general, in the abstract. But this time it was specific. I wanted you.'

Stephanie laughed. 'You sound like a man.'

'Exactly.'

'I wanted you too, Jacqui.'

'Do I have to feel guilty?'

'About what?'

'Usually if something feels this good in life you have to feel guilty about it.'

'That's up to you. I told you, it doesn't mean you'll suddenly lose interest in men. There's a whole range of sexual experiences isn't there? It just means you're broadening your vocabulary. There are other things you can learn here . . .'

'What other things?' Jacqui asked eagerly.

Stephanie didn't want to introduce the subject of the cellars just yet.

'All in good time.'

'Stephanie . . .' Jacqui said earnestly. She held out her hand and touched Stephanie's cheek tenderly.

'Yes?'

'I'm not finished, are you? I mean . . .' She smiled a wicked, knowing smile. She wanted more.

Stephanie got up from the lounger and held her hand out

to help Jacqueline up too. Keeping hold of her hand she lead her back into the bedroom. She stripped the counterpane off the bed to reveal the white silk sheets.

'Lay here,' she said firmly. Now it was her turn to take the initiative.

Jacqui lay on the bed, her long supple legs stretched out, her heavy tits pulled over to the side by their weight, their nipples corrugated by her passion, her slim waist in contrast to the fullness of her hips. Her legs were open slightly; the short blonde hair of her pubis looked as though it had been combed into a strict pattern, every hair pointing inwards and downwards to the apex of the V-shape made by the creases at the top of her thighs.

Stephanie stood looking at her for a moment. It was, comparatively speaking, such a short time since she had first taken pleasure in a woman's body, that she still felt an excitement at the newness of it all. She shivered as she remembered the orgasm this woman had just given her.

Sitting down on the edge of the bed, Stephanie's began to caress Jacqui's smooth calf and slim ankle using both her hands. Jacqui opened her legs wide, pulling her free leg up and bending her knee. Stephanie could see the whole of her sex. The folds of her labia were quite thin but on either side of the long slit that ran between her legs, her flesh was swollen and puffed up, making the valley seem deeper and darker. Here her pubic hair was virtually non-existent, the thinnest possible covering of downy short hair.

Jacqui grasped her own breasts in her hands, kneading them, pushing them together, then holding them apart, making circles on her chest with them. As if the idea had just occurred to her she tried to get her left nipple into her mouth. It was not difficult. She sucked it eagerly. Then she fed the right breast up to her mouth and pinched at its nipple with her teeth.

Stephanie could see her excitement, the excitement of doing something for the first time and discovering it was pleasurable, better than pleasurable. Sex was inextricably involved with self. Discovering an aspect of sex was the pleasure of self-discovery. Stephanie had experienced it so recently herself that she could remember the feeling in detail. It was a feeling, a whole set of feelings, she would never forget.

Kneeling up on the bed, Stephanie moved her hands up Jacqui's long thigh. She caressed it, working all the time higher, until she could feel the heat of Jacqui's cunt radiating from the long open slit of her sex.

With the tip of her forefinger she found Jacqui's clitoris buried in what looked almost like the padded flesh of her genitals.

'Yes . . .' Jacqui moaned enthusiastically.

Stephanie tapped it.

'Suck it, suck it!' Jacqui begged.

Stephanie was only too happy to oblige. She bent forward and gathered the whole of Jacqui's labia into her mouth, then prised her tongue on to her clitoris. She heard Jacqui moan.

Slowly Stephanie nudged the bud of nerves with her tongue, making it wet, circling it, wanking it. She could feel Jacqui's reaction to these tiniest of movements, which were amplified and magnified by every nerve in her body, all in harmony with her clit, all ready to join in the chorus of whatever it was feeling.

'Oh God . . . It's so good. I had no idea it would be this good.'

Stephanie could feel the rhythm and pulses of her body, the waves of feeling emanating from what was, at least for the moment, the centre of her world. Every time she pushed the clitoris up with her tongue Jacqui's body pushed up too, arching off the bed. It came down as Stephanie's tongue licked down. Up and down. Up and down. Jacqui's whole body poised on the tip of Stephanie's hot, knowing tongue.

Stephanie knew Jacqui was starting to come. She could feel it so accurately it was as though she was coming herself. It was almost like masturbating. Doing the right thing, the pace, the pressure. Exactly right.

At the last moment Jacqui grapped her own tits again squeezing them so tightly they reddened, as though she were afraid they would escape the feeling that was welling up inside her. She looked down her body and saw Stephanie's head bobbing between her legs and knew it was that image, that thought – a woman sucking her off, a woman! – that made her come as fiercely, as hard as she'd ever come in her life. Every nerve exploded. She felt her eyes roll back in her head, her world go black, deep, deep, space black, and a sudden rush of wetness, like a river, gush out of her.

Stephanie waited for the explosion to subside. Then she kissed Jacqui's labia just once as though kissing a mouth, a paternal, gentle, comforting kiss. She was about to pull away when she heard the voice.

'What the hell do you think you're doing with my wife?'

Terry Clarke stood in the middle of the bedroom in a white towelling robe over his bathing trunks with a white towel wrapped around his neck like a boxer. His expression of surprise, disbelief and disgust was written on his face as if in ten-foot letters of flashing neon.

Stephanie hadn't the slightest idea of what to say. She kicked herself mentally for not locking the bedroom door. This was going to be a great start to their supposedly dream weekend. Far from being enamoured of Devlin and what he could offer, Terry Clarke would never want to hear his name again.

'Fuck me, Terry.' It was Jacqui's voice, calm, level and unwavering.

'What!' he exploded.

'You heard. Fuck me. I need your cock. Look at me for Christ's sake. Look at me. Can't you see how much I need it?'

'She's just . . .' he stuttered, his mind telling him one thing while his body reacted differently. The sight of two beautiful women, naked, lying in a pool of sexual passion was too much for his body to ignore. The towelling robe had fallen open. Stephanie could see his erection bulging from the tight material of his trunks. But he still hesitated.

'You've just been fucked.' He was trying to sound angry, to renew his shock. But the moment had passed. His body was demanding other priorities.

'Terry . . . please,' his wife begged. 'Fuck me.'

His eyes were riveted on his wife's cunt. It glistened with juices, her own and Stephanie's. He had never seen her look so wild, so wanton, so open. Her eyes were sparkling with excitement, her mouth slack with passion.

And there was the other woman. Naked too. Naked and available. Her thickly matted cunt in such contrast to his wife's.

His body won the internal argument. In a frenzy of movement, he tore off his robe and pulled his trunks down. Belying his appearance in clothes, Terry's body was hard and muscular. His stoutness was the result of muscle not fat, his nascent paunch less noticeable.

Ignoring Stephanie for the moment, he knelt between his wife's legs and thrust his fingers into her soaking wet cunt. They went right up to the knuckle. Jacqui moaned.

'You bitch,' he said. Stephanie wasn't sure if he meant her. She made to get up off the bed.

'No,' Jacqui said immediately. 'Stay, stay please. I want her to watch, Terry. I want her to watch you fucking me.'

That was the end of his control. He could no longer think of rights and wrongs, of shoulds and should nots, of blame or anger; he could only think of lust, passion, sex. He threw himself down on to his wife's supine body. His cock slid into her instantly, her cunt so wet it created no friction. At once he started to ram it home. There was no subtlety, no finesse. There was nothing but his remorseless need. He would show her what a man could do. No woman could give her this, he repeated in his head. This, this, this, he told himself ramming forward harder and deeper each time.

Jacqui was crying out, gasping, moaning, fighting to get her breath. His first assault had made her come, and she was coming again and again, clinging to her husband's muscular body as her orgasms broke over the head of his cock. She could feel him so deep he was at the neck of her womb. She wrapped her legs around his back.

'Oh Terry, Terry . . .' She managed to open her eyes and saw Stephanie watching, saw lust in her face too.

'You bitch!' he screamed driving into her as though the

39

strokes of his cock should be a punishment instead of the ultimate pleasure.

Unconsciously Stephanie began to finger her own clitoris.

'Terry, Terry . . .' Jacqui had come enough. 'Save some for her. Don't you want to fuck her. I want to see it.'

'What?' he said not believing what he'd heard.

'Fuck her, Terry. I want to see you fuck her.'

He stopped his rhythm entirely and looked down at his wife's face as though he were looking into the face of a stranger.

'Have you gone mad?'

'Yes, yes. For God's sake Terry just do it for me.'

He looked over at Stephanie. His eyes went from her face down to her tits and over her navel until they rested on the fingers that had teased out her clitoris from the forest of pubic hair. He pulled his cock from Jacqui's cunt. It looked as angry as his face, red and glistening wet, his foreskin pulled right back, the little slit of his urethera leaking a tear of his own fluid. Once again lust won over anger. It was as though he had been plunged into a dream when he'd walked through that bedroom door after he'd listened in the corridor to the moans of pleasure. Plunged into a long wet dream of cunts and tits and unbridled lust.

Stephanie looked into his eyes. He stared back at her. She would see his confusion but most of all she saw the flames of desire.

'Are you going to fuck me? I need a cock as much as your wife did.'

Still on her knees, she turned away from him, pointed her tight sharp arse at him, then leaned forward supporting herself on her hands on all fours, her back straight, her hairy sex opening as she eased her knees apart. Swivelling her head over her shoulder, she looked back at him.

'Fuck me,' she said unnecessarily.

'Do it,' his wife urged.

That was too much for him. If he had any control it was gone now. He pulled away from his wife and sat up on his knees.

'I want to see it,' Jacqui said.

He needed no further encouragement. He twisted round on his knees and nudged his cock, already wet from his wife, into Stephanie's arse. It found the target immediately, plunging into Stephanie's sex so rapidly, it took her breath away. His cock felt like his body, hard and muscular and strong. She pushed her buttocks back at him as he pumped into her, matching his strokes with her own, feeling his navel on her arse.

'You bitch,' he said. Stephanie knew he meant her this time. Not that she cared. She didn't care about anything now. She was coming, the heat and urgency of his cock too extreme for her body to ignore. He reached forward and around her thigh until his hand covered the delta of black pubic hair and his finger found the wetness of her labia. With no gentleness at all he probed until his fingertip was on her clitoris. Then he began to wank it, hard and fast, like he was strumming the string of a guitar. Stephanie groaned but not with pain. He was making her come, everything he did was making her come.

Jacqui was not going to be passive. Squirming round on the ruffled sheets she positioned herself so that her head was between her husband's calves. Then she worked herself back until her face was up under his arse, until she could see, inches from her face, his balls banging against Stephanie's bottom as his cock pistoned forward. His balls were big, hairy and sensitive. She knew better than to kiss them yet. Instead she levered her head up off the bed to get her mouth on Stephanie's clitoris, sucking and licking her husband's fingers.

It was this double action that took Stephanie over the edge. The feeling of Jacqui's hot mouth and tongue working through to her clitoris while it was still being wanked – somewhere deep in her mind did she register the thrill that this was the first time Jacqui had ever done this – sucking and nibbling while Terry's fingers sawed away at it too, and his cock reamed into her cunt.

Stephanie screamed as she came. There was so much sensation, so much nerve-shattering feeling that she could not tell whether her orgasm broke over cock, or finger or mouth. It was as though she came in all three places at once, her whole body shuddering until she could feel nothing but black ecstasy.

Jacqui felt her come. Immediately she turned her attention to her husband. It was his turn now. She moved her head down to Terry's balls. At first she just licked them with her tongue, gently, carefully. He reached instantly with a moan but did not stop his rhythm. Slowly the licking turned to sucking. She closed her lips around one drawing it into her mouth. He moaned louder. At home it had been his favourite thing – to wank while she sucked on his balls. He'd knelt above her face. She'd suck at his balls and he'd wank until his hot sperm splattered over her magnificent breasts. They hadn't done that for years.

Now it was the same thing except he wasn't wanking, he was fucking, fucking another woman. He knew he couldn't hold back any longer. Only his anger had allowed him to go on for so long. Now he had to come. His wife, beneath him, was reeling his other ball into her mouth. When she had them both, she sucked gently like she used to do. It was enough. He looked down at the trembling woman in front of her, her long back, and sharp rounded arse and pushed one last time into her wet tight cunt. He buried his cock deep in the hot tunnel of Stephanie's sex and waited for the spasm that would jet spunk out into the dark cavern he had found. He felt his wife's tongue playing with his balls. It felt like her tongue was inside his cock, right inside it. His mind was full of images. But most of all he saw his wife's face lying on the bed when he'd come into the room as the black-haired temptress sucked at her cunt. He saw the look in her eyes as she told him to fuck her. He had never seen her so turned on. He had never felt her cunt so hot.

His cock spasmed. In his mind he saw his white hot spunk erupting into the slippery walls of Stephanie's grateful cunt. The spasms went on forever. He thought they were never going to stop. So much spunk.

No one wanted to move. They disentangled themselves

slowly. Stephanie rolled on to her side, Terry on to his back and alongside his wife.

'My God . . .' he said finally.

'Don't be cross,' Jacqui said.

'How could I be cross now?'

'It was good, wasn't it?'

'What have we been missing.'

'Do you want me to go?' Stephanie asked.

'Of course not,' Jacqui said, touching Stephanie's arm affectionately.

'I didn't know you were into women,' Terry said.

'Neither did I.'

'We were experimenting,' Stephanie tried to explain. 'We were lying out in the sun and it just happened. Your wife is a very beautiful woman. And very sensual . . .'

'You're a lesbian?' Terry asked directly.

Stephanie laughed.

'If I were do you imagine I'd have let you fuck me? Do you think I'd have come like that?'

'No. No I suppose not.'

'Sex isn't a matter of labels. It's what feels good.'

'It felt wonderful,' Jacqui said, then turned to her husband. 'But it made me want cock. I don't think I've ever wanted cock more in my entire life. God I was hot, wasn't I?'

'Yes.'

'Are we going to get our sex life back, Terry?' Jacqui said, quietly pressing herself into her husband's body, one of her large breasts resting against his chest, its nipple still erect.

'I hope so,' he said kissing her on the cheek.

Terry got up off the bed. 'I need a drink,' he announced looking round the room.

'There's a bar set in the panelling over there. Next to the fridge.' Stephanie said pointing to the silk panelled door that concealed all the accoutrements of a bar.

Terry poured himself a brandy and soda. Knowing his wife's taste, he made her a gin and tonic. He got ice from the fridge.

'Do you want anything?' he asked Stephanie.

Stephanie shook her head. Terry handed his wife her drink. She sipped it eagerly.

'Well,' Jacqui asked, 'what other surprises have you got in store for us?'

'Other surprises?' Terry echoed.

'Stephanie says there are all sorts of things in the castle we might want to get into.'

'What sort of things?'

'After dinner.' Stephanie said firmly.

'I can't wait,' Terry said.

'And is this all part of Devlin's weekend?' Jacqui asked.

'Only if you want it to be,' Stephanie replied.

'I think we do, don't we darling?' Jacqui turned to her husband who had sat himself on the edge of the bed.

'If you want a sensible answer you'll have to ask me again in a while. When I've come down. I'm still floating.' He let himself lie back on the bed, his glass balancing precariously in his hand.

'So what am I going to wear for dinner?' Jacqui asked. 'That's what I came in here to find out.'

'Oh yes, I forgot.' Stephanie smiled. So much had happened since Jacqui had knocked on her bedroom door. 'You can wear anything you like, as dressy as you like.'

'Great. I feel like getting dressed up to the nines.' Jacqui got up from the bed. Her heavy tits bounced firmly. Then she had another thought. 'Can you lend me a pair of stockings and something to hold them up with?'

She saw the look of surprise on her husband's face.

'Black preferably,' Jacqui said looking into her husband's eyes. 'And very sheer . . .'

She saw her husband's cock stir.

'I think we're going to go to our room now and have a little lie down before dinner. Don't you, darling?'

'What a good idea,' Terry said reaching for a towel to cover his growing enthusiasm.

THREE

The powerboat nosed its way into the jetty for the second
time that afternoon. As it approached Stephanie could see
Mrs Agnes Bloom sitting in the transom on the striped
canvas padding that formed a long bench seat. She was not
smiling. A broad-brimmed straw hat and a pair of elabo-
rately decorated sunglasses covered most of her face.

The servant, who waited on the jetty with Stephanie, tied
the boat's forward line to the clets in the dock while the
boatman secured the aft line.

'Welcome,' Stephanie said holding out her hand to help
Mrs Bloom ashore. 'I hope you had a good journey.'

'No, I didn't as a matter of fact,' Mrs Bloom said, taking
Stephanie's hand to steady herself as she stepped from the
bobbing deck of the boat. Her hands were both bejewelled
with rings, every finger ringed, some with two or three
rings. The fingers were long, thin, bony. 'The Italians,
everything is *domani, domani*. I don't know why I bother to
set foot outside the States. Europe is so damn inefficient.'

Mrs Bloom set off up the stone steps. She knew the way.
She had been to the castle many times before. Stephanie
followed in her wake as the powerboat was quickly
unloaded and untied, to return to the mainland for another
cargo.

Inside the castle Mrs Bloom walked determinedly into
the main salon, very much as if the castle was a hotel.

'I need a drink,' she said.

Stephanie summoned a waiter.

'Dry martini,' Mrs Bloom instructed as though speaking
to a small child. 'Very dry. *Secco. Comprehende?*'

'*Sì, signora,*' he said and scuttled off.

Mrs Bloom took a pack of Lucky Strikes from her Hermes handbag and lit one with a Cartier gold cigarette lighter. She inhaled the smoke deeply, then blew it out in an unwavering straight line.

'You're new,' she said sitting on one of the large sofas and crossing her legs. She was wearing a white suit, the jacket heavily decorated with two rows of bright gold buttons bearing some sort of Roman insignia. Her legs, in common with the rest of her body, was overthin and over tanned. Too many years of strict diet and concentrated sunbathing had left her bony and hard with a skin as dark as a tanned hide of leather. Her hair was blonde, a whitey blonde, brittle and coarse, the bleach bottle taking its toll on the natural sheen of the hair.

She dumped her hat and sunglasses on the sofa beside her. She had light green eyes. Her face was attractive, symmetrical and well-proportioned; only her nose was slightly too big for the rest of her features.

'I've been here for awhile now,' Stephanie said, sitting in a chair opposite.

'So what? You're the brothel keeper now? What happened to Bruno? He been pensioned off?'

'He's still here.'

'Well you sure look good. If I were into women I'd want to fuck you myself.'

'I take that as a compliment,' Stephanie said finding it hard to like Mrs Bloom.

'But I'm strictly into cock.'

The waiter came back with a silver tray on which was perched a triangular martini glass, frosted with condensation. He set the glass down on the table in front of the American. She sipped it tentatively.

'Well at least you can mix a decent martini, Gino,' she said. 'Now go and be a good boy and get me another, *pronto.*'

Bowing slightly to indicate he understood, the waiter went to get her second drink. By the time he'd gone the first had all but disappeared.

'So what? You're one of Devlin's pack of thieves are you? On the take and got caught?'

'No,' Stephanie said calmly, her dislike for the woman growing by the minute.

'No, I thought . . .'

'I'm a free agent, Mrs Bloom,' Stephanie said sharply.

'Okay, okay. Don't get antsy with me. I'm only asking. I like to know where I am, is all. So what time's dinner?'

'Eight. We have two other guests. Mr and Mrs Clarke.'

'Well I'm sure you've got enough to go round. I want two of the best sent up to my room right after dinner. Right?'

'Anything you want,' Stephanie replied.

'And make sure they're real athletic. They're going to need to be.'

The waiter returned with the second martini and removed the empty glass.

'So what's the story?' Mrs Bloom continued.

'What story?'

'With you? You've got your hooks into Devlin have you? I don't blame him, you're a real piece of work.'

Stephanie didn't reply. Mrs Bloom downed the second martini.

'So what. Keep it to yourself. I should care. I'm not here for the conversation. You can show me to my room now. I'm done here.'

She stubbed the cigarette out in the large glass ashtray on the coffee table and stood up. She brushed cigarette ash off her suit.

Stephanie led the way up the sweeping marble staircase and down the corridor to the room that had been prepared for Mrs Bloom. Fortunately it was on the other side of the castle from herself and the Clarkes. She wanted to have as little to do with Agnes Bloom as possible.

By the time she got back to her room Stephanie could hear the powerboat approaching across the lake again. Mrs Bloom had not been the only passenger aboard Devlin's Learjet flown in from London that afternoon.

Stephanie had worn a tracksuit to greet Mrs Bloom.

47

Stripping it off, she went to the wall of wardrobes to find an outfit a little bit more suitable for her next visitors. It did not take her long to find what she was looking for. She had bought it in Rome at the special shop she had found. The jodhpurs were made from leather, with a blouson type leather blouse worn on top. The blouse had long puffed sleeves and a high collar.

Stephanie sat on the bed and pulled the jodhpurs up over her legs. They were a tight fit. She buttoned up the leather blouse and found a pair of short high-heeled boots which she zipped on to her feet. Gloves were essential too. She found a pair that matched the dark brown of the rest of her clothes.

She looked at herself in the mirror. A picture of authority she thought smiling back at her own reflection. Her black hair streamed over her shoulders. She brushed it quickly and tied it loosely at the back.

For some reason, when the castle had been built a staircase had been constructed that led directly from this room down into the cellars. What purpose this served the original fourteenth-century proprietors Stephanie could only guess at – perhaps they had gone to watch enemies and religious heretics tortured as a prelude to a night of sexual excess – but whatever the reason Devlin had had the staircase restored and, on occasions like this, it was ideal. Remembering the first time she had opened the small door hidden in the silk panelling of the room, on the first night she had spent with Devlin in the castle, she picked her way down the circular steps, holding on to the rope that formed a handrail, and going slowly in the high-heeled boots.

At the bottom of the staircase she unbolted a small wooden door that had been newly built into the corridor of the main block of cells. The cells lined the brick-vaulted cellar, identical individual cubicles with thick wooden doors and circular viewing ports that could be opened by drawing back a rotating steel plate. As yet the cells were empty; the slaves had not returned from their duties in the gardens.

Stephanie walked to the end of the row of cells and

through a door into an entirely different arrangement. Here there were a suite of rooms, two large bedrooms with adjoining bathrooms as luxuriously appointed as any of the rooms upstairs – a full bar, a video system, a large double bed – and a third room altogether less comfortable. This room was more like the cells, its walls the stone of the original castle, its floor stone too. Here, in what was called the bondage room, there was every conceivable piece of sexual equipment to satisfy every conceivable sexual taste. There were punishment frames, pulleys, sets of rings secured to the wall, even an iron cage suspended in midair in one corner of the room. There were wardrobes of clothes too: rubber, leather, women's underwear and women's clothes in sizes that would fit men as well as women. There was a rack of wigs, a shelf of high heels again in sizes that would fit men and women. Hanging from hooks on one wall was every type of instrument of flagellation from a coiled bull-whip to a leather tawse, wooden paddles, crops, tiny whips with multiple thongs, whippy schoolmaster's canes and even whips made from rubber.

Whatever the guest's requirements, whatever fantasy he wanted to create, he was unlikely to be disappointed in the bondage room.

It was here that Stephanie found Bruno and the rest of the Learjet 'cargo' – two new slaves, a man and a woman. As she approached Bruno, mute since birth, and still harbouring a resentment over Stephanie's new position in the castle, superceding him in charge of the cellars, grunted but did not stop what he was doing.

In London the slaves had been packed into padded wooden crates after being tightly bound inside canvas 'body' bags. The crates, marked agricultural equipment, were then loaded aboard the jet. None of the slaves ever knew where they were being taken, nor, when they got to the castle, where it was. Transported as they were, they had not the slightest clue.

Bruno had humped the body bags out of the crates and they now lay side by side on one of the punishment frames, bed-like structures made of slatted wood. Unzipping the length of the bag, he pulled each slave out in turn, the man first and then the woman. They were still unable to move, their bodies bound by thick straps made of nylon webbing, their mouths gagged with tape. Bruno unbuckled each strap in turn starting with the woman. He worked up from the ankle, ripping off the tape from her mouth last. He repeated the process with the man.

In the canvas bags there had been no need for blindfolds. Now as their eyes blinked to get accustomed to light again Stephanie saw them trying to work out where they were. It was several minutes, after the long period of enforced darkness, before they could properly see their new surroundings.

Bruno ripped the tape off the man's mouth.

'You may go now, Bruno,' Stephanie said.

He grunted again but obeyed immediately, the keys on his thick leather belt which he wore over a black tunic like a medieval executioner, jangled as he shuffled out.

Stephanie turned her attention to the new arrivals and they sat massaging the circulation back into their atrophied limbs.

'Not a pleasant way to travel, is it?' she said. 'Stand up when you can.'

The man tottered to his feet.

'What's your name? Christian name only. That's all we use here.'

'Andrew,' he said hoarsely not having used his voice for several hours.

Stephanie went over to a small metal chest on a shelf by the door. Inside was a selection of metal discs all enscribed with various names. She found 'Andrew' and clipped it to a thin metal chain.

'Put this round you neck. It's to be worn at all times. Is that understood.'

He nodded as he hung the chain around his neck.

'And you?' Stephanie said to the woman.

'Grace,' she said timidly. Stephanie found the corresponding disc, clipped it to a chain and handed it to the woman who immediately put it around her neck.

50

'Now take off your clothes and put them in the boxes over there.'

Bruno had prepared two cupboard boxes. Grace and Andrew stripped off their clothes and packed them away in the boxes.

'Not bad,' Andrew said looking at Grace's naked body.

'Shut up,' Stephanie snapped.

Andrew was not tall and though he was not fat, his skin was swallow and his muscle tone nonexistent. As feeling had flooded back into his aching body so had a definite cockiness. Andrew, Stephanie could see, regarded himself as a jack-the-lad, the cock of his particular walk.

Grace, on the other hand, could not have been more pliant. She packed her clothes away neatly, item by item, skirt, blouse, a cream bra and matching knickers. Her body was distinctly plump, not fat in any particular place but covered in a thin layer of fat all over. Though she was short her body was well proportioned. Her breasts were firm, her legs shapely. Her nudity clearly embarrassed her.

Stephanie slid the lid on the boxes.

'You'll get these back at the end of your stay.'

'So what happens now?' Andrew said jauntily. 'Do we get whipped before or after dinner. Or is there some randy bird wants to use me first?'

'Speak when you're spoken to,' Stephanie said.

'Sorry darling, you're the boss.' Stephanie could see his cock was starting to become erect as his eyes darted between Grace's nakedness and her own leather-clad body.

'You both know why you're here.'

'Yes,' Grace said quickly not looking at Stephanie directly.

'We have only one rule. Obey everything you are told to do immediately. That is all. If you do that you won't have any problems.'

'And if we don't?' Andrew said his eyes focused on the tight leather that covered the junction of her thighs.

'Then you are given a simple choice. We can send you straight home to face the criminal charges that you would have faced in the first place . . .'

51

'Or?' Andrew prompted.

'You can ask to be punished.'

'Ask to be?'

'Put this on.' Stephanie picked up the hard leather covered metal pouch worn by all the male slaves. Bruno had laid it out next to the boxes. He was very efficient, she thought. Never forgot a thing.

'I'd rather not,' Andrew said.

'I told you to obey immediately.'

'Looks like a boxer's jockstrap,' Andrew said taking it from her hand. For a second Stephanie could see he was deciding what he was going to do. Then he stepped into the chains and pulled the pouch over his now semi-erect penis. Stephanie cinched the chains tight and padlocked them in place with the small lock that fitted the links where the chain rising between his buttocks was attached to the one around his waist.

'This isn't very comfy,' he said trying to work the chains out from the crease of his thigh.

'So what is your choice, Andrew?'

'Can't you loosen this a bit?'

'I asked you a question, Andrew.'

'What choice?'

'Do you want to be sent straight back home or be punished?'

'Punished for what?'

'I told you to speak only when you are spoken to.'

'Oh come on.'

'I don't think you've understood properly, Andrew. I think I should send you straight back, don't you? You're not suitable. How long do you think you'll get? I haven't seen the file. How many years?'

For the first time she saw the cockiness go out of his eyes.

'Bruno . . .' Stephanie called. He had been waiting outside. He lumbered back into the room, his keys ever jangling. 'This gentleman has decided he doesn't want to stay.'

'No,' Andrew said quickly.

'No.'

'No. I don't want to go back.'

'What then?'

'I'll stay.'

'What then?' Stephanie said firmly again.

Andrew looked her in the eyes but this time there was no defiance and meekly he looked down to the stone floor.

'Punishment,' he mumbled.

'What did you say?'

'Punishment,' he repeated louder. He wanted to call her a bitch and tell her what she could do with this lousy place but he dared not. He did not want to be sent back. At all costs he didn't want that.

'Please, say "please madam".'

'Please, madam,' he repeated.

'Bruno take Andrew away and give him what he's asked for.'

Bruno stepped forward and pulled Andrew by the arm. He did not look at Stephanie but as he got to the cell door he could not help himself from reasserting his independence.

'It's been fun,' he said under his breath.

'What did you say?' Stephanie snapped.

'Nothing.'

'I think your attitude will have changed the next time I see you, Andrew. I hope so for your sake or your time here is going to be very unpleasant.'

Stephanie signalled for Bruno to continue and turned to Grace as Andrew was led out of the room.

'I hope you're not going to give me any trouble, Grace,' she said.

'No, no madam.'

'Good.'

'May I ask you something, madam?'

'Yes what?'

'I'm not very . . . I mean . . . I have . . . I'm not very sexually experienced.' She was looking around at the equipment in the room. 'It's expected, isn't it?'

'What did you do, Grace?'

'I was embezzling, madam. Not a lot. Well I supposed it was a lot over the years. It mounts up.'

'And you chose to come here?'

'I'd certainly have gone to jail. It wasn't my first offence. I couldn't have stood that. It's only I know we've got to be available, sexually I mean. It's just that I've never had much sex and I don't think I'm very good at it.'

Grace looked as though she were about to burst into tears. In the high-heeled boots Stephanie towered over her. Grace was not more than five feet tall. She was pretty Stephanie thought. Despite her subcutaneous fat her breasts were not large, they were wide and wedge-shaped. But her apple-shaped bottom and rounded navel were appealing.

'Some men like that, Grace,' Stephanie assured her. Grace was definitely not going to be a troublemaker.

'Do they?'

'Have you ever been with a woman?'

'No.'

'You may have to.'

'I don't think I'd mind that.' The tone of Grace's voice had become suddenly more up-beat.

'Have you thought about it then?'

'Yes . . . I think I'd like it.'

'Just do as you're told and you'll be fine.'

'Thank you.'

Grace cast her eyes to the floor and stood waiting for what was, in effect, her sentence to begin. As the leather-clad woman strode from the room she felt a sensation of foreboding but at the same time, if she were honest with herself, it was mixed with a strong measure of excitement too.

The thick glass-topped dining table had been set for four people. It could have seated thirty. As usual the table was bedecked with flowers, a massive arrangement in its centre and a small sprig of orchids on the napkin of each place setting. Georg Jensen silver, Czechoslovakian handmade glasses and fine white German crockery completed the picture.

Stephanie had changed into a short black strapless dress,

a satin silk with a subtle sheen. It was too short for a suspender belt so she wore hold-ups with lacy tops that matched the black lace of her panties and strapless bra. She had pinned her hair up so her long neck emphasised the bareness of her shoulders and her breasts, arched up by the bra and pushed into a deep cleavage.

The Clarkes were the first to join her. Jacqui, too, was wearing a strapless dress, but in red. It clung to the slim curves of her body to spectacular effect. Like Stephanie she had pinned her long hair up so her shoulders were bare. Her cleavage, the dark channel formed by her two heavy breasts pushed together by the material of the dress and its carefully engineered underpinning, looked so deep and dark a man could drown in it. The dress fitted tightly until it reached the top of her thighs, then flared out into a mass of pleats. As it was full length it gave no hint of what Stephanie knew she was wearing underneath.

Terry looked dapper in an evening suit and black bow tie. What little hair he had was neatly brushed. He held his wife's hand as they walked in.

The waiter poured champagne into the crystal flutes and they all clinked glasses. There was a definite conspiratorial air. As the two women stood together in red and black, a blonde and a brunette, Stephanie could read the look in Terry's eyes as he glanced from one to the other. He was remembering the afternoon, remembering how the two women had looked naked, as he'd fucked them both in turn. He was wondering, no doubt, if he would get another opportunity. Before he could even hint at such subjects Mrs Bloom marched in.

'Hi, there,' she said. She came up to the fireplace where a big log fire had been lit and warmed her hands. Even in the summer the thick walls of the castle let little heat into the main building.

Stephanie made the introductions. Mrs Bloom was wearing a green velvet suit with a white blouse under the jacket, and curiously, a black bra which was clearly outlined under the silk. A heavy gold chain hung down between her small breasts, a gold brooch glittered on her jacket and she wore gold bracelets on both her wrists. She had taken none of the rings off her fingers. She even wore a little gold chain on both ankles under the tanned nylon of her stockings, and her shoes were embossed with gold medallions.

Stephanie offered her a glass of champagne.

'Jesus, no,' she said, 'It gives me gas. I need a martini. Where's the guy who made my martini?'

A servant was despatched to get the necessary drink.

'You from England?' she said to the Clarkes.

They chatted about nothing in particular while Mrs Bloom consumed three large martinis in quick succession one after another, the waiter being told to fetch another immediately he had delivered the first.

The dinner was made up of local specialities, fish caught from the lake that afternoon, Umbrian lamb with rosemary, a local goat's cheese made no more than ten miles away on the mainland, a homegrown salad, and a dessert of raspberries soaked in sponge and sweet wine. There was Frascati with the fish and Barolo with the meat. A delicate vino Santo was served with *biscotto*. Stephanie had taken to the local custom of dunking the biscuits in the wine.

Mrs Bloom drunk no wine. She stayed on martinis throughout the meal, eating the twist of lemon that came with each one by nibbling it between her front teeth. Apart from the lemon peel she ate little, pushing each course away after no more than a mouthful and calling for another martini. The more alcohol she consumed the louder she got.

'See,' she told everyone over the dessert, 'sex is like food. You ought to taste everything so you know what you really like best. I mean if you've never eaten chocolate how do you know whether you're going to love it or hate it? I mean sex isn't just straight up and down, is it? I mean that's what the animals do 'cause they don't know any better. Jesus that's so boring.'

'You must draw the line somewhere though,' Terry said.

'Oh sure. Listen I don't want some guy peeing over me to get his rocks off. I can do without that.'

'What?' Jacqui sounded astonished.

'You hadn't heard that one honey? Oh it's common enough. Works the other way too. I mean women want to pee on men and men want to be peed on. If that's what turns you on.'

'People really do that?'

'It's not my bag. But anything else. Oh except animals. I draw the line at animals, definitely. You've never had animals in the cellars, have you?'

'No,' Stephanie said. She had been hoping Mrs Bloom wouldn't mention the cellars. It was a subject she wanted to bring up with the Clarkes herself.

'Everything else though. I mean some of the guys down there. Wow . . . I suppose they get a lot of practice is all. But I tell you these guys know how to give a girl a good time. A real good time. You'll have a ball, honey, take it from me. And I'm a veteran.' She patted Jacqui's hand as it lay on the table. 'Can't speak for the women,' she said turning to Terry. 'I've never been into women. Oh like I said I tried it once. Sure. I came here one weekend and got two of those slaves girls to do everything a woman could do to another woman, I mean licking and sucking and diddling in every orifice. Well it was okay. I mean I wasn't lying there thinking I'd left the cooker on or nothing. But I didn't get no real fireworks. Not like with a cock.'

'Slave girls . . .' Jacqui sounded bemused.

'Perhaps you'd like some coffee,' Stephanie said trying to change the subject at least for a moment.

'I'd love some. Do you have expresso?' Terry asked.

'In Italy it's obligatory.'

'Of course.'

But Mrs Bloom was in full flood and not to be put off. 'I even tried both together. A man and a woman. There's a lot of combinations, believe me. Need to be a geometry teacher. You can have anything you want. That's what I mean. I tried everything. But I can tell you for me it's men. I know what I want. I know exactly what I want. Talking of which I hope you've got two live specimens for me.' She was looking at Stephanie.

'Everything's taken care of, Mrs Bloom,' Stephanie said.

'Two real athletes that's what I need tonight 'cause I'm as horny as a rattlesnake and twice as mean. Matter of fact,' she said grabbing Terry under the table by the knee, 'I nearly made a play for your husband over the main course. You wouldn't have minded would you, honey, long as we did it out in the open so you could get an eyeful. This is one big table. We could have done it at the other end. Hell with a glass top like this you could have all watched from underneath.'

Agnes Bloom laughed loudly and finished another martini. Their was an expression of disbelief on both the Clarkes' faces.

'Don't worry big man,' she said getting to her feet, not before tweaking Terry's knee one last time, 'I've got enough to satisfy me upstairs. They've never let me down yet. That's why I keep coming back.'

She marched to the door remarkably steadily considering the amount she had drunk. At the door she paused.

'Don't forget the cameras will you, sweetie?' she said to Stephanie.

'It's all arranged,' Stephanie replied. Devlin had left her instructions. Mrs Bloom always returned to America with a full video tape recording of all her activities, no doubt to be played and replayed until her next visit.

'I'll say goodnight then. Have a good time. Fill your boots. There's plenty for everyone. And if you want to look in be my guest. I'm not shy.'

'Look in?' Terry said.

'Sure, I like an audience. Why not?' She winked one heavily mascaraed eye.

With that Mrs Bloom walked out of the dining room, closing the door behind her.

Terry took a large swig of his wine.

'What is all this? Slaves, cellars, cameras . . .'

'I told you there were other . . . experiences. I'd hoped to explain it to you a little bit more subtly.' Stephanie said.

'Go on,' Terry prompted.

58

Stephanie sipped the small glass of vino Santo. 'Well . . .' She told them everything. She told them about the cellars, about the slaves and the way they were recruited, even about her own introduction to the castle. After their initial surprise Stephanie thought she sensed not shock but a frisson of excitement.

'And cameras?'

'Oh apparently Mrs Bloom likes a video of her activities. Her bedroom's wired with cameras.'

'That's what she meant by looking in,' Jacqui said.

'There's a monitor in the cellars, yes.'

'That I'd like to see,' Terry added.

'I didn't know you were a voyeur, darling,' his wife said playfully.

'I didn't know I'd be turned on by seeing you in the arms of another woman until this afternoon, but I was.'

'I didn't know I'd like to be there . . .'

'Exactly. So what happens now?' Terry asked.

'If you like I could show you around. If you're sure that's what you want.'

Terry turned to his wife. Stephanie could see the excitement in his eyes. Fortunately for him – and for their marriage – it was matched by the look in Jacqui's eyes. What had happened in the afternoon had broken the ice: now they were keen to jump into the water.

'Jacqui?' Terry said.

'Like Mrs Bloom said we should try everything at least once, shouldn't we?'

'Exactly.'

'In the cellars we can cater for every possible sexual fantasy. That's what Mrs Bloom meant. Anything you've every wanted, or imagined. We can make it come true.'

'What sort of fantasy?' Terry asked.

'You'll see for yourself. A brandy first?' Stephanie suggested.

Neither of them wanted anything else to drink.

FOUR

Stephanie pulled aside the corner of the vast modern tapestry that covered the stone wall beside the marble staircase in the vestibule of the castle, to reveal a solid wooden door.

'Very mysterious,' Jacqui commented. She felt a peculiar mixture of trepidation and excitement; if she were honest with herself there was a strong element of real sexual arousel too.

'Be careful,' Stephanie warned leading the way down the stone steps, the women's high heels echoing through the vaulted cellars.

At the bottom of the stairs she lead them across the stone floor, passed the wine racks and discarded detritus of the years, to the door of the slave's quarters.

Terry looked at his wife in the dim light. 'Are you excited?' he asked squeezing her hand.

'I don't know what I feel,' she said honestly.

The heavy wooden door swung open in response to Stephanie's knock. Bruno stood aside to let them in. Terry and Jacqui eyed his bizarre costume.

'This is Bruno, keeper of the keys. He's a mute, I'm afraid. And effectively a eunuch.'

'A eunuch,' Jacqui's voice sounded momentarily alarmed.

'Oh not deliberate.' Stephanie laughed. 'He had an unfortunate accident.'

'What a relief,' Jacqui said laughing too.

Stephanie had made some changes in the cellars since she had taken over responsibility. Previously all the slaves had been kept – once returned from the garden, showered and fed – in their individual cells where they were restricted by a chain attached to their ankle and locked to the floor. A guest would go from cell to cell to make his or her choice. But Stephanie had decided it would be better if all the slaves were seen together, whenever there were guests, and only returned to their own cells after the choice had been made. In this way guests could make comparisons more easily.

It was not a change the male slaves had welcomed. Chained into their metal pouches surrounded by naked and often attractive females made their lives distinctly more uncomfortable.

At the far end of the corridor containing the cell cubicles a large area had been cleared. The slaves were now all chained here, not, as before, by the ankle, but by a short chain from a thick leather collar around their necks. This, in turn, was attached to a metal ring set into the stone wall. The chains were not long enough for any of the slaves to be able to touch each other.

Stephanie lead the way along the corridor. Bruno brought up the rear.

'These are the individuals cells,' she said indicating the doors along the corridor. 'And these,' she said as they got to the end of the passage, 'are the slaves.'

There were ten slaves in the stiff leather collars standing tethered to the wall, six women and four men. Two of the collars hung empty, their occupants already sent up to Mrs Bloom.

'My God,' Terry whispered. Though he had been told what to expect upstairs in the dining room the reality took him completely by surprise. His wife had the same reaction. They stood mouths open hardly believing what they saw. But as their eyes roamed the naked, in the case of the women, and near naked, in the case of the men, bodies their astonishment was superceded by a stronger reaction.

They were still holding hands. Jacqui squeezed her husband's hand strongly. She could feel his surge of lust like the tingling of electricity. It perfectly matched her own.

Whereas Grace was chained to the wall with the other

slaves, Andrew, the other newcomer, was spread-eagled against the opposite stone wall, his wrists and ankles strapped into leather cuffs, which, in turn, were chained to metal rings in the stone work. The chains were short and his stomach was pressed against the rough stone, his face turned to one side. He was gagged by a hard ball of leather held in place by a black leather strap.

It took little imagination to guess that he had been whipped. Bright red welts crisscrossed his firm but very white buttocks.

'What's he done?' Jacqui asked, her voice betraying her excitement, suddenly pitched high and reedy.

'Andrew thought that this was the easy option,' Stephanie explained. 'I told you they were all thieves. This isn't meant to be a holiday.'

Jacqui walked over to Andrew her silk dress russling as she moved, her high heels clacking on the stone flags of the floor.

'Can I touch?'

'You can do anything you want,' Stephanie assured her.

Jacqui extended her hand tentatively at first. When it was still inches from Andrew's arse she felt the heat it was radiating like an electric fire.

'It's so hot,' she said. She touched his buttock, rubbing it with her hand. She looked into his eyes. Her touch felt cool on his tortured flesh. He pleaded with his eyes for her to caress all of it, soothe it. 'So hot,' she said almost to herself.

Moving forward again, she pressed the silk of the dress against the tortured flesh. The silk was so cool he could not suppress a moan of pleasure behind the gag. 'More please,' he tried to say with his eyes. But that was not what Jacqui had in mind. Instead she stepped away and raised her hand to slap it down firmly on his buttock. He winced through the gag.

'Do you mind?' she asked Stephanie.

'I told you . . .'

But before Stephanie could finish Jacqui's hand had delivered another blow, harder this time, her palm tingling from the impact. The thwack of flesh on flesh echoed through the vaulted cellar.

Terry came up behind his wife. His erection, already growing at the spectacle of the slaves, hardened by the sight of his wife, her eyes wild with excitement, slapping the helpless man. He pressed himself into her back and ran his hands up to squeeze both her large breasts under the strapless dress.

'You're very excited, aren't you?' he whispered into her ear.

'Oh yes, yes,' she replied turning her head so she could kiss him on the mouth and pressing herself back on to him at the same time, feeling his hardness between her buttocks.

'Could we take him somewhere private?' she asked Stephanie.

'Anything you want. But he is on punishment. He is not allowed to have a good time.'

'Don't worry. That was not what I had in mind,' Jacqui said, her tongue unconsciously poised between her lips. She rubbed Andrew's hot arse again. 'I don't think he'll imagine being here is an easy option when I've finished with him.' There was a hard edge to her voice Stephanie had not heard before.

'We'll put him in the bondage room – through here. I'll show you.'

Stephanie opened the door into the other suite of rooms. She showed them the two bedrooms and bathrooms and then the bondage room. The latter produced another astonished reaction. Almost as if they were in a dream they toured the room picking up various pieces of equipment as if to assure themselves they were real, fingering the straps on the punishment frames, looking in the wardrobes at the bizarre collection of clothes.

Suddenly Jacqui started to laugh.

'God this is going to be fun,' she said. 'Mrs Bloom was right.'

'Talking of Mrs Bloom,' Stephanie said, 'why don't we see what's going on upstairs? There's a monitor in the bedroom.'

63

'Good idea,' Terry said enthusiastically.

'Where do you want him put?' Stephanie asked.

'What?'

'Andrew.'

'Oh.' With all the new attractions Jacqui had temporarily forgotten the slave outside. She looked around and considered the possibilities, seeing, in her mind's eye, the man strapped into the all the various pieces of equipment. Her eyes lighted on a pair of leather cuffs hanging from a nylon rope and attached to a pulley in the ceiling. The rope was tied off at a cleat on the wall.

'Put him in these,' she said.

They walked back into the bedroom and Stephanie turned on the television monitor while Terry said he had to pee and went into the bathroom.

'Unzip me, darling,' Jacqui said.

Stephanie pulled the long zip of the dress down into the small of Jacqui's back. It fell away from her body like the petals of a tulip. She stepped out of it, picked it up and arranged it on a chair. The black satin basque she wore underneath fitted her perfectly, the big cups of its bra supporting her large breasts, the subtle boning following the slender line of her waist, while its long black suspenders snaked over her strong thighs to pull the black stockings up into sharp peaks on her creamy flesh. Stephanie had leant her matching panties too, but Jacqui was not wearing them.

'You look so sexy,' Stephanie said.

'I have to tell you Stephanie, I have never felt so sexy in my entire life. I practically came when I slapped that man.'

Jacqui turned to look into Stephanie's eyes. She put her hand out to touch her cheek then moved it round to the back of her neck so she could pull Stephanie's mouth on to her own. She kissed hard, her tongue probing into Stephanie's mouth as she felt her breasts crushing into Stephanie's firm tits.

'I love that. I love it,' she said breaking the kiss finally. 'It feels so naughty, kissing a woman. It feels so . . .'

Wicked?'

'Yes. And I've got to thank you.'

'What for?'

'Terry and I haven't really made love for years. You know it's all been perfunctory. He'd lost interest in me. I'd lost interest in him. But this afternoon . . . We did it again after we went back to the room. It was so . . . My God . . .' she said interrupting herself.

Jacqui had just caught a glimpse of the picture on the television monitor. In astonishment she sat down heavily on the edge of the bed. Stephanie, equally surprised, sat down next to her. Even after months at the castle she had never seen anything quite like it.

On the large double bed in Mrs Bloom's bedroom – brightly lit for the camera – lay the two male slaves. Both lay on their backs. They had little choice. From the bottom of their ankles to the very top of their shoulders each man was bound with black leather straps, at regular intervals no more than an inch or two apart. The straps were of different widths, thin around the legs and broad around the torso. The slaves had been made to lie with their legs together, their arms at their sides, their hands open against the side of their thighs. Mrs Bloom had started at the bottom and progressively clinched the belts around their ankles, calves, under their knees, over their knees, over their thighs and hands, their navels and wrists, and then, with the widest straps of all, over their arms and chests right to their shoulders. Each belt, on both men, had been pulled so tight the flesh bulged out on either side of the leather like a budding Pirelli man. There was no way the men could move even a fraction of an inch.

Poking vertically between the leather around the upper thigh and the belt strapped around the lower navel, the men's cocks were fully erect. They appeared huge, swollen and red, perhaps enlarged by the construction, their balls trapped under the tight bindings.

Mrs Bloom was standing by the bed, naked except for a pair of brown riding boots, proper reinforced hard-shelled riding boots, short leather riding gloves, and, strangely, her rather plain black bra. Her body was as tanned as her face. She was bony and angular with little flesh covering the protuberance of bone at her pelvis and ribs. Her pubic hair was sparse but what little there was of it was incredible long and wavy. The top of her thighs seemed almost concave. With her legs closed there was a gap at the very top of her thighs big enough to insert a fist.

Terry came back into the bedroom. He had stripped off his clothes and was wearing a white towel wrapped around his middle.

'I'm . . .' he began to say when he saw the women's attention focused on the television screen. Sitting down next to his wife, he put his arm around her shoulder and gave her a big hug. 'What's this?'

'Mrs Bloom,' Jacqui said.

On screen Mrs Bloom had picked up a riding crop in her gloved right hand.

'Now which of you is going to get it first?' Her voice was distorted slightly by the microphone. She trailed the tip of the whip all the way up the bonded thighs of the man nearest to her and then flicked it lightly on his chest, catching one of the exposed bulges of flesh. The man winced.

'Don't be such a baby. That didn't hurt.' Mrs Bloom chided. 'What about you, are you a baby too?' She turned her attention to the other man, running the whip along his body then flicking it down on his chest. He remained silent.

'You first then,' she said, flicking the whip down again and again getting no verbal response.

'This is better than *The Stud*,' Terry said. He moved back on the bed indicating for his wife to join them so they were more comfortable. He pulled the pillows from under the counterpane and they propped themselves up against the headboard.

Stephanie stood up and pulled down the zip at the side of her dress. Stepping out of it she folded it neatly on top of Jacqui's.

Terry didn't know where to look next – at his wife's long legs sheathed in sheer black stockings, her body held tight by the satin and lace basque; at Stephanie, the lacy-topped stockings matching her bikini briefs and strapless bra, her high heels tipping her perfectly rounded bottom into an inviting pout; or at the television screen where Mrs Bloom was kneeling on the bed beside her two captives.

Stephanie moved around the bed and propped herself against the headboard on the other side of Terry. There was a distinct bulge in the white towel.

'You don't need this do you?' Stephanie said, pulling at the towel.

'No.' Terry arched himself off the bed as Stephanie pulled the towel away. His rigid cock stood at a right angle to his body.

On the screen Mrs Bloom knelt on the large bed, the whip still in her leather-gloved hand. Between her open legs the long strands of pubic hair pointed down to her knees. She was running her fingers over the mouth of the man who had not winced, pushing his lips into distorted patterns. She put her fingers inside his mouth and pinched at his tongue. He tasted the leather of the glove.

'Try to struggle,' she ordered her fingers still in his mouth.

With all his strength he tried to escape his bonds. His body rocked slightly on the bed, he was able to raise his legs an inch, but that was the extent of his freedom.

Mrs Bloom swung her leg over the bound body and dropped her skinny bum down on his leather covered navel. His hard erection nudged her backside.

'Ahmm,' she said wriggling her arse against the hot sword of flesh. 'Are you ready to fuck me, big boy?'

He said nothing.

She removed her fingers from his mouth. They were wet with saliva. She inched them up his cheek to his eyes, using two fingers to close each eye in turn, the wet saliva leaving a trail over his face like the wake of a slug.

She raised herself on her haunches and moved back along his body until her sex was poised over his throbbing erection. He could feel the long pubic hairs tickling his glans. Reaching behind her she took his cock in her gloved hand and guided it into the folds of her labia. Suddenly she plunged herself down on him, all the way down, dropping on to him and not coming up again.

Jacqui leant forward and wrapped her hand around the firm stem of her husband's penis. There was a tear of fluid at its tip. She wanked him slowly, moving her hand up and down the shaft with the lightest of pressure. Stephanie had put her hand down to his thigh and pulled his leg up off the bed slightly so she could insinuate her hand down under his balls, cupping them in her hand.

None of them took their eyes off the television screen.

Mrs Bloom was moving now, up and down, on the captive cock. After a few minutes of this, accompanied by a soundtrack of 'mms' and 'ohhs' she stopped. Pulling her knees up to her chest, she began to turn herself round, rotating on the man's cock, like a wheel on its axial. She went all the way round, three hundred and sixty degrees and then round again. On the third turn she stopped halfway. Now she was facing the man's feet and the camera. Perhaps that was her intention as she looked straight up into the lens. Her face was slack with passion.

'Now,' she said loudly. She reached over to the other man on her left side and took his cock in her gloved hand like it was the lever of some machine. 'You know better than to come boys, don't you? You spunk and I'll whip you so hard there won't be one place you can find to sit on for a month.'

Sitting astride one, her hand wanking the other, Agnes Bloom began riding the cock inside her as though it were an unbroken rodeo pony, slamming herself down on it, each stroke harder and faster, while her left hand mimicked the movements on the other cock, wanking it for all she was worth.

She was moaning, crying out loud, whooping like a cowboy. Occasionally she shouted words – 'fuck me', 'do it' – but more often the sounds were incomprehensible. Her right hand was not passive either. Using the whip, it flicked her captive's flank just as if he were a horse. The microphone picked up the smack of leather on flesh when it struck a bulge poking out between the straps, or leather on leather, but it mostly hit against the man's incredibly tight bonds.

Without her eyes leaving the screen Jacqui slid down her husband's body, nibbling at his chest with her lips, pinching his nipples with her teeth, licking along his navel until she reached the stem of his erection. She wrapped her lips around it and heard him groan. Stephanie tightened her grip on his balls ever so slightly and felt his whole cock pulse. He moaned again.

The cries of Mrs Bloom were reaching a crescendo. She was coming. They watched as she stopped slamming herself down on her captive cock. Instead she pushed herself down, deep down, as deep as she could go so the cock was buried inside her, right up to the hilt. In the same way she stopped wanking the other cock but held it tight instead, so tight its tip suffused a dark purple red. They saw her eyes close. Her body ground itself down on the cock, her clitoris actually touching the leather strap that bound the top of the man's thighs. Her body shuddered. She gasped once, an almost animal sound, produced by her nerves all keening for attention.

Jacqui slipped the tip of Terry's cock into her mouth. Only the tip. She sucked on it hard. Her mouth was hot. He groaned.

Mrs Bloom was not one to rest on her laurels. She opened her eyes as soon as her orgasm had run its course and looked up into the camera. She lifted herself off her captive's erection. It glistened under the bright camera lights. With no ceremony she swung herself astride the other slave, guided his cock between her labia with her gloved hand, and sunk herself down on to him until the whole shaft was buried inside her cunt.

Jacqui sucked the bulbous tip of Terry's cock again but did not take it deeper into her mouth. Her hand still held its stem, Stephanie's hand still on his balls.

Mrs Bloom grasped the cock she had just vacated to repeat the procedure exactly, though this time she had swivelled round and was facing away from the camera, her eyes towards her stead's head. She rode her new charge just as energetically, whipping his flanks with one hand while the other wanked the cock she had just left. Her glove was wet from her own juices.

She looked at the slave she was wanking.

'I want to see you come,' she said. 'Come.'

If it were possible she rode the cock faster and harder than before while her gloves hand wanked the other cock so fast it appeared like a blur of action on the screen. As before she stopped suddenly, planted herself down one final time so the cock was as deep as it could possibly go, and stopped wanking, holding the cock in a grip of steel.

'Come!' she screamed.

Remarkably he did just that. His cock spasmed, fighting to eject its spunk passed the rigid grip. In one mighty effort it succeeded and a string of white spunk spat out into the air, arching out from his cock to land on his thighs and navel. Mrs Bloom managed to keep her eyes open long enough to see it but then her body convulsed, her eyes closed and she trembled to her second orgasm as she squashed herself down on the hard hot erection still deep inside her.

'Wouldn't you just love to do that darling?' Jacqui asked, looking up at her husband as she felt his cock pulse in her hand.

'Oh yes.' His voice was hoarse.

'In my mouth?'

'Anywhere,' he said truthfully. He was desperate. He had never wanted to come so much in his life. If he hadn't been watching the scene on the monitor, the two beautiful women playing with his cock and balls – especially his balls which always drove him wild – and dressed so provocatively, would have been enough to send him into ecstasy. He could feel their bodies, the shiny feel of satin and silk, the harshness of nylon, breasts and thighs pressed into him. But what he had seen had driven him higher. His urgency now was extreme.

'Shall we let him come?' Jacqui said in a teasing tone.

'Perhaps we should strap him up.' Stephanie said indicating the screen. 'Make him wait.'

'What a good idea. Isn't that a good idea, darling?' Jacqui said, her hand wanking his cock teasingly slowly.

Mrs Bloom had got off the bed and taken a Lucky Strike

from the packet on her bedside table. She lit it and drew smoke deep into into her lungs. She stood at the foot of the bed, her back to the camera, blowing smoke out in a long stream, and looking down pensively at the long neat bundles that she had made out of the two men.

'You're going to come in my mouth,' Jacqui said matter-of-factly. She kissed the thick stem of Terry's cock. Stephanie knelt up on the bed still cupping his balls in her hand but leaning forward to put her mouth on his cock too. For a moment they played a game, trying to kiss each other, trying to touch lips, with Terry's cock firmly between their mouths. They squirmed and turned their heads to get their lips to meet. Both could feel the hot cock throbbing.

Jacqui pulled her mouth away and looked into her husband's eyes. 'So many new experiences . . .' she said almost to herself.

He knew he was going to come. He was surprised he'd been able to hold out until now, surprised he hadn't spunked as both their mouths encircled his cock. Now there was no way he could hold back, not with all this stimulation. Not with his mind full of images of sex, of this afternoon, of now. Not with Stephanie's mouth nibbling at the base of his cock while her hands played with his incredibly sensitive balls; his wife sunk her mouth down over his cock and swallowed it into her throat.

He was simply out of control. He looked down at the two women, their bodies encased in tight black satin and silk and lace, their legs moulded in sheer black nylon, their heads working together on his cock, and he came, spurting his spunk into his wife's mouth so hard and so long that, for the second time that day, he thought it was never going to stop.

Jacqui took it all, all his jetting spunk. She swallowed some. But Stephanie wanted her share too. She tilted her head up and kissed Jacqui full on the lips immediately penetrating her mouth with her tongue eagerly searching for the taste of his spunk.

Mrs Bloom put out her cigarette and climbed on to the bed again. She knelt beside the bed of the slave who had not come.

Stephanie sucked spunk into her mouth then probed for more.

Mrs Bloom sat astride the slave's face, the whip back in her hand. She was facing his feet. She poised her labia above his mouth.

'Make it good,' she said flicking his erection with the whip then aiming a much harder blow across a strip of flesh that bulged from the straps around his thigh.

The slave's tongue started to lick. It could only just reach her labia. Her long pubic hair was wet.

Stephanie was no longer watching. Her mouth slipped from Jacqui's lips to her neck, down her arched breast. Jacqui lay back on the bed.

Mrs Bloom flicked both her captives with the whip.

'Harder, make it wetter,' she ordered gradually allowing her cunt to rest on the slave's mouth. His tongue found her clitoris.

Stephanie's mouth ran down Jacqui's navel, down over her soft pubic hair into the slit of her sex. But teasingly she licked lower, down Jacqui's long thigh, down to the welt of her stocking, then slowly, so slowly, up again.

Mrs Bloom kept up her tirade of instructions. 'Higher. There. There. Do it there. Suck it. Harder.'

Stephanie's mouth climbed to Jacqui's labia. It was soaking wet. Using just the tip of her tongue she found the swollen bud of Jacqui's clitoris. Like a tiny cock it was hard and erect.

'Yes there, there,' Mrs Bloom shrieked over the television as the smack of the whip accompanied her voice.

'There, there, don't stop,' Jacqui cried as Stephanie's tongue worked on the centre of her nerves.

'Oh my God . . .' It was Mrs Bloom's voice. The whip sang out once more as Mrs Bloom came on her captive's tongue, sinking her sex down on to his mouth, unable to think of anything but her own exquisite pleasure.

Stephanie moved her body alongside Jacqui's so they lay end to end. She kept up her pressure on Jacqui's clitoris hoping that she would take the hint. Stephanie's need was great too. Up to now she had concentrated on being the hostess, making sure her guests were well looked after. But now her own desire was running away with her. *She* needed to be looked after too.

Jacqui was not slow to respond however. Stephanie felt her hand pulling on her ankle to open her legs. Stephanie came up on to her knees poised over Jacqui's face while Jacqui's hands snaked up around her thighs. She used her fingers to pull aside the silk crotch of Stephanie's knickers.

As Stephanie locked her mouth on Jacqui's cunt, Jacqui levered herself up off the bed to imitate the action. Both their needs were urgent. Both were fired up. They had the taste of spunk in their mouths. They had both seen Mrs Bloom's multiple orgasms raking through her body, using the two men as if they were nothing more than animated dildos. It had excited them, stoked the fires that seemed to be consuming their cunts. Their cunts were wet. Their mouths were wet, drenched with each other's juices as they eagerly lapped each other's sex.

If it were possible to come exactly together they did. Jacqui did everything to Stephanie that Stephanie did to her, probing her clitoris with her tongue, licking the whole slit of her sex, pushing her tongue into her vagina. Every sensation she got from Stephanie she gave back. She knew it because she could feel it. It was impossible to separate their coming. Stephanie felt it in her cunt just as she felt it in her mouth. They were locked together in a tryst of passion. The trembling contractions were shared, experienced and felt at one and the same time. multiplied and amplified and echoed until they had no control, until both mouths could do nothing but cling on and let the explosion of feeling wreak through their bodies, until it finally died away releasing control to their minds once again.

Jacqui opened her eyes. Over the sharp slope of Stephanie's bottom she could see her husband's eyes watching her. She looked at his cock. It was already beginning to stir into life again.

Mrs Bloom, though nobody was watching now, was riding the tongue of her strapped and helpless victim. She had come once in his mouth and wanted to come again.

73

'There, there, there,' she screamed. His tongue lapped the spot she had selected. Then she came, hard and sharply, a final slash of the whip across the captive's thigh the last thing she could do before her body, too, lost control of everything except its ability to feel profound pleasure.

FIVE

Both of the bedrooms in the suite were equipped with bars, just like the rooms upstairs. Stephanie slid off the bed and took a bottle of champagne from the bar fridge. She wrapped the cork in a linen cloth and opened it, twisting the cork out without allowing it to pop.

'I need this,' she said. 'Anyone else?'

'Yes, please,' Jacqui said eagerly. She was laying on her side in her husband's arms, one of her long legs wrapped over his thigh, her hand cupped over his genitals.

Terry accepted too. Stephanie handed the glasses round and turned off the television monitor.

'Here's to Mrs Bloom,' she said raising her glass.

'What an inspiration,' Terry said sipping the wine.

'What a woman.' Jacqui added. 'She certainly seems to have inspired you.'

'Oh come on. With you two. Look at you both. I don't think I could have imagined anything more sexy. Let alone what you're wearing. It's not exactly the nuns' night out is it?'

'I think we've got some habits in the wardrobes,' Stephanie said laughing.

'But what a woman. I mean all that stuff over dinner. She actually meant it. Finding out what she wants and sticking to it. It must be difficult to get volunteers.' Jacqui took a large swig of the champagne.

'Oh I don't know,' Terry said. 'It might be a bit uncomfortable but you saw how that guy came. You can't say he wasn't enjoying it.'

'Yes, I suppose you're right,' his wife conceded.

75

Stephanie sat on the edge of the bed. The champagne had energised her again.

'So what happens now?' Jacqui said.

'Whatever you want,' Stephanie replied.

'No, I mean to Mrs Bloom.'

'I've no idea. Do you want to watch? Sorry I thought . . .'

'No, no enough's enough,' Terry said.

'She had one erection left at the last count, didn't she? I'm sure it won't go to waste,' Stephanie said.

'And with us?' Jacqui asked.

'Do you want to call it a night.'

Both Terry and Jacqui said 'no' at exactly the same time.

'Definitely not, the night is young,' Jacqui was very definite.

'New experiences,' Terry added.

'I wouldn't want to disappoint that nice young man,' Jacqui was smiling a wicked smile.

'Okay. I'll go and see that everything's been arranged then.'

Stephanie got up. Jacqui's eyes were wide with excitement. Her husband's erection, under the gentle ministrations of her hand was nearly as hard as it had been a few moments before.

In the bondage room Andrew was standing with Bruno. His gag had been removed. Bruno held the chain from the collar around his neck firmly in his strong hand. When Andrew saw Stephanie, he smiled, his eyes lecherously roaming her lingerie-clad body.

'You've been having a good time then. I should think the whole castle could hear you. I like it loud myself.'

'I see you haven't learnt your lesson.'

'What lesson was that. A few taps on the arse? Come on I'm a big boy. I had girlfriends who used to hit me harder than that. I like it. If you'd take this bleedin' chastity belt off I'd show you, especially with that gear on. You look a right tart.'

Stephanie caught Bruno's eye. She tapped the leather cuffs on the pulley hanging from the ceiling and indicated

Andrew. Bruno pulled Andrew by the chain from the leather collar until he was standing under the leather bindings. He went over to the cleat in the wall and lowered the cuffs until they were at chest level.

'What's this then?' Andrew asked.

'You do want punishment, don't you, Andrew?'

'Anything you say. You look a treat in that gear. All that black. I prefer suspenders myself mind.'

Bruno strapped his wrists into the padded leather cuffs. Andrew gave no show of resistance. By the cleat Bruno pulled the rope through the pulley until Andrew's hands were high over his head. Stephanie saw his cockiness evaporate as the idea occurred to him that he was going to be hung in midair. Bruno tied the rope off again just before Andrew's feet left the ground.

Stephanie went back into the bedroom where she left the Clarkes. They hadn't moved, Jacqui lying in her husband's arms, her hand loosely wound round his erect cock, her head resting on his shoulders.

'Everything's ready,' Stephanie announced. Her hair, she noticed in the mirror, had almost escaped its pinning. She pulled the rest of the pins out and let it fall free, brushing it out with her fingers.

Jacqui got up. She straightened and stretched her stockings which had wrinkled under the strain, and re-fastened them. 'Are you coming to watch darling?' she asked her husband.

Terry nodded and got up too. He tied the white towel around his waist again but the bulge of his cock was only too obvious.

'Just remember he's on punishment,' Stephanie warned not wanting Andrew to be given any favours after his latest insolence.

'Oh I will,' Jacqui said smiling. 'Don't worry about that.'

Jacqui strode into the bondage room. She felt alive and alert, fully enjoying the role she had been given to play. Bruno had vanished.

'Now that's really something,' Andrew said immediately. 'Look at those legs.'

'Shut up,' Stephanie said, following Jacqui into the room with Terry behind her.

'That's all right,' Jacqui said. 'I'm sure I can find a way to quieten him down. Actually I always thought my tits were my best feature.'

Slowly Jacqui eased her left breast out of the bra of the black basque. She flatten the cup of the bra underneath it so it was still supported but now completely exposed. She followed the same procedure with her right breast. When they were both exposed she pinched their nipples between her thumb and forefinger and lifted them into the air, holding her breasts up by them.

She stood in front of Andrew. With her high heels she was virtually the same height. She looked into his eyes and felt a frisson of pleasure shudder through her body centred on her tortured nipples. She let go of both simultaneously. Her breasts dropped back on to the flattened bra cups quivering massively. She could not help but gasp.

'I've never beaten a man before,' she said, her eyes staring at Andrew, her tone husky with passion.

Andrew, for the second time, felt his assurance desert him. Jacqui's eyes were a delicious shade of blue. Her long body was simply magnificent in the tight basque; she was the picture of an erotic dream. But there was something in those eyes, something hard and black, that told him this was not an experience he was going to enjoy.

Terry sat on one of the punishment frames in the corner. Stephanie sat down too, quite content to let Jacqui be the ringmaster of this particular circus.

Jacqui walked over to the wall of whips aware that Andrew's eyes were following her. With no knickers her ripe arse was unobstructed. He watched the way it swayed as she moved. She unhooked several of the instruments, weighing them in her hand, swishing them through the air, before she made her selection. She chose an old-fashioned cane like the sort that had been used in schools.

'We like to have them ask to be punished,' Stephanie said. 'So they have a choice.'

78

'So ask . . .' Jacqui picked up the name tag around Andrew's neck, 'so ask Andrew.'

He said nothing, his cockiness disappearing rapidly as he watched the cane being flexed in Jacqui's hands.

'Ask,' Jacqui snapped.

'Or do you want to be sent home?' Stephanie prompted.

'Please pun . . .'

The first stroke landed on his naked arse, immediately followed by a second and a third. Three red welts appeared across Andrew's white buttocks. He wanted to swear at her, curse her, tell her what a bitch she was but, for once in his life, he dared not.

'Can I take this off,' Jacqui said, tapping the hard metal pouch that covered Andrew's genitals with the tip of the cane. A set of keys were kept in every room of the suite, each key tagged with the name corresponding to the circle of metal around the slave's neck. Stephanie found the right key and handed it to Jacqui who snapped open the little padlock in the small of his back. The pouch fell away. Almost instantly his cock, freed of its long constriction, sprang up.

Jacqui took it in her hand, examining it as though it were a curious medical specimen. Her other hand stroked the three red welts she had created on his arse, feeling their heat and the way they seemed to throb.

Stephanie watched her intently. She could see the light and shades of excitement crossing her face like clouds scudding over a bright sun.

Jacqui let his cock go. She turned her back on him so she could rub her naked arse against the hard erection. By contrast to the tight black basque above it, her buttocks seemed incredibly white and plump. She pushed it back, wriggling it from side to side. Forgetting there was nothing behind him for support, she pushed back again so he was swept off his feet, hanging by his hands, virtually lying on her back, his cock buried in the deep cleft of her arse.

He moaned with a mixture of pleasure and pain. Pain from his wrists, pleasure from his cock.

Jacqui moved forward again allowing Andrew's feet to

touch the floor. She circled his cock with her hand and started wanking it slowly.

'Are you going to come for me, Andrew?' Jacqui said.

'Oh yes.'

'Good. That's good.'

Jacqui's hand moved progressively faster.

'Is that nice, Andrew?' she teased.

'Oh yes.' He felt his spunk coursing into his prick.

'But Stephanie says you're not to be allowed anything nice.'

Jacqui let go of his cock.

'No,' Andrew said in horror, realising what she intended. He bucked his hips, trying to fuck the air.

'Yes, Andrew. When I was at school I was the number one prickteaser. I had such a reputation. All the boys used to want to get me to wank them. I seemed to have this sixth sense. I could always tell when they were going to come. Then I stopped. I didn't want all that mess over my hands. After the first two or three they stopped pestering me.'

'I bet.' Stephanie said.

'It was unerring. Just a knack I suppose you'd say.'

Jacqui went over and sat on her husband's knee. Terry had watched his wife without saying a word. His cock was hard, as much from her excitement as his own. This was like nothing he had experienced before. There were no rules, no standard behaviour, no guides to what he should or should not be feeling. Just the experience. Jacqui kissed him hard on the mouth, grinding her lips against his, forcing her tongue deep. Her mouth felt hot. He could feel the heat between her legs too.

'I want you to fuck me so badly,' she whispered so only he could hear. 'I want to make him watch. Is that a good idea, darling? Does that turn you on too?'

He had no need to reply.

She got up, winked at Stephanie and went back to the helpless Andrew still bucking his hips rhythmically as though fucking some phantom woman.

'This time, Andrew. This time you can do it.'

'Please . . .'

'Please what?' Stephanie said.

'Please, mistress, madam, please.' Andrew had never wanted to come so much in his life, his whole body, his whole existence seemed to be centred on the huge sword of flesh that stood out at right angles to his body. He could see it, red and swollen. But he could not touch it.

'Pretty please.' Jacqui stood in front of him.

'Please, madam.'

'You see you can be good.' Jacqui grasped his cock again. He moaned ecstatically.

'I'll do anything, anything! Just let me come. Please,' he said desperately.

'Of course you will. So come for me then.'

Jacqui wanked him again, a slow even pace. He moaned. It was heaven. 'Yes, yes . . .' he said, his spunk on the point of exploding.

'That's enough, just now,' Jacqui said, walking away.

'No!' Andrew shrieked entirely forgetting his subservience. He pulled at his bound hands trying to break away. He was about to call her every name under the sun, to swear and curse her. Something stopped him. He stopped struggling and was silent.

Jacqui sat on her husband's knee. She kissed his ear, put her tongue inside it exploring the orifice as though it were some strange organ of sex. She blew hot breath into it. She pushed her thigh against the hardness of his cock under the towel.

Then she went back to Andrew. She felt her excitement surging through her. In a way she was teasing both men. It had all come back to her; she remembered how she loved to tease, how wet it had made her, how she'd had to go to her bedroom and play with herself just thinking about it.

'This time, Andrew, will I let you come this time?'

'Please, madam,' he said but he was not really pleading now. He knew she wouldn't let him, that this was his punishment.

Jacqui's passion flared. Instead of grasping his cock again, she picked up the cane and stroked his arse twice in rapid succession. She saw his cock surge with excitement, harder and redder as the blood rushed to the new welts.

But he said nothing. His mind was full of things he wanted to say but he remained silent. Jacqui threw down the cane and grasped his cock. It was as hot as a poker left in the fire. Red hot.

'Not so cocky now,' Stephanie observed.

'No madam,' was all he dared to say.

Jacqui wanked him hard, viciously almost. He tried to ignore it, tried to think of something else, but it was impossible. Every nerve in his body begged for release, every nerve on edge, strung out. He wanted to plead with her. He said nothing.

She left it to the last possible moment, till she knew one more stroke would bring him off, then pulled away, as he knew she would. He moaned but did not speak. He had learned the lesson of the castle. Why had he been so stupid he asked himself? It wasn't worth this.

Jacqui dipped her hand between her legs. Her cunt was liquid. Now it was her turn. She had created her need with all the teasing. She could feel her juices seeping down her thighs.

She stood in front of her husband and pulled the towel away from his loins. Straddling his lap she had no need to guide his cock into her sex. It slid in as though part of a machine, right up to the hilt, until she could feel it at the neck of her womb while her clitoris was crushed by his pubic bone. There was no time for thought now, only action, man and woman joined in a mutual and desperate need. Jacqui rode up and down on the shaft of flesh, no subtle progression, starting slow and gradually; just hard, fast, frantic strokes. She had never come so quickly in her life. In seconds that hot cock inside her was bringing her off, taking her over the edge. Inside her she felt as though her waters had broken, a flood of her juices cascading over his prick and down her cunt to match the flood of sensation that hit every nerve in her body.

Its intensity made her scream. It was so wet. So hot. And then she felt the cock spunking too. Hot spunk jetting into her. She swore she could feel it, feel each pulse of his cock

as it spate the spunk into her. She could see it in her mind's
eye, the spunk hitting the walls of her cunt. She would
never have believed she could go any higher but the spunk
set her off again, an orgasm more shattering than the first,
an orgasm that felt like it touched every nerve, nerves
already raw with feeling.

'Darling,' she managed to whisper as the waves of sensation ebbed away.

'Oh Jacqui,' was all that Terry could say.

Stephanie saw her guests out of the cells. They were both
elated and exhausted by their experience and asked not to
be woken until late. Stephanie was tired too but there were
still things to be done.

Back in the bondage room Andrew still hung from the
pulley.

'Well, Andrew, I hope you have learnt your lesson?'
Stephanie said.

'Yes mistress,' he replied. There wasn't the slightest tone
of sarcasm in his voice. He did not look at her.

Stephanie unwound the rope from the metal cleat on the
wall and lowered the cuffs that held his hands above his
head. She unbuckled the cuffs and he rubbed his shoulders
and wrists energetically.

'Put the pouch back on,' she ordered.

If his rebelliousness was going to flare again it would be
now. But without a word he picked up the pouch from the
floor and drew the chains back into place around his thighs
and waist. His erection had diminished sufficiently for this
not to be too difficult as the metal shell slotted over his
cock. Stephanie tightened the chains and snapped the tiny
padlock into place.

She led Andrew out into the corridor. All the other
slaves had been returned to their cells. Bruno waited
patiently outside the suite door. Stephanie watched as he
took Andrew to a cell.

'Goodnight, Andrew,' she said for no particular reason.

'Goodnight, mistress,' he said still not looking at her, his
voice quiet and subdued.

Stephanie opened the door to the private staircase to her room and began to walk up the stairs. She realised that nothing had been done about Amanda and her insolence in the gardens. But it was too late now. It would have to wait until tomorrow. Another thought occurred to her. She stopped and smiled to herself. A secret smile.

The door of the cell swung open. Andrew lay on his bed, his ankle attached, like all the slaves, to a ring in the floor by a long chain. The cell was dark, the only light from the corridor outside.

This was some new torture he thought.

Bruno grunted, indicating with sign language for Andrew to sit up. Andrew obeyed. Bruno held a leather hood in his hand. He quickly pulled it over Andrew's head. There was a long opening for the mouth but none for the eyes. It was laced on tight, the leather pressing into Andrew's cheeks. He could see nothing now. He heard Bruno walk out and the cell door close. In the blackness behind the leather he thought there was a slight lightening as though the cell light had been turned on.

He heard the cell door swing open again and then close. There were footsteps but whoever had come into the room was not wearing shoes. He thought he could smell perfume but it was difficult to distinguish it from the aroma of the leather hood.

A smooth hand touched his arm. It wanted him to turn over, lie on his stomach. He obeyed. He heard a key inserted into the tiny padlock at the top of his arse and felt the pouch being pulled roughly away. The hand caressed the welts on his buttocks. It felt deliciously cool. His cock surged to erection on the mattress. It was another torture, another teasing torture.

The hand wanted him to turn on to his back. He shuffled round. His erection was so hard it was painfully, his balls ached too. His mind filled with images of what he had seen, of the two women, of what had been done to him.

Suddenly he felt his body being straddled. He felt the rasp of nylon against his skin. In the same second he felt himself impaled in a cunt, a wet, hot cunt. He heard a gasp of pleasure. He felt himself being used, the woman riding him, fucking him, taking him. He could feel her thighs at his side, feel the soft flesh above the tops of the nylon. Most of all he could feel the incredible heat as the woman's body shuddered to a climax, moaning with pleasure as she pushed herself down on his cock until it would go no deeper.

He lost control, he spunked with her, at long last allowed to vent his lust, into the silky wet body he could not see. He could not see her smile either. A secret smile.

SIX

It was going to be a hot day. At this time of year the temperature varied more than when Stephanie had first come to the castle, as the sun was lower in the sky, but today the weather was coming from the south, from the continental heat of Africa, and it was going to be hot.

Stephanie had woken late, showered and rang down to the kitchen to say that she would taken her breakfast on the main terrace with guests. According to the staff, none of them had surfaced yet.

Pulling on a towelling robe she walked out on to the terrace of her bedroom and stood by the stone parapet to gaze over the calm waters of the lake. The sun reflected off the surface making the water look as though it were a sheet of polished gold. Yesterday, she thought, had proved a success. She could not imagine the Clarkes would turn down the opportunity of being associated with Devlin after what they had experienced. From what Jacqui had said it looked as though their sex life had needed the spur of adventure that the castle had provided.

As she watched a flight of grebes winging their way across the water towards the mainland, flying into the sun, like the final touch to complete a perfect landscape painting, Stephanie remembered what her life had been like before she had known all the beauty stretched out before her. It seemed a long time ago. Another life. In the last year her life had changed completely. Of course the change in her circumstances had been dramatic but the most fundamental change was in her attitudes and most particular in her attitude to sex.

She remembered George, good old dependable George. She hadn't thought of him for months despite the fact that they had gone out together for nearly two years. Another life. She saw herself laying underneath him, watching his buttocks rise and fall as he sawed into her as he conscientiously tried to make her come. He had rarely succeeded. If she was in a good mood she'd fake an elaborate orgasm for him; if she was not she'd do nothing, letting him use her as a receptacle for his spunk. Sex had been so unexciting, so dull.

That was before Martin. That was before she'd bought the first book, the first of her library of books: books that described a different world of sex, a world of imagination, a world where sex was not ordinary, limited, routine. The books had opened her eyes and then she had met Martin. If she wanted to believe in fate meeting Martin was a prime manifestation. Fate had provided her with a man who knew how to tap into her sexual psyche, to release an energy, a huge well of suppressed sensuality, a whole section of her mind that, until she met him, had been as dormant as an extinct volcano. But once he'd released it, once the heat in its depth had found a route to the surface, there had been no turning back: the hot lava flowed, melting and burning everything in its path.

What if she hadn't met him? What would she have done? Would she have lost interest again, stopped reading the books and buying new ones? Or would she have gone out to find someone? Perhaps unconsciously she had gone out and found Martin, sensed what he was capable of? In which case it was not fate at all.

In her mind's eye she could see every detail of the hotel room where he had tied her to the chair in her white silk underwear. She could feel the coarse rough tweedy material of the seat of the chair on her bottom, feel the leather straps binding her arms to the arms of the chair, her ankles to its legs. She could feel the woman's mouth on hers, the woman Martin had brought to the room, feel her hands kneading her breasts, her fingers exploring her clitoris. The first time she had been kissed by a woman, touched by a

87

woman. And she remembered being freed, the straps falling away, to release her into a tangle of cock and cunt and tits, a living sculpture of raw sex. She would never forget it; not a moment of it.

She felt herself shudder at the memory. It would always produce that reaction, she thought. It was, after all, the beginning Martin had lead her to Devlin, to Devlin who, when she had first met him had only been able to fuck her in his bedroom so he could see a huge oil painting dominated by a woman with a crimson cunt. Only that made him hard, only then could he come.

Devlin had brought her to the castle. And just as Martin had tapped her sexual depths, so she, in turn, had tapped into Devlin's, tapped deep, where no one had been before. Instinctively she had found a key, and released a sexuality he was completely unaware of. She had turned the master into a slave, her slave.

Stephanie felt a pang of hunger breaking into her reverie. She walked back into the bedroom to change for breakfast. But as she pulled on a white sleeveless leotard to be worn with a pair of skintight white leggings, her mind was still full of memories. How Gianni, the first guest she had encountered at the castle, had persuaded Devlin – whose whole business empire appeared to be precariously balanced on the succss of a deal with Gianni – no, had forced Devlin, to let him use and abuse her. That too had been an extraordinary experience. It too sent a shiver of pleasure through her body.

She had got her revenge. Ultimately. She could not help smiling. In fact, she laughed out loud as she always did when she thought of what they had done to Gianni, the indelible marks they had left, literally, on him.

Smoothing the leotard over her body and adjusting the leggings she combed out her long hair leaving it to flow loosely on her shoulders. Her hunger was too great to ignore now and she headed down to breakfast.

Mrs Bloom was sitting on the terrace in a one-piece orange swimsuit under a multi-coloured flower print wrap, her straw hat tilted down over her eyes against the glare of the sun. She was already smoking a Lucky Strike.

'Morning,' Stephanie said asking the waiter to bring fresh coffee.

'Some night,' she said, 'Did you watch?'

'For a while.'

'I think those boys'll only be fit for light duties today. I gave them quite a hammering.'

'They can take it.'

'Did that couple look in?'

'They found it quite . . . inspiring.'

Mrs Bloom laughed, a croaky frog-like sound, her voice effected by too many cigarettes. 'Open their eyes did it? Broadened their horizons?'

'Something like that.'

As the servant arrived with the coffee so did the Clarkes, hand-in-hand and looking surprisingly fresh and chipper.

'Beautiful morning,' Jacqui said.

'Sure thing,' Mrs Bloom said looking at Terry's bathing trunks under his robe. 'You going to swim? I'll join you.'

'Coffee first,' he said.

A fresh basket of croissants and brioches arrived and was quickly demolished by all but Mrs Bloom who ate nothing, but smoked one cigarette after another. The sun filtered through the trees. The terrace was partially shaded in the morning. Mrs Bloom moved her chair to be in the full sun.

'How'd you get on last night then. Hope you made full use of all the facilities.'

'You could say that,' Jacqui said winking at Stephanie.

'Well I certainly did.'

'We saw.'

Mrs Bloom stubbed out her cigarette. 'Time for action.' She got up, 'Coming?' she asked Terry.

'Great,' he said.

They walked off the terrace and down to the jetty. In minutes two figures swam out into view under the canopy of trees, Terry waving before turning on his stomach and falling into a regular almost mechanical stroke.

'So how do you feel this morning?' Stephanie said.

'Wonderful,' Jacqui replied firmly. 'I'm turning into a male chauvinist.'

'What do you mean?'

'Well don't they say all women's problems can be solved by a good seeing to. I think they're right. Judging from how I feel this morning i.e. one hundred per cent great. A bit sore in places, mind you.'

Stephanie laughed. 'Well you certainly seemed to be enjoying yourself last night.'

'Ourselves. That's what's so good. Terry hasn't been so turned on since we first met. But we're going to relax today. Give it a rest. Until tonight. We can go down there again tonight, can't we?' she said suddenly, horror in her voice, in case Stephanie were to say no.

'Of course.'

'Oh good. We were talking about it this morning. Terry's got something in mind.'

'You do whatever you want. That's what the weekend's for.'

'Great.'

Jacqui put her hand on Stephanie's knee. She was staring into her eyes. Stephanie stared back and saw a look of intimacy mixed with a definite streak of lust.

'God, I feel so sexy,' Jacqui said.

'I thought you wanted to relax until tonight.'

'I do. Actually I think I better had. My clitoris needs a rest. Weeks of abstinence and then this!'

The white jacketed servant came out of the castle to tell Stephanie there was a telephone call for her. Stephanie excused herself and walked inside as Jacqui rearranged herself in the chair Mrs Bloom had dragged into the sun. She picked up the phone by the large window that had been cut into the thick castle walls to give a view of the terracotta-paved terrace and the lake beyond.

'Hello.'

'It's me.' The 'me' was Devlin. He sounded depressed.

'You don't sound very jolly.'

'I'm not.'

'Why's that?'

'This deal.'

'Not going well?'

'Not going anywhere. Just an impasse. I think it's all going to be a waste of time.'

'Oh dear.'

'Can't be helped. Some you win, and some you meet a bastard who can't see good sense when it's two inches in front of his face.'

'Isn't there anything you can do?'

'I don't know. Doesn't look good. Listen, I had an idea. Why don't you come over. To New York, I mean. At least we could make the best of a bad job.'

'I'd love to.'

'That's settled then. I'll get the plane to pick you up at the lake this afternoon, say six o'clock, and you can take the first Concorde in the morning. You'll be here for breakfast.'

'Sounds wonderful.'

'I need it,' he said earnestly. 'How are the Clarkes?'

'At least that's good news.'

'What?'

'I think you'll find they're are going to be ultra co-operative from now on.'

'Really?'

'Oh yes. In fact I'm sure of it.' Stephanie looked out of the window at Jacqui. She had taken off her peachy silk robe and sat in the sun in a miniscule black bikini, its tiny bra barely containing the weight of her heavy breasts, its knickers no more than covering Jacqui's downy pubic hair. 'The Clarkes are having the time of their lives. Mrs Clarke particularly seems to have discovered a penchant she can indulge.'

'Great. See you tomorrow then.'

'Devlin,' Stephanie changed the tone of her voice very deliberately, 'haven't you forgotten something?'

'What's that?' Devlin was still playing the master, still in business mode, wheeling and dealing, controlling his fortune, a long way from the castle and his mistress.

'You need to be told, do you? You've forgotten so quickly have you?'

She could imagine him standing in his hotel suite, the phone in his huge hand looking like a piece of doll's house furniture in proportion to his fingers, papers spread out all around him.

'No,' he said meekly.

'No what?'

'No, mistress.'

'That's better. So you forget so quickly do you, Devlin? Well I can see I'm going to have to give you a lesson you won't forget, aren't I?'

'I didn't mean to,' he stammered.

'Aren't I?'

'Yes, mistress.'

'Are you hard now? Is your cock hard?'

'Yes, mistress.' His cock had sprung to erection the moment he had heard her voice change tone. She could imagine it bulging monstrously, out of his flies.

'Well you'd better be hard for me tomorrow, hadn't you?'

'Yes, mistress, I will be.'

'You will be. Because I shall need to be serviced. And I can think about it all day, can't I? What exactly I'm going to have you do?'

'Yes, mistress.'

'That's better.'

Without a word she put the phone down, smiling to herself. She looked at her watch. It was nearly twelve. Plenty of time to pack and make the other arrangements.

'I've been called away,' she told Jacqui walking out on to the terrace.

'Sounds interesting.'

'Devlin wants me to join him in New York.'

'That's nice.'

'You'll be all right on your own won't you, now you know all our little secrets. I'll make sure Bruno gives you carte blanche.'

'Of course.'

Mrs Bloom and Terry headed up the terrace steps from the courtyard, towelling themselves dry as they walked.

92

'Wonderful,' Terry said. 'The water's so soft. And the fish don't seem to mind. They swim right up to you.'

'Makes you feel good,' Mrs Bloom added taking a cigarette from her bag and lighting it with her gold lighter.

'Stephanie's got to leave us,' Jacqui told them.

'Oh really,' Mrs Bloom said.

'New York. I hope you don't mind.'

'As long as we can get into the cellars you can fly to the moon for all I care. Have a good time,' Mrs Bloom replied.

'Bruno will look after you.'

'You bet he will,' Mrs Bloom commented sucking on the Lucky Strike. 'So what's for lunch?'

Stephanie packed more clothes than she would need and a great deal more lingerie. She packed some of the more unusual items too, remembering her promise to Devlin, and all the accoutrements that went with them. She wanted to be prepared for everything and anything. Most of the clothes she had bought in the designer shops of Rome, when she had gone to take her revenge on Gianni. The thought of Gianni, which had once made her boil with anger, now almost made her laugh out loud.

She folded all the silks and satins and lace carefully and selected accessories to match each outfit. It did not take long to fill three large suitcases. She packed a smaller bag for her overnight stay in London.

There was a timid knock at her bedroom door just as she was finishing.

'Come in,' Stephanie shouted.

'Hi.' It was Jacqui.

'Been sunbathing?'

Jacqui was still wearing the miniscule black bikini.

'Yes. But I don't want to burn.'

'You've got a good tan already.'

'I cheat.'

'Cheat?'

'Solarium. I hate looking like a white worm.'

Stephanie folded the final items for her overnight bag. 'So what can I do for you?'

'What time are you leaving?'

'The plane's coming at six.'

'It's nearly four. Have you packed?'

'Last items.' She put the clothes in the case.

'There's time then?'

'What's all this leading up to?' Stephanie asked, knowing perfectly well by now what the answer was. Jacqui sat on the edge of the bed, her ankles crossed, her hands flat on either side of her thighs.

'I just thought . . .'

Stephanie zipped up the make-up case and put it into the overnight bag.

'You just thought what, Jacqui?'

'That, if you had time . . .'

'Well? Are you going to say it?' For some reason she wanted to make Jacqui ask, to hear her say the words.

'We could fuck . . . That's not really the right word, though, is it?'

'It's good enough.'

'And you haven't got time?'

'Did I say that?'

'No, but.'

'Take your bra off, Jacqui,' Stephanie's voice was commanding, not asking. Without a word Jacqui reached behind her back and unclipped whatever held the bikini top in place. The thin straps and tiny black triangles at each breast fell away, relieved of their task. Jacqui had obviously been sunbathing in the nude as there was no corresponding paleness where the triangles had been on her fleshy tits.

Stephanie looked down at the woman sitting on her bed and felt a surge of undiluted lust. It never ceased to amaze her, over her months at the castle, how her sexuality seemed to have increased. In years gone by she had gone weeks without any sex, even forgetting to masturbate for days on end if she wasn't in the right mood. There had been no need, no desire, no yearning. Now she seemed always to be in the mood, to always need and desire and yearn. She was insatiable.

Jacqui's breasts were magnificent. Though they were large and heavy, they did not sag at all but jutted from her chest, the upper slopes arched out, the effects of gravity somehow miraculously defeated, or, at least, postponed. Her tits were not pendulous either; they were perfectly round globes, topped by the pink cherry of her nipples surrounded by a dark brown circle of areola. Stephanie lowered her gaze to Jacqui's lap, where the tiny triangle of the rest of the bikini barely covered the delta of fine pubic hair and its thin straps followed the creases at the top of her thighs.

'So you want to fuck?' Stephanie made her voice deliberately hard and crude.

'Yes,' Jacqui said quietly. She wanted to explain, wanted to tell her she could think of nothing else, that her mind was full of images of their bodies locked together, of feelings she'd never felt before or even imagined. But there was no point in saying anything. Stephanie could see it all in her eyes.

'Pull my leggings down,' Stephanie ordered moving so she could reach. Jacqui's hands snaked up her hips to the elasticated waist and pulled from both sides, down over the tanned flare of her hips, down until the thick bush of Stephanie's pubis was uncovered, its black curls springing up as they were released from their constriction, down over the long thighs and slim calves. Stephanie raised each foot in turn so Jacqui could pull the leggings away.

'Unfasten this,' Stephanie said indicating the clip of the leotard between her legs. Jacqui's hand caressed her thigh briefly before freeing the three press studs. She could feel the heat and softness of Stephanie's labia underneath. The last stud snapped open and the two halves of the leotard sprung free. Stephanie pulled the garment off over her head.

She stood in front of Jacqui naked. For a long moment neither woman did anything. They only breathed. They could smell and taste and see each other's lust.

'I'll give you want you want,' Stephanie said quietly.

Roughly she pushed Jacqui back on to the bed. For some

reason she was not in the mood for soft, gentle, feminine sex, sex of whispering silk, breathless touches and crushed petal tenderness. She was in a mood to fuck.

Jacqui shimmied out of the bikini knickers. Almost before she had thrown them aside Stephanie pushed her on to her back again and mounted her, mounted her like a man, pressing the whole length of her body down on top of her, using her knee as if it were a cock, pushing it up between Jacqui's legs and feeling instantly her wetness and need.

'You're so wet, you little bitch,' she said. It sounded like something a man might say. She had been so careful with Jacqui yesterday, so tentative. All that had gone. Now she did what she wanted to do.

'Wet for you,' Jacqui moaned. She thought she was going to come on Stephanie's knee she felt so turned on.

Stephanie ground her knee into Jacqui's soft labia. Using both her hands, she took the great gourds of her tits and kneaded them hard, feeling her own passion increase as she felt Jacqui's body respond so readily.

With her fingers she found Jacqui's corrugated nipples and pinched them using her fingernails. Jacqui gasped but it was the pleasure of pain, driving her on, increasing the temperature, *her* temperature. Her nipples had never felt so sensitive, so alive.

'Oh yes,' she said as Stephanie pinched again.

'You like that,' Stephanie said. It was not a question. Immediately Stephanie buried her head between the huge mounds of flesh using her hands to push the flesh into her cheeks so she was surrounded by a mass of flesh. Her mouth found a nipple and sucked it in, her teeth biting on it. She felt Jacqui's whole body arch in ecstasy again.

Without changing her position, her mouth still firmly clamped on Jacqui's breast, Stephanie's hand groped out towards the bedside table. Using her sense of touch she managed to find the handle of the drawer and pull it open. Her hand delved inside sorting through the objects in the drawer until it lighted on the cold smooth head of the vibrator. She pulled it out. Jacqui did not see. Her eyes were closed.

They had not kissed. Now Stephanie moved, taking her knee away, kissing her way up to Jacqui's neck, feeding the vibrator into the wetness between Jacqui's legs. The coldness of the hard plastic made Jacqui open her eyes.

'What is . . .'

But before she could finish the question Stephanie's mouth covered her lips, Stephanie's tongue plunged into her mouth just as the vibrator plunged between the lips of her cunt. Stephanie felt her body shudder, her gasp gagged by Stephanie's mouth.

Jacqui's body arched off the bed again. Stephanie pounded the vibrator deep, with no thought of anything but to get it in as far as it would go. She continued the kiss and squirmed her firm breasts into Jacqui's, so she could feel her hard nipples buried in the mountain of flesh.

Twisting the gnarled ring at the bottom of the vibrator, Stephanie turned the strong motor on. A hum, muffled by the folds of Jacqui's cunt, filled the room. Stephanie held the vibrator deep in Jacqui's body, pressing it into her tender flesh. She broke the kiss and watched instead as Jacqui began to quiver too, her nerves tuning themselves to the vibrations, until she was quite out of control, the insistent, endless vibrations, right in the centre of her being, forcing her to abandon everything but her feelings. She started sobbing, little animal sounds, arching herself further off the bed, bent, like an archer's bow, every muscle locked by the tension in her nerves. Her body went rigid, shook from end to end one final time as she moaned, a long, long wordless moan . . .

Stephanie watched as slowly Jacqui's body lost its tension and she relaxed back on to the bed. She turned the motor of the vibrator off but did not pull it out. Gradually the muscles of Jacqui's cunt contracted against the intruder and millimetre by millimetre it was expelled, like giving birth to some strange cylindrical alien creature. Its final 'birth' produced a new wave of sensation in Jacqui, an aftershock of orgasm that made her nerves spasm uncontrollably again.

Stephanie kissed Jacqui on the cheek. The first tenderness. But tenderness was not the mood.

Jacqui opened her eyes to find Stephanie looking down at her.

With a completely unexpected surge of energy Jacqui rolled over on to Stephanie forcing her back on the bed, pushing her knee into Stephanie's sex, as wet now as her own had been, aping Stephanie's action.

'Now it's my turn,' she said.

Before Stephanie could say anything, Jacqui's mouth pressed down on her lips, her tongue prying between them. She reached behind her to find the vibrator, searching the sheet with her fingers outstretched, until they happened on the plastic, wet with her own juices.

Jacqui pulled her knee away from Stephanie's labia and replaced it with the head of the vibrator but she did not push it deep. Instead she turned the gnarled ring to bring the motor to life and, with the rounded but sharp end of the cream plastic, parted Stephanie's cunt lips just enough to find the nodule of her clitoris. The room was filled with a much louder humming now, nothing muffling the vibrator's raucous noise. As the tip nudged against Stephanie's already engorged clit, she moaned into Jacqui's mouth. Watching Jacqui's body come, feeling it come as she had, Stephanie was already on the brink, her body clock well into its counter-down. Now as the hard plastic vibrated her most sensitive nerves, as sensation spread through her body in huge waves to suck in all her nerves, she was out of control in seconds. She broke the kiss, needing air, out of breath from so much breathless sensation.

Jacqui's mouth moved to her breast. As Stephanie felt the vibrations taking her over completely, Jacqui's mouth sunk on to her breast and then her teeth, aping Stephanie's actions again, bit into the puckered flesh of her nipple. The vibrator was remorseless, almost too much, almost giving too much pleasure as Jacqui held it right up against the tender pink knot of Stephanie's clit.

Stephanie squirmed herself down on it. That was the last thing she could do. Her orgasm enveloped her, filled her, overwhelmed her, flung her body in a chaos of directions to meet its own hungers, satisfy its own longings as though nothing to do with her and then, satiated, threw her aside like a floppy rag doll.

Jacqui turned the vibrator off. Looking straight into Stephanie's eyes, she brought it to her mouth and licked the glistening juices off its plastic stem.

'Oh,' she said, 'nice.'

'You're a quick learner.'

'When it's something I want to learn,' Jacqui smiled.

'Did you get what you wanted?'

'Yes.' Jacqui put the vibrator down and sprung off the bed full of energy. 'Exactly what I wanted thank you. How quickly things can change.'

'What do you mean?'

'If you'd done that to me yesterday I'd have run a mile.'

'And now?'

'Now it gives me a bloody great climax and . . .'

'And?'

'Makes me hot for tonight. Now I want cock. God, Stephanie, I don't believe myself.'

'I thought you were going to save yourself for tonight.'

'I was. But you're going away. I didn't want to miss the chance.'

'Are you sore?'

'Yes. But it's delicious. Every time I close my legs it reminds me of all this pleasure. I'd never have believed myself capable of this. I don't just mean having sex with you. I mean everything. Last night. And every time I come it seems to get better and better.'

'I know exactly what you're feeling.'

'Do you?'

'The more you have the more you want.'

'Seems so.'

'It must be like a muscle. What do they say? If you don't use it you lose it? Well the opposite of that is the more you use it, the more you want to use.'

'And now I want to use all my other muscles. I'm going to have a long hard swim. I've go to do something to cool off.'

'Where's Terry?'

'On our terrace in the sun, why?'

'I want to see you both before I go. There's something you can do for me tonight. Terry in particular.'

'Sounds intriguing.'

'You go and swim. I'll see you in about forty minutes.'

Jacqui picked up her discarded bikini and walked, naked, out of the bedroom.

It took a little longer before Stephanie was ready. She wore a yellow jersey dress that was too hot for the Italian sun but would be good against the chill of London, and relatively sensible yellow shoes.

The powerboat had arrived and all the luggage loaded aboard. She had heard the Learjet circling the castle to make its final approach to the landing strip on the mainland.

At exactly half past five, as instructed, Bruno tapped on the door of her private staircase from the cellars. Stephanie opened the latch and he came in leading Amanda by a chain attached to a black leather collar strapped tightly around her neck. Apart from this and a pair of black court shoes, she was naked.

Bruno let the chain fall between her breasts and turned back down the staircase without exchanging a grunt or a look with Stephanie.

'Well Amanda, we forgot about you last night, didn't we? Perhaps you thought you'd got away with it.'

Amanda said nothing but her light brown eyes were blazing with undisguised contempt. Naked, her body looked bigger than one would expect from her appearance in clothes, but it was not fat. Though she was not tall Amanda's body gave the impression of strength, her arms and legs well muscled. Her breasts were full and firm, her buttocks long and plump but, once again, firm from muscle not flab. Her most notable feature, naked, was her waist. Despite her well developed musculature, her waist was hour-glass thin, emphasising thereby, the flare of her hips underneath.

Stephanie picked up the chain from between her breasts and lead Amanda over to the bedside table. From the drawer she took out the nipple clips she had used on

100

Devlin. She opened the jaws and sunk the serrated edges into Amanda's already erect nipples. Amanda appeared not to react.

'I always keep my promises, Amanda,' Stephanie said.

'Yes, madam.'

'Do they hurt, Amanda?'

'Yes, madam.' She did not add that it was the most delicious hurt she had ever felt in her life and that she could feel her sex juicing with the pleasure.

Stephanie picked up the chain again. As she lead Amanda forward the chain brushed one of the clips and Amanda felt another frisson of pleasure-pain boil through her body. Stephanie pulled her into the corridor and down to the Clarke's bedroom. She knocked on the door. It was opened by Terry.

'Present for you,' Stephanie said, handing Terry the chain from Amanda's collar.

'What?' he said laughing, his eyes devouring Amanda's naked body.

Stephanie walked into the bedroom. Jacqui was lying on the bed in her peachy silk robe reading. They exchanged 'hellos', as Terry lead Amanda towards the bed.

'Amanda needs special attention. Since your wife was so good with Andrew last night, I thought you might like to work the same trick on this young lady, who is equally obstreperous.'

'What a good idea,' Terry said. Stephanie could see from his eyes that he meant it.

'She's pretty,' Jacqui said, getting up off the bed to examine the naked girl. 'What are these?'

'Nipple clips,' Stephanie explained. 'I should have used them on you, shouldn't I?' Stephanie's hand rubbed the silk covering Jacqui's bottom as she passed.

'I don't know.'

Jacqui appeared fascinated by the clips. With the tip of her finger she flicked at the imprisoned nipple. Amanda winced but Jacqui could see the wave of pleasure in her eyes.

'I want to try them,' she said opening the jaws of one and

101

releasing the tender flesh. Amanda winced again, the pain of having them removed greater than merely wearing them. Jacqui opened her robe.

'Do it for me, darling,' she said to Terry.

'It'll hurt.'

'I know,' Jacqui said eagerly.

He took the clip and positioned it over his wife's hard nipple. The serrated edges sunk into her flesh.

'Oh,' she moaned. It was pain but a pain that seemed to go straight to every sexual nerve in her body.

She pulled the clip off. Another surge of passion. For a moment Jacqui was completely lost in the sensations her body was producing in reaction to this tiny stimulus. Then, quickly, she replaced the clip on Amanda's nipple and wrested herself back to some sort of normality. There was plenty of time for passion later.

'So what has she done?' Terry asked.

'She has a discipline problem, don't you, Amanda?'

'If you say so,' Amanda said sullenly.

'And she needs to be made to realise that in her time at the castle she needs to alter her attitudes. Don't you, Amanda?'

'If you say so.'

'Or perhaps you'd rather come with me. I'm going to London. Would you rather go home? I could ring ahead and make all the arrangements. Get your file out.'

'No,' she said.

'The more I think about it, the more I think that would be the best solution.'

'No.' For the first time there was genuine fear in her voice.

'No what?'

'No, madam. Please don't send me back.' She tried to say it with all the sincerity she could muster.

'So what do you think I should do instead?'

'Leave me here, please, madam.'

'And?'

'You know bloody well.' Amanda's temper flared out of control again.

'She is naughty isn't she?' Terry said.

'I'm sure we can do something with her,' Jacqui said, sitting on the edge of the bed right in front of Amanda.

'So would you like to help me out?' Stephanie asked.

'Oh yes,' Terry said. His hand was stroking Amanda's bottom.

'Great. Well I'll see you again I'm sure.'

'You can count on it. And tell Devlin to call us next week. We've been talking about it, the business I mean. Will you get him to call as soon as you get back?'

'First thing,' Stephanie said smiling inwardly to herself.

'Bye then.'

'And thanks for everything,' Jacqui said meaningfully.

Jacqui got up and kissed Stephanie on both cheeks looking into her eyes, deep into her eyes, to try to tell her exactly how she felt. Terry kissed her too.

As Stephanie got to the bedroom door she saw Terry drawing the thin belt out of his trousers while Jacqui sat back on the bed pulling Amanda's head down into her lap by means of the chain hanging from the collar around her neck. So much for waiting till tonight, Stephanie thought.

SEVEN

The Learjet stood waiting at the landing strip, its engines on, the passenger ramp extended. The Mercedes drove right up to the ramp and the driver raced round to the rear door to open it for Stephanie, his eyes locked on her long elegant legs as she swung them out of the car.

Susie, the Malaysian flight attendant on the plane, waited at the top of the steps, the *kheong-sam* she was wearing, in the darkest navy blue raw silk, split almost to the top of her thigh.

'Good evening, mam,' Susie said in her light lilting voice as Stephanie stepped aboard the plane. Stephanie handed her the fur coat she had decided to take against the cold of New York. Devlin had brought it back from Russia for her on a trip last month and she had never really had a chance to wear it.

'Good evening, Susie.'

Stephanie selected one of the large, comfortable leather armchairs and fastened her seat belt, as Susie retracted the passenger ramp and sealed the pressurised door. The note of the engine changed as the captain saw the light that indicated that the door was closed wink up on his instrument panel. The plane began to nose forward.

'Can I get you anything, man?' Susie asked.

'A dry martini, very dry with a twist. Wait till we've taken off though,' Stephanie said as the plane turned to point down the runway.

As soon as they were airborne Susie mixed the cocktail and poured it into a triangular glass frosted by condensation, as it had been kept in the fridge.

'The captain says we're going to be a little late in. There's a lot of traffic over London,' Susie said as she served the drink.

'I'm in no hurry,' Stephanie replied sipping the cold viscous liquid. 'Is Norman aboard?'

'Yes, mam.' The slightest suggestion of a frown crossed Susie's Oriental features. Perhaps she was remembering the first time Stephanie had been aboard the plane, when there had also been another passenger.

'Good.'

'Is that all, mam?'

'For the moment.'

Susie went back to the forward cabin. As Stephanie gazed out of the circular window, the sun was setting rapidly in the west but still radiating enough light for the coast of Italy to be plainly visible, a band of foamy white between the blue of the water and the beige of the sandy beaches, where the waves broke on the shore.

Gradually, as the light faded, the panorama closed in, until, as the plane headed up over Milan to the Alps, there was nothing to see from the windows but monstrous shapes of black, white and grey in the darkening clouds beneath them.

Stephanie unbuckled her seat belt and stood up. Immediately Susie appeared.

'Anything I can get you, mam?'

'No,' Stephanie said sharply not wanting to be shepherded around the plane. 'Go back to your seat.'

Susie looked unhappy but obeyed nevertheless.

Stephanie walked down to the door in the bulkhead at the back of the plane. The door was locked but the small brass key was in the keyhole. Stephanie turned the key and unlocked the door.

The wooden crate lay on the floor of the cargo compartment. Stephanie knelt, unfastened its steel latches and swung its lid open. Norman was neatly parcelled inside a black nylon body bag – exactly as the newly arrived slaves had been except that on departing from the castle it was not deemed necessary to bind the slaves as well as zip them into

105

the bags. They were gagged, however, but not blindfolded. No light could leak through the thick black bag. There was no way he would ever know where he had been. Not even a general direction.

'Well, Norman, nearly home.'

Stephanie saw Norman's head move in reaction to her voice. Still kneeling she eased the zip of the body bag down over his head. Underneath he was naked, the pouch removed in the cellars. His clothes would not be given back to him until he was in the warehouse in London. There he would get his belongings and his freedom. A job, though not the same job, would be waiting for him in one of Devlin's companies. After a spell at the castle it had been found that the slaves made extraordinarily industrious workers. They were watched carefully obviously, but so far not one had re-offended; quite the opposite, they proved to be models of efficiency.

The zip sung as Stephanie pulled it down to his ankles.

'Get up,' she ordered.

What on earth was she doing? she suddenly thought. She was supposed to be having a quiet flight to London, enjoying the luxury of the plane, drinking her martini, relaxing, not interfering with one of the slaves. Was she insatiable? She answered her rhetorical question with a smile. It appeared so.

Norman was getting to his feet, extracting himself from the tight nylon bag.

'I'm going to take the gag out.' Stephanie unstrapped the leather gag and pulled it from between his lips.

'Thank you, madam,' Norman said not looking at her but staring at the floor. He had learnt his lessons well.

It was completely dark outside now. There was no way for him to get a clue as their direction. Not that it really mattered if he did. No one would ever be able to find the castle. It was a very small needle in a very big haystack.

'Did you enjoy your stay at the castle, Norman?' Stephanie said leaning against the side of a packing crate.

'No, madam.'

'Do you remember oiling me in the mornings? Rubbing the sun screen on to my body?'

'Yes, madam.'

'All over my naked body. You had a good touch.'

His penis began to unfurl. It always gave Stephanie a thrill to watch the effect she could have on men: it was the thrill of power.

'Did I feel good?'

'Very good.'

'Come closer. Can you smell my perfume?'

'Yes . . .'

'Do you like it?'

'Yes.'

She reached out and touched his chest. His chest was hairy, thick black hairs. She let her fingernail trail across to his nipple. His cock reacted with a surge of blood, hardening by the second.

'You're getting excited, Norman. Why is that? Do you find me attractive?'

'Yes, madam. Very.' He managed to choke off the rest of what he wanted to say to her. Of course he was excited he wanted to say. What did she expect, sitting there in front of him, her skirt hitched up on her thighs, the soft jersey dress clinging to those firm round breasts he had massaged so often.

'You've got a nice cock, Norman. Very smooth.'

But she didn't touch it.

For a moment she did nothing. She was listening to her body, trying to work out its needs. What did it want from her? To go back into the cabin, have another martini and read the English newspapers that the crew had brought from London? Or something else? Was her excitement, the little trills of pleasure playing at her nerve ends, something she could ignore? Or had the experience with Jacqui this afternoon left its residue in her body? Was there a need?

'Ms Curtis,' a tinny, distorted voice called over the plane's public address system, 'I'm afraid we're estimating a further half-an-hour delay on our flight time due to air traffic control problems.'

Stephanie laughed aloud. It seemed fate had made up her mind for her.

'Well, Norman, it looks as though you're in luck.'

Norman daren't allow himself to imagine he might actually have any luck. Too many times, at the castle, he had served the guests' sexual needs while his own had been deliberately left unsatisfied. That was, and remained, after all, the ultimate punishment. In the hard metal pouches it was one he had suffered in silent agony.

'You don't look very happy about it. I'm going to let you fuck me, Norman,' Stephanie said. It hadn't occurred to her that that was what she wanted until she said it. But it was. After her experience with Jacqui this afternoon she wanted cock, just as Jacqui had expressed the same desire. (By now Jacqui probably had it too with her newly energized husband.) She felt a hard pulse of excitement. It wasn't the first time she had been fucked at 35,000 feet doing 650 m.p.h. in this very place. The memory of the first time – when everything had been so new to her – increased her desire.

Standing, she hitched up the dress and pulled down the little white panties she was wearing underneath. Norman's eyes followed every movement.

'Do you want to fuck me, Norman?'

'Yes, madam,' he replied quickly. Yes, madam, he thought, but you won't let me, will you. This is the last punishment, the final teasing, to remind me of all the other times. That was what he wanted to say.

Stephanie ran the tip of her finger over the top of his circumcised cock, moving it in little circles around the slit of his urethra. A tear of fluid had appeared but her finger did not disturb it. Despite the air conditioning of the plane, the jersey dress felt uncomfortably hot. She pulled it up over her head.

Her breasts quivered, she was naked apart from the yellow shoes. She cupped her breasts in both her hands to stop their movement.

'Remember, Norman.'

'I could never forget,' he said sincerely. It was true. He

would never forget her marvellous body, its lines so firm and smooth, her round tits, hard nipples, the pert thrust of her arse, the long endless thighs and that forest of black pubic hair extending right down over her sex like the fur of an animal. She was an animal, a sleek, feline, sexual animal.

In all his time at the castle Norman had played it by the rules. He had only been whipped twice and both times that was for the pleasure of a guest. He'd obeyed. He'd taken his punishment. He tried to take this punishment too.

Stephanie slipped her hand down between her legs, searching in the dark forest until her fingers found the opening and delved into her cunt. It was wet. She pulled her finger out again.

'I'm wet,' she said sucking at the finger at though it were coated with honey, looking him in the eye, watching him watching her.

It was then that he lost control, totally and abolutely. After three months of constriction at the castle, three months of rigid obedience, three months of acute frustration, something inside him snapped, snapped so decisively, so finally he was surprised it wasn't audible, that the plane wasn't filled with a noise like the breaking of a string on a violin. His string had finally broken. He felt free. He didn't care anymore, didn't care what they did to him, didn't care if they sent him back to the castle for another three months. He had to have her.

Stephanie was no more than a step away. In one fluid motion he pulled her towards him and wrapped his strong arms around her long back, forcing his mouth down on hers, his tongue probing between her lips, his penis flat up against her belly. He wasn't going to be teased again.

Stephanie was too taken aback to struggle. The power of his embrace had literally taken her breath away. Norman was pulling her down on to the hard metal floor. Before she could recover he had forced her to her knees and then down on to her back and he was on top of her.

But by then she had regained her senses and her breath. She started hammering on his back with her fists and screaming, 'Let me go, let me go.' Not that she wanted him to. She wanted him to do precisely what he was doing, to fuck her hard and crudely; but she was determined to play the game.

'You bastard get off me.' One by one he caught her wrists in his hands and forced them down on to the metal floor on either side of her head.

'You bitch,' he hissed, with the pent-up emotion of months of having to hold his tongue.

'I'll have you flayed for this,' she threatened struggling and bucking her hips. It only made him harder. It only made her hotter.

He worked his thigh down between her legs, prying them open. She could feel his erection on her belly.

'Don't you dare put that thing in me.' She was saying the exact opposite of what she meant. Not that it mattered. He was taking no notice. He worked his other thigh between her legs, then spread his thighs to force her legs apart. His penis nudged the soft folds of her labia.

'Please, please don't.' The words thrilled her. She could feel the vibrations of the plane's engines through the metal floor. The metal was cold, dimpled with little domes to improve friction. The domes were uncomfortable on her back and arse as his weight pressed down on her. But she was incredibly turned on.

Norman pushed the tip of his cock forward. She struggled again trying to raise her arms off the floor, trying to sit up. He slammed her back down again. She tried to raise her legs so she could attack him with the heels of her feet but the movement only changed the angle between their bodies, making a channel for him to plunge his cock all the way into her wet, tight cunt.

The feeling of his thrusting cock, its heat, its rabid eagerness, was too good for Stephanie to keep up the pretence. Instead, she wrapped her legs around Norman's back and levered herself deeper down on to him.

There was no subtlety, no tenderness. He was reaming in and out of her as though he had never had a woman before; he was using her, using her to escape the frustrations of three months of naked women all around him, all untouchable, unfuckable.

'Yes,' he said to himself as, at last, he felt a cunt wrapped around his cock. He couldn't have cared less about her. He couldn't care less whether she came or didn't come. He made no attempt to please her, to touch her breasts or clitoris, to lick or suck her. He wanted only for himself. He powered on and on and on, feeling his spunk coursing into his cock, filling it, swelling it, defining his need.

Under him Stephanie was coming, coming as violently as he was fucking, a different kind of orgasm, sharp, almost painful, but no less intense, no less exquisitely thrilling as it broke over the head of his cock and plunged her into a blackness of sensation her body spasming out of control.

He felt her contractions, heard her moans, saw her tossing her head from side to side. Still holding her hands fast above her head, he raised himself on his arms and looked down between their bodies so he could see his cock thrusting in and out of her cunt, wet with her juices. That made him come. That picture. He fought to keep his eyes open but could not. All he could do was abandon himself to his orgasm as he felt the spunk lash out of him and into her. Even then he did not stop hammering into her, like some automaton, on and on, feeling the wetness of his own spunk inside the tight tunnel of her vagina.

Despite the discomfort of the floor neither of them moved until his prick had softened and slipped from the soaking nether lips. It was only then that he rolled off her, only then he felt the soreness of his knees, and Stephanie, the numbness of her bottom. As she sat up the numbness turned to pain, the hard metal dimples having left their mark on her soft, pert arse.

Norman too regained his sense of reality. He would be sent back to the castle, he was sure, back to obedience and frustration, weeks more of service in the cellars, of endless titillation – months probably. All because he'd lost control an hour before he was due to be free.

But he didn't regret it. He would do it all again. If he had to spend more time at the castle at least he would have the memory, the feeling, the image in his mind of Stephanie's body as he lay on top of her fucking her for all he was worth.

Stephanie stood up a little unsteadily. She picked up her panties from the floor, stepped into them and pulled them up over her legs to cover the wetness of her crotch.

Norman did not look up. He sat, his knees drawn up to his chin, his face set in an expression that was a peculiar mixture of depression and despair.

It did, of course, occur to Stephanie to be angry, at least to pretend to be angry, just as she'd pretended to be raped. It could hardly be real anger. Norman had filled her, physically and emotionally, made her come exquisitely, done what had not been done to her sexually for some time, literally sweeping her off her feet. He'd taken control. Temporarily. But she was back in control now. And she had to decide what to do. Pretend anger. Send him back to the castle. Or . . .

'Get back into the body bag, Norman,' she said with no emotion.

'I didn't mean to . . .'

'Shut up and do as I say.'

Norman scrambled back into the crate. He slipped his feet into the tough nylon tube at the bottom of the bag and then lay back, his hands pressed to his sides in the proscribed manner. He couldn't believe his luck.

Stephanie pulled the fat zip all the way up his body, watching the nylon mould itself to all his contours, effectively binding all his limbs. He was helpless again, a tightly wrapped parcel. Hers.

Of course, he thought suddenly, this didn't mean she was letting him off. Not necessarily. Perhaps she was sending him back without a word. He looked into her eyes searching for some clue as to her intention. There was none.

She picked up the leather gag. He followed her with his eyes, her breasts swaying as she moved, her tight arse bisected by the little white panties. As she turned he could see the crotch of the panties were wet, sticking to her, sucked up into the slit of her sex, a long undulation in the material.

'Open your mouth, Norman,' she ordered.

'What are you going to do with me?' Norman said pathetically. Being physically helpless again made him emotionally vulnerable. His bravado had disappeared with his erection. He was her chattel again.

'Gag you,' she said knowing perfectly well that was not what he had in mind.

'Please don't send me back. I didn't mean . . .'

'Why should I send you back?'

'I just thought . . .'

'Nothing happened here, Norman. Nothing. Just remember that. If I find out you've told anyone different then I will have you sent back.'

'Oh thank you,' he said so pathetically she thought he was going to cry.

'Now open your mouth.'

She crammed the leather gag back into his mouth and buckled it tightly around his head. It had the effect of forcing his mouth open like some hideous gargoyle. She zipped the body bag over his head.

She stood up. He was exactly as she had found him. Nothing had happened.

Taking her dress over her arm, she locked the bulkhead door again and walked back down the plane to the bathroom. Susie came from the forward cabin to see if there was anything she wanted. The dark eyes of the Malaysian woman scowled a look of disapproval at Stephanie's semi-nakedness but she knew better than to make any comment.

'Just been checking the cargo,' Stephanie said to further annoy her. 'It appears to be in very good condition. Can you get me another martini?'

'Right away, mam.'

In the plane's bathroom Stephanie showered and towelled herself dry. Her knickers were too wet and uncomfortable to put on again so she went without, pulling the jersey dress down over her head and smoothing it on to her body.

Back in the main cabin she sipped the martini that awaited her and felt good. Deep down inside her there was a residue of still delicious tangible pleasure.

113

The captain announced that they were starting their decent into London, once again apologising for the delay. After a few minutes the plane broke through the covering of cloud and Stephanie saw the lights of London spread out before her. The orange lights gave the city a surrealist glow, almost as though it was not London at all but some strange planet of perpetual night.

She was glad she had bought the fur with her. London was cold and damp. As she walked across the tarmac the cold seeped into her bones and she wrapped the coat around herself more firmly. After going through immigration control and customs, she was glad to see the Mercedes coupé waiting for her outside the tiny terminal building of the private airfield. She was even more pleased and surprised to see Venetia.

'I thought you were in the States,' she said kissing her on both cheeks.

'I had to come back to sort out some contracts. Devlin asked me to pick you up.'

'You look great.'

It was true. Venetia's blonde hair was pinned up. She wore a plain black suit with a very short skirt. Her legs, clad in the sheerest black nylon were long and shapely, firm thighs, slim calves, pinched ankles.

Hurriedly Stephanie stripped off the fur, threw it into the back of the car and strapped herself into the passenger seat. The car was pleasantly warm.

'Devlin suggested you use the London house. But if you'd prefer a hotel . . .'

'What a good idea,' Stephanie said, and meant it. It would certainly be interesting to see the house. A lot had happened since her last visit there.

Stephanie could not suppress a shiver.

'Are you cold?' Venetia drove the car through the gates of the airfield and on to a busy main road.

'Freezing. It's not that cold is it? Must be all that Italian sun, lowered my resistance.'

Venetia turned the heating up full. The noise of the

114

heater fan filled the almost silent car and a big wave of heat flooded from the dashboard vents. The chill Stephanie felt rapidly disappeared. She was surprised at herself. The cold of London had never bothered her before; it was obviously the price of her sybaritic life.

'How's Devlin?' she asked.

'Not a very happy man at the moment. He's used to getting his own way.'

'At least in business.'

'He misses you. He talks about you all the time.'

'Does he?'

Venetia smiled. 'He's smitten.'

Stephanie relaxed into the big leather seat of the car. She remembered the first time she had been in it, the first time she had been driven by Venetia, Devlin's girl Friday. She turned off the fan of the heater as soon as she began to feel genuinely warm. Watching Venetia drive, her left leg resting, her right darting between accelerator and brake, its muscles tensing under their nylon veil, Stephanie could hear the rasp of nylon on nylon, just as she had that first time, when Venetia had taken her home with Devlin's invitation to come to the castle.

She could remember that night after all. It was the first time she had been with a woman. Martin, all those months ago, had brought her a woman, of course, but that was different: she could pretend to herself that what she had done with Alice was for Martin's sake, to please Martin, to turn him on. *Ménage à trois*. The male fantasy. But when Venetia had taken her home, when Venetia had stripped off her clothes and lain naked on her bed, when she had kissed and embraced her, there could be no such pretence. It was only for her. Her passion. Her discovery.

Venetia was wearing her hair pinned up. Her long neck was sinewy and elegant. Under the buttoned jacket of the suit she was not wearing a blouse. Stephanie could see the delicate lace of a black bra. Venetia's breasts needed the support of a bra.

The journey did not take long. Venetia drove the Mercedes into the gravel driveway of the house where

Stephanie had spent her first time with Devlin. She hardly remembered the outside of the house at all, but she knew she would remember the inside. She would remember the bedroom. She would remember the huge oil painting that dominated it.

Almost before the car had stopped a man appeared from the front door and came out to the car. Pulling her fur back on, Stephanie stepped out into the cold.

'Just the small case,' she said as the man lifted the lid of the boot.

There hadn't been any servants when she had been to the house before. Devlin must have given them the night off.

Inside Stephanie recognised the layout, the immaculately decorated and designed interior, the modern furniture, wooden floors, concealed lighting and numerous works of mostly contemporary artists. She was surprised to find that the artist whose work was so predominantly displayed in the master bedroom was also featured downstairs, though these oils were certainly less erotic, but no less vivid in their use of colour.

'Were these always here?' Stephanie asked.

'As long as I've been coming here, yes,' Venetia replied.

'I've put your case in the master bedroom, madam,' the man said, who from his manner, as well as his jacket and striped trousers, appeared to have the rank of a butler.

'Good. That's what I wanted.'

'Will you want to have dinner, madam?'

'No.' She thought for a moment. 'No, we'll go out, won't we?'

'Anything you want,' Venetia said.

After eating at the castle Stephanie felt like going to a busy crowded London restaurant by way of contrast.

She went upstairs to change. The butler had left the case on the large double bed, its counterpane folded back already. Her memory had not exaggerated the drama of the oil painting that dominated the room: the tangle of limbs, two women and a man, somehow centred on the crimson vulva of one of the women. The crimson seemed to throb, to be alive. Stephanie found it difficult to tear her eyes away.

They attracted a lot of attention, Stephanie and Venetia, two beautiful women alone together. But Stephanie was not in the mood for another liaison. She wanted an early night. She had never been on the Concorde before and was determined to be well rested for the experience. They ate and talked. They ignored the rather obvious approaches from at least two groups of men.

Back at the house they sat in the living room in front of the black iron fireplace of a futuristic design, watching the beech logs burn and sipping brandy which Stephanie though would help her sleep.

Venetia sat at Stephanie's feet, on a rug with a modern geometric design. They talked more, of the castle, of their lives. They laughed about Gianni, replaying together his final downfall when they had left him, helpless, in the Excelsior hotel in Rome.

Then it was time for bed.

'I want to sleep alone tonight,' Stephanie said bluntly, knowing that Venetia would be expecting them to sleep together.

'Oh.'

'I have to get up early.'

Venetia looked disappointed. Not that it mattered. Venetia was a slave like all the others, Stephanie reminded herself, a thief caught embezzling. She had been useful to Devlin; he trusted her now, but in the end – though she roamed the world as Devlin's assistant – she was still as much a part of the castle, and the cellars, as Norman had been.

Stephanie got up and helped Venetia to her feet. She kissed her briefly on the cheek.

She had no need to say anything, explain anything but she found herself saying. 'When I get back from New York.'

'You always make me feel so . . .'

'So what?'

Venetia tried to think of the right word. 'Liquid,' she said finally.

Stephanie looked into her eyes and for half a second thought about changing her mind, thought of how that magnificent body would feel pressed against her own, how Venetia's expert mouth would . . .

'Goodnight,' she said firmly walking away.

Upstairs she showered quickly in the *en suite* bathroom, an interior designer's invention of black slate and white marble with elaborate chrome taps. Back in the bedroom, wrapped in a bath towel, she lay on the bed without getting between the sheets. She stared at the oil painting, remembering with a shiver of pleasure, how Devlin had fucked her for the first time, how his monstrous cock had filled every corner of her sex.

The painting seemed to be alive. It was impossible to look at it without looking at the crimson vulva. The vulva seemed to fluoresce, as though it were full of feeling, as though it had experienced what Stephanie had experienced so many times since that first night with Devlin – that peculiar soreness, a mixture of pain and pleasure, that comes only after prolonged sexual encounters, of multiple orgasms. It was as near as a painting would ever get to describing an orgasm.

In the central heating Stephanie's body had dried rapidly. She stripped off the towel and got into bed. Unfortunately for her plan to have an early night, she was not feeling particularly sleepy. She looked around the room for something to read and noticed some books supported by granite bookends on a chest of drawers. She hadn't noticed the chest of drawers before. It was, like most of the furniture in the house, of a modern design, beautifully constructed in yew, with inlays of satinwood around the outside of the drawers. But the drawers were very small, not bigger than the size of a paperback book. Too small for clothes. Stephanie counted seventy drawers, seven stacks up and ten across.

Getting out of bed she first looked at the books. They were all classics. Emily Brönte, Charles Dickens, Zola, and Joseph Conrad, all bound in leather with titles picked out in goldleaf. She selected *Thérèse Raquin* and was about to take it back to bed when curiosity, her most enduring quality, got the better of her. Each drawer was opened by a small hinged brass ring, set flush into the solid yew. Stephanie pulled a drawer out by its ring. It was empty. She tried the one immediately underneath. That was empty too. And the next one.

She was about to give up when she tried the fourth drawer. Here, neatly stacked, their size exactly matching the internal dimensions of the drawer, were dozens of white envelopes, heavy vellum envelopes, divided by file cards, each file card flagged alphabetically; this drawer contained a sequence from BA to CO.

Stephanie picked out an envelope from a section marked BA-BE, propping the next envelope to it at an angle so she could fit it back into the right place. The envelope was typed with the letters BA in the top left-hand corner. She opened the flap of the envelope. Inside was a white card. The card was neatly typed with a number, 2351, and a name, Arabella Bannerman. Underneath the card was a colour photograph of a woman's face. Stephanie recognised the background of the photograph immediately. It was this bedroom. The picture looked as though it were taken from a full-length shot, enlarged to show just the face. It did not take much imagination to see that the woman's face was flushed with excitement. This was not a carefully posed portrait. Underneath this photograph the envelope contained a whole set of pictures. The next was the same shot enlarged, now showing just the left eye. The next was of the right eye. Stephanie laid them out on the top of the chest of drawers. Next came a nose but this was not taken from the first picture. It was a different angle altogether, not straight on but looking up so the nostrils were clearly visible. Next was a photograph of the mouth, then one of the left ear, then the right ear.

The next in the pack was of her breasts. First a photograph of both breasts together – just the breasts, the shot cut off at the neck and diaphragm – then one of each breast individually. By this time Stephanie knew what to expect. The next picture was a shot of the labia. The next of the crinkled corona of the arse.

There were twelve more shots in the envelope. There

was a full-length picture of her completely nude standing by the bed with a champagne glass in her hand. Her other hand was squeezing one of her small, rather flat breasts as though trying to make it look bigger. There was a shot of her on her knees on the floor her mouth wrapped around a massive cock. Though the owner of the cock was not visible Stephanie had no trouble recognising the huge phallus as belonging to Devlin. The other ten shots were all of various sexual positions, each different, each with the male partner's face obscured.

In the last one the woman was on her knees on the bed facing directly into the camera. Behind her Devlin's cock was buried as deep as it would go in her sex. The expression on her face, the look of total sexual abandonment, sent a sudden thrill through Stephanie's body. She knew exactly how the woman felt.

Carefully Stephanie replaced the photographs in the envelope, and put the envelope back in its place in the drawer. She flicked through and chose another at random from a division marked CA-CO. The neatly typed card read, '1268, Rita Camrani and Nina Singh'. The pictures were the same, in exactly the same order – face, eyes, nose, mouth and sexual organs, all taken from larger photographs, all with this bedroom as their background, but in the corner of each of the prints were typed the letter 'R'. A second set of facial and sexual organs followed in the corner of which was typed the letter 'N'. Then followed twelve other photographs. The first six were of the two dark skinned and small Indian women in a variety of lesbian activities. One of the women, Rita, appeared to be quite slim and fit; the other, Nina, was grossly overweight with rolls of fat around her belly and on top of her hips. It was Nina who seemed to be dominating the lesbian encounter. The second six showed them with a man. His face was never in the shot but the huge phallus belonged to Devlin.

The last shot in the pack had Nina lying on her back. Her head was lying between Rita's legs as Rita knelt facing the fat woman's feet. Nina's legs were raised and bent back over her body until her heels rested on Rita's shoulders.

Rita held them there, her arms looped around Nina's calves. The rolls of fat on Nina's body strained to escape, but the slit of her sex, fringed by a garland of black pubic hair, was completely exposed. Stephanie could see Devlin's unmistakable finger pressed into Nina's vagina while immediately underneath it the tip of his cock had been inserted into the puckered ring of her anus.

Replacing the photographs and the envelope, Stephanie opened another drawer, selected another envelope at random marked HA. The card inside read '1762, Philip Harrison and June Elliot'. The photographs were in the same order, the woman's features first, then the man's, typed with the letter J then P respectively, and followed by twelve shots of sexual activity. But this time the background was not this bedroom. Perhaps it was not even this house, though the modern furniture, made her think it probably was one of the guest rooms. Devlin was not involved in this tryst. The images were of the man and woman fucking in a series of conventional positions. There was no oral sex, at least, none in the photographs.

It was quite obvious from all the photographs, from the sometimes awkward angles and the expression on the faces of the participants, that they had been taken unposed, and probably without the knowledge of the models.

Presumably, Stephanie mused, someone had gone through a mass of photographs from each session and selected not only which ones to reproduce but given detailed instructions as to which should be used for enlargements of each feature. It must have been a time-consuming job.

Stephanie opened the drawers until she found a file card marked BA-BO and flicked through until she came across an envelope marked BL. Inside was, as she'd expected, a card typed, '2131, Agnes Bloom'. She had not expected it to say, also, Douglas Bloom. Mrs Bloom's face stared back at her from the first photograph. She looked much younger than she had at the castle. Skipping through the pictures of her features, Stephanie reached the first photograph of her husband. Douglas Bloom looked as though he had once been a heavyweight boxer. His nose had been broken several times and he had scar tissue above his left eye. Surprisingly, considering Mrs Bloom's activities at the club, the shots of sex were all straight sex with Mrs Bloom being licked and fucked by her husband. All except the last in the set where Mr Bloom, his large bulky body thick with muscle, stood over his wife, who lay face down on the bed, with a thin leather strap in his hand. From the colour of his wife's backside he had been using the strap on it for some time.

Once again in this sequence Devlin was not involved and once again the background was another room. This time Stephanie was sure it was not in this house.

Stephanie replaced the photographs in the envelope and slipped them back into the file. She found a section marked CO-CU and flipped through the envelopes until she found the letters CU. Sure enough inside the envelope was her name, Stephanie Curtis, and a number, 2491. The first picture of her face contained a fragment of the red dress she had worn that night, the night she had come to the house alone. Fascinated she laid each picture out on the chest of drawers. Her eyes, her mouth, her nose, her hairy labia. And then the shots of Devlin fucking her from behind, his big hands holding her by the hips, or wanking her with his finger.

She had a very clear memory of that night. She looked at the photographs carefully. When Devlin had used those huge fingers to bring her off they had been downstairs not in the bedroom. Quickly she opened more envelopes, flicking straight to the back and ignoring the sexual gymnastics, looking only at the backgrounds. Sure enough, though most were taken in the bedroom, there were some in the living room too and even one in the kitchen. Not only were the bedrooms wired for photography, the whole house was rigged with hidden cameras.

Stephanie replaced all the photographs except those of herself. She closed the beautifully made drawers, then collected all the photographs she had arranged on the chest of drawers and took them over to the bed. She placed herself

122

in the exact same position as the position she was in in the photograph, which was bent over the bed. She then looked round, estimating the angle where the camera would have to be placed. She saw it immediately. There on the opposite wall was an elaborate mirror. It was one of the few things in the house that was not modern. The camera must be hidden behind the mirror.

Stephanie went over and levered the mirror away from the wall. Sure enough clamped to the back of the glass was a big sophisticated looking camera complete with zoom lens, and recessed into the wall. She could see what were obviously the control cables leading from the camera back into the wall.

Still naked Stephanie climbed back into bed. She looked at the photographs again. The sensation of Devlin's monstrous cock sinking into her sex was something she would never forget; nor early on that night when he used his finger. The photographs brought it back vividly. She felt herself getting aroused, her sex beginning to churn.

She picked up the photographs and was about to put them back into the vellum envelope when she noticed another set of letters and numbers printed on the white card. In the bottom right hand corner was typed CD167. What did that mean? Once again her curiosity overtook her faint desire to sleep. She went back to the chest of drawers and systematically opened every one. They were either empty or full of the alphabetically ordered envelopes. Taking out a couple of envelopes she confirmed that every card had a marking in the right hand corner all prefixed with the letters CD.

But there was no clue as to what that meant.

The furniture in the bedroom was minimal: the large bed, the chest of drawers, and the two bedside cabinets, together with a Le Corbusier chaise longue, and a discreet but large black television mounted on the wall; that was about it. All the clothes and accessories were kept in a dressing room next door.

The only logical place Stephanie had to search was the bedside cabinets. On the left hand side the drawers contained a bottle of baby oil, some small leather straps, the sort used at the castle for strapping up a cock, and two vibrators, one larger than the other. There were some items of lingerie, a mauve suspender belt, a pair of grey stockings, crumpled and laddered, and two pairs of panties. One of the pairs was stained with the hard white dryness that spunk leaves. The lingerie smelt heavily of perfume.

The right-hand cabinet was entirely different. When Stephanie drew out the top drawer, all the drawers opened. In fact the drawers formed a false front, presumably to match both sides. There was only one large, deep receptacle and it contained what looked like the controls of a hi-fi. Some of the controls, power, volume, balance, were clear. Others were unlabelled.

The anodized steel lever marked 'Power' was obviously the first stage. Stephanie threw the switch.

Several things happened at once. The lights in the room dimmed while the control panel blinked with colour lights, each indicating a different function. The television screen came to life too, though the screen was blank. Fascinated Stephanie stared at the controls. On one side was a keyboard, like the numbered pad of a calculator. Above it was an LED display. Stephanie punched in the number 2. Nothing happened other than a 2 appearing in the green LED display. She punched in 3. Again nothing happened other than a 3 appearing next to the 2 on the display. She added a 4. The 4 appeared in the display which then began flashing the word 'ENTER'. Stephanie found a rectangular button marked 'ENTER' and pushed it.

A series of mechanised clicks began. It took ten seconds. The picture of the television screen flickered and Stephanie recognised the bedroom she was in. The camera was pointing at the large bed. In the middle of the picture was a woman, a huge fat woman, naked apart from a gold chain around her neck. She was about to get on to the bed. Her flesh wobbled as she moved.

'Do you like this?' her voice said over the picture. She was cupping one of her mammoth tits in her hand and feeding it up to her mouth until she could suck on her own nipple. At the same time she opened her legs and moved her other hand down between the folds of her fat thighs until it could wank her clitoris. The fat folded back on itself. It was impossible, even with her legs spread wide, to see the slit of her sex or even the triangle of her pubic hair. All that could be seen was rolls of fat.

Devlin walked into the shot. His face was turned away from the camera. His cock was flaccid . . .

Stephanie punched three more numbers into the control panel. The picture on the screen went blank as she punched 'ENTER'. Ten seconds later the screen lightened. A man lay on his back in the middle of a bed, not this bed and not this room, playing with his erection. He was a young man, good-looking, well endowed, and fit.

'I want to fuck you,' a female voice said.

'Come here then,' the man said.

A woman, small, short, dark, with a not stunning body, walked into the shot.

'Devlin will hear. He's next door.'

'You'll have to keep quiet then,' the man said.

'I can't, you know . . .'

But before she could finish the man had pulled her down on to the bed and smothered her words with a kiss. His cock was inside her body instantly. And instantly she started moaning, loud desperate moans.

Stephanie picked up the card with her name typed on the top. She was feeling more aroused than ever, her cunt throbbing. This was Devlin's wanking pit. Go to the file, select a woman, or a couple, and then lie here and play it all back, no doubt wanking himself silly while the images flickered on the screen. The ultimate wanking pit. Well, Stephanie thought, what's sauce for the goose . . .

She punched the numbers 167 into the control panel. The screen cleared. Then she saw herself standing in front of the oil painting. She opened her legs and dipped her fingers into her cunt, not at all surprised to find it wet, while she watched herself on the screen, taking Devlin's cock for the first time. She heard herself moan on the sound track. It was an extraordinary feeling, seeing what she had remembered so graphically, reliving the experience as though it were happening again. Almost without being conscious that she was doing it, as she watched the screen intently, her hand had found her clitoris and was wanking it aggressively while her other hand pressed into her cunt.

She watched as Devlin pulled his cock from her cunt. She remembered how it felt. Exactly how it felt. She remembered what they'd done next. He'd taken her over to the bed. She watched as he lead her over to the bed, her hand in his looking so small against his massive fingers.

'Will you come?' she heard herself saying, her voice deep and husky with sex.

'Yes.'

'In me?'

'Will you let me do what I want?' he asked.

'Yes.'

She remembered what he'd done. He'd knelt on the bed between her thighs and taken his monstrous prick in his own huge hand. She watched as her memory was confirmed. She watched him wank, as she'd watched then. She heard his little moans and gasps of pleasure as her hands worked between her legs. She wanted to come as he came, wanted to match her body to his, wanted to climax as she saw his spunk brimming out over his hand as she knew it would do any minute.

It was going to be easy, so easy. She was so turned on, so hot. This was like being able to play back your wettest dream, see it all in detail. Her juices made her fingers slippery, sliding over the bud of her nerves so deliciously, driving her to orgasm.

Devlin's hand wanked faster on the screen. She remembered he'd glanced at the painting just as his spunk flowed over his fist. And she came too, pushing her fingers, two, three, perhaps even four fingers, deep into the silky wet walls of her cunt, her finger pulling hard at her clitoris, jamming it against her pubic bone. She arched off the bed, her nerves locking every muscle of her body. She could

126

almost feel, as she'd felt that night, the hot spunk from Devlin's cock, lashing down on to her body.

The television screen went blank. Stephanie slowly, very slowly recovered her senses. She was almost surprised not to find her thighs and navel covered with spunk.

She flicked the power switch off and closed the drawer. The lights came back on and the television switched itself off with a loud clunk.

Stephanie packed the photographs back into the envelope and climbed between the sheets her body still prey to the little shocks and tremors of the aftermath of orgasm.

She had discovered another of Devlin's secrets, the secrets of his complex sexuality. She had no idea how all the video linkage worked, but she could well imagine Devlin lying where she lay now, wanking slowly to whatever scene he had selected from the catalogue he had acquired over the years. She made a mental note to check whether he had the same set-up in his bedroom at the castle.

Well she would certainly have something to upbraid him with in New York. She smiled to herself. Not that she really needed an excuse.

EIGHT

The fur was taken away by one of the steward's in the Concorde lounge. Despite the fact it was early in the morning Stephanie accepted the proffered champagne. Her coat, the steward assured her, would be put aboard the plane, and returned to her on arrival in New York.

Stephanie sipped the champagne and glanced through the *Vogue* that she had picked up from a huge variety of reading material on offer at the reception desk. There was not much time to wait. They were boarded almost immediately, walking down the long tunnel at the gate and on to the sleek white airplane. As flying Concorde was such an existing experience Stephanie had dressed carefully, more as if she were going to a party than flying the Atlantic. She wore a simple red dress, a dark moody red, cut to fit every contour of her body, tight to the breasts, her slim waist, and especially over the pert curves of her buttocks. The skirt was just long enough for her to wear beige stockings, held up by the tiniest suspender belt she possessed. Her panties too had to be slender; she wore only the smallest of G-strings. Any other knickers would have shown under the smoothness of the dress. A diamond had been cut away just above the bosom of the dress and revealed the foothills of Stephanie's breasts, unrestrained by a bra. If anyone looked carefully enough and long enough they would see the thin line of the suspender belt, the little dimple of the suspender button at the top of her thigh. If anyone watched her sitting down or getting up they would catch a flash of her stocking tops, too, no doubt. She didn't mind. Let them stare.

Her first impression as she walked down the aisle of the Concorde was how small it was. With only two seats on either side of the aisle and little more than twenty five rows of seats plus the galleys, the plane seemed tiny in comparison to the vast jumbos she had been on before.

A stewardess took her boarding card and indicated her seat two rows in front of a bulkhead in the middle of the plane. She had the window seat. A young boy, no more than eighteen or nineteen, she guessed, already sat in the aisle seat.

'Excuse me,' she said. 'Can I get by?'

She saw the look in his eyes as he turned towards her. It was as though all three symbols on the fruit machine had all just clicked into line.

'Sure thing,' he said at once leaping to his feet to let her passed. His accent was American and his mouth was open as he stared at her, his eyes devouring every inch of her body in the clinging red dress. As she sat down he was looking at her legs. He saw more than he bargained for. His mouth opened wider and she heard him swallow hard as she pulled her skirt down over her thighs and made herself comfortable in the seat.

'I'm Oscar Caplin,' he said extending his hand as he sat back in his seat.

'Stephanie Curtis,' she took his hand and shook it lightly hardly gripping it at all.

'First time?'

'Sorry?'

'First time on Concorde?'

'Oh. Yes it is as a matter of fact.'

'Great, isn't it? This thing flies faster than a bullet, did you know that? 38,000 pounds of thrust with reheat, 4,000 mile range. It burns 5,368 gallons of fuel an hour. We travel twenty-miles every sixty seconds, that's over a mile every three seconds.'

'Really?'

'They say that there isn't a fighter plane in the world that could scramble and catch up once we're airborne. They'd run out of fuel. We cruise at 42,000 feet. Another mile and we'd be in outer space.'

'Amazing.'

'Am I boring you? Would you rather I shut up? I know you Britishers like your privacy. I won't say another word.'

'No please. I think it's really interesting.'

'So are you.'

'Sorry?'

'Well interesting isn't the right word. You're exceptional. Beautiful, I mean. Perhaps I shouldn't say that.' Suddenly he blushed.

'Well I'll take it as a compliment.' Far from finding the boy irritating Stephanie enjoyed his enthusiasm.

'It was one.'

For a second he just started at her, the blush gradually leeching out of his cheeks. His gaze was interrupted by the stewardess bearing a tray of glasses.

'Would you like a glass of champagne before take-off?' she asked. 'Or we have bucks fizz. Or plain orange juice?'

'I'll have champagne,' Stephanie said feeling definitely festive.

'I'll take the orange juice,' Oscar said.

'Cheers, Oscar,' Stephanie held out her glass to be clinked. 'Nice to meet you.'

'And you,' he responded immediately. 'Here's to your first trip at twice the speed of sound. See that?' He indicated a rectangle LED display set into the bulkhead in front of them. 'That's the air-speed indicator. We go subsonic until we're clear of the land. Then they kick in the after burners and we're off like a bat out of hell.'

'You've done this a lot then?' she asked.

'Pa is rich. Seriously rich. He likes me to come home every term. I'm at Oxford reading English.'

'And you always go Concorde?'

'Well he sends me the ticket. Who am I to complain? It'll probably turn me into a spoilt brat of course. I'll be impossible to live with, but what can I do?'

'Sit back and enjoy it, I'd say.'

'What about you? What do you do? You must be a model.'

'No. I used to work in advertising. Now I've sort of

'retired.' She could hardly tell him what she really did.

'Are you married?' Stephanie saw the way his mind was working; she had 'retired' because she'd found a rich husband.

'No, Oscar,' she wiggled the third finger on her left hand 'I'm unattached.'

'Sorry,' he said sensing a reluctance to discuss the matter further. 'None of my business.'

The plane had taxied to the runway and was now rolling gently forward to turn into take-off position. Stephanie heard the engines being throttled up and the plane accelerating. In seconds the plane was airborne and banking to the west. From her window she saw London stretched out beneath her.

A few minutes later, after the captain's announcement that their flight to New York would take three hours, they reached the coast of Somerset.

'He'll turn the after burners on in a minute now. Watch the air speed.' Oscar said quietly.

The plane was still climbing. As the coastline disappeared behind them Stephanie suddenly felt another surge of power, not as strong as take-off but a definite kick nevertheless. The figures on the LED display quivered at MACH 0.89 and then, in seconds moved passed MACH 1.00, flickering and changing constantly until, no more than five or six minutes later, the display was reading MACH 2.20.

'Twice the speed of sound,' Oscar pronounced unnecessarily.

'Amazing.' She meant it.

'I never get used to it,' he said.

'Don't think I would. It's so exciting.'

More champagne was served and a delicious meal. Though it was only breakfast time the meal was in fact a lunch. Oscar chatted pleasantly and since Stephanie was too excited to sleep or read, she was glad of his company. His eyes frequently drifted to the diamond-shaped opening in her dress or down to the hem of her skirt and her slender long legs.

131

'So how does your father earn his money?' Stephanie asked as they were served coffee. She refused the offer of liqueurs. It was, after all, only eleven o'clock. When they arrived in New York it would still be eight-thirty in the morning.

'He's something big on Wall Street. He was in commodities but now he's changed to stocks. Apparently he made most of his money out of junk bonds, then got out before they all blew up.'

'I thought they were illegal.'

'Not exactly. Anyway no one ever pinned anything on him.'

'And what about women, Oscar? Have you got a girlfriend. The way you've been looking at me I'd say you haven't had sex in a month.'

Oscar blushed again, this time spilling his coffee in the process. A stewardess appeared immediately.

'It's all right,' he said waving her away, 'I'd drunk most of it.'

'Shall I get you another cup, sir?'

'No. No thank you,' he said recovering his composure though his face was still the colour of a beetroot.

'I don't mind you looking,' Stephanie said putting her hand on his knee. 'In fact I find it very flattering.'

'I didn't mean to . . .'

'I like it.'

'Do you?'

'Why shouldn't I? You're an attractive man.' It was true. Oscar had thick curly hair, a firm strong chin and dark brown eyes. He was obviously fit. He was tall. And he was young.

'I can't remember being this close to anyone as great looking as you. I guess it makes me stare. It's just that you've got such a great bod.'

'Thank you.'

'I don't suppose you'd like a date. I could show you New York.'

'I've seen New York, Oscar.'

'Yeh, but I bet I could show you places you haven't seen.'

132

'I bet you could'

The stewardess cleared away the coffee and Stephanie folded the table back into the seat in front. She crossed her legs. Half an inch of stocking top slid out from under the hem of the skirt. Oscar's eyes flitted over it. He tried to concentrate on her face.

'You didn't answer my question,' she said.

'What question?'

'Do you have a girlfriend?'

'No one steady. Do you really want to know when I last had sex?'

'Not especially.'

Stephanie looked out of the window. They were so high the clouds below seemed a long way down. She could actually see the curvature of the earth, or was that her imagination? The sky up here was so blue, a pure almost azure blue. Perhaps it was the height, or the speed, or just the pure wonder of it all but she felt peculiarly coquettish, capricious, flirtatious and wicked. Not only was she high, she felt it.

'What would you do?' she said smiling.

'Sorry?'

'If you took me out. What would you do to me, Oscar? Would you fuck me?'

It was a good job the coffee had been taken away or it would have hit the ceiling. He looked at her open-mouthed.

'Do you know what I like?' She leaned her head back on the seat so her mouth was close to his ear. 'I like to be fucked slowly, really slowly, for a long, long time. Would you do that for me?'

'Yes,' he managed to speak.

She put her hand on his knee again and this time squeezed it hard.

'Would you lick me?'

'God, yes . . .' he said in the same strangulated voice.

'You're making me hot,' she said. She uncrossed her legs and opened them slightly, no more than an inch.

'Am I?' he said.

'Stewardess?' Stephanie called as an attendant walked by.

'Madam?'

'Can I have a blanket?'

'Certainly madam.' The stewardess reached into the overhead locker and extracted a small red blanket. Thinking it was for Stephanie's exposed legs she arranged it over her lap. The moment she had gone Stephanie threw the blanket over Oscar's lap and tucked it into the waistband of his trousers.

'What are you doing?'

'I know what I'd like to do.'

Under the blanket she reached up to the flies of his trousers. His cock was already hard.

'You can't do that here,' he whispered in alarm.

'I'm doing it.'

'People will notice.'

'That doesn't seem to be putting you off, Oscar. You're very hard.' She found the zip of the flies and pulled it down. His penis had already forced its way out of the front of his boxer shorts. Her hand closed on his throbbing erection. He moaned loudly. It sounded like a moan of pain.

The couple in the seats across the aisle heard the noise and both looked at Oscar to see what had caused it. The man in the window seat was in his sixties, portly, with an almost completely bald head and piggy eyes. His wife, assuming the large gold ring she wore on her finger had been given to her by him, was blonde, bleach-dyed blonde, and in her early fifties. She was wearing a tailored pinstriped suit with a frothy ruched white blouse. Her legs were crossed. She had good legs.

The bald man went back to his newspaper. The woman pretended to go back to her book but Stephanie could see her eyes glancing at the bulge in the blanket.

'You'd better keep quiet,' Stephanie said squeezing his cock firmly.

'What are you doing?'

'Isn't it obvious? Do you want me to stop?'

'Yes. No.'

'Make up your mind.' She loosened her grip on the tumescent flesh.

'No.'

Stephanie moved her hand up to the tip of his cock and ran her finger round the rim of his glans. He moaned again.

The woman across the aisle looked up from her book more surreptitiously this time. She crossed and recrossed her legs and shifted in her seat. Stephanie had turned to her side and was looking straight at her. For a moment their eyes met. Then Stephanie saw her eyes drop to the bulge in the blanket. The very smallest of smiles flickered over the woman's face.

Stephanie pressed the hard cock into Oscar's belly. Rather than circling it with her hand she rubbed it up and down with her palm.

'Oh that's good,' he whispered. 'Why are you doing this?'

'It's an experiment.'

'Oh, oh . . .'

The woman across the aisle looked up again.

'An experiment?' Oscar hissed.

'To see what it's like to come at twice the speed of sound.' She rubbed harder. The blonde woman could see the bulge in the blanket moving up and down, like an animal burrowing in the ground.

'Oh . . .'

'Be quiet.'

'I can't.'

She felt his cock beginning to pulse, his spunk rising. She increased the pressure, moving her hand faster.

'Eargh . . .' he moaned loudly as she felt her hand covered in hot sticky fluid. 'Eargh,' he repeated as if the first cry hadn't made everyone in the plane look round to see who had made the noise. Oscar was, once again, blushing beetroot red.

The woman across the aisle caught Stephanie's eye. She made a circle with her thumb and forefinger and moved it up and down in the air a couple of times. Stephanie nodded. The woman smiled, a knowing, conspiratory smile.

'Sorry,' Oscar said. 'I've always been noisy.'

'Have you got a handkerchief?'

Oscar extracted a handkerchief from his pocket without disturbing the blanket. Stephanie cleaned her hand and wiped his cock dry. She stuffed it unceremoniously back into his trousers and zipped him up. There was a wet stain on the blanket.

'You're an extraordinary woman.'

'I know,' she said.

Stephanie relaxed back into the seat and watched the world rushing by the window. The fact that she had just wanked a perfect stranger, the fact that it had even occurred to her to do it, worried her not at all. Sex used to be surrounded by taboos and inhibitions. It was inextricably intangled with emotions, relationships and problems and obsessions. It meant more than it actually was. But her experience with Devlin had changed that. Sex for her was just sex and no more. It was simple, straightforward. She took what she wanted when she wanted. She was in control.

It was a wonderful freedom. Stephanie was not going to bow to inhibition or guilt or any other obsequies. It was like exercising a muscle that had been allowed to atrophy for a long time. Gradually the strength of the muscle increased until it felt strong and powerful. It energised all the other muscles and made the body feel strong. And the Greeks had been right. A strong body meant a strong mind.

The slight forward pull indicated that the sleek white plane was decelerating. The captain announced that they would be landing in twenty minutes and the MACH meter dropped to 0.89 again.

'We're coming in,' Oscar said nervously not at all sure what Stephanie expected of him now.

'I know. The captain just said so.'

'Listen. I really must see you again.'

Stephanie smiled. 'Must you?'

'I mean I would like to. Really, really like to. Take you out. I've never met anyone like you.'

'I should hope not,' Stephanie teased.

'Don't tease me,' Oscar said sharply.

'I like teasing.' That was true she thought.

'Do you?'

'Yes. It turns me on.'

'Will you come out with me please?'

'I'll think about it.' That was not a tease. Stephanie had no idea whether she would have any time for Oscar.

'I'll do anything. My father is very rich.'

'What's that got to do with it?'

'Nothing. I just meant.'

'That you could buy me. I'm not a whore. Do you imagine that every woman who is sexually,' she searched for the right word, 'direct, is a whore?'

'Oh god no.' Oscar was desperate. He had no idea how to entice Stephanie with words. He was confused. 'I just . . . I can't . . . It's just that I . . .'

Stephanie took pity on him.

'It's okay. Calm down.'

'I can't.'

'Give me your number. I may call you. No promises though. You understand. No promises. I'm going to be busy. I may not have the time.'

'Oh, thank you.' He took out an Asprey's gold-cornered notepad and scribbled his number on one of the white cards. 'Day or night. Anytime.'

'Okay. We'll see.'

'Stephanie,' he said seriously.

'Yes?'

'Even if you don't ring I'll never forget you.' He looked disconsolate and was trying to put a brave face on it without much success.

'Oscar, I like you. Do you think I'd have done what I did if I didn't like you. I don't suppose I'll ever forget you either.'

Privately she decided, if time permitted, she would call the boy. She genuinely liked him. It would be interesting to see more of him, and to take further what she had already begun. But she had no intention of telling him that for his own sake.

They fastened their seat belts as instructed and heard the

137

four Olympus engines change tone as the plane dived into the thick cloud over Manhattan. A few minutes later they landed faultlessly at J. F. Kennedy airport in New York. It had taken just three hours and thirty-five minutes to cross the Atlantic.

Devlin, in a black astrakhan coat with a fur collar, waited on the other side of customs. Stephanie bounded up to him, delighted, as always, to see his ugly, misshapen form. She kissed him on both cheeks and took his arm as they walked through the busy terminal to the waiting limousine, a redcap following with Stephanie's luggage.

'Pleasant flight?' Devlin asked.

'It was sensational. That plane is wonderful. And look at the time. It's still only eight thirty in the morning.'

'I'm glad you enjoyed it.'

'I loved it,' she said squeezing his arm tightly.

It was cold outside and Stephanie was glad of the fur as they waited for the chauffeur to bring the stretch Cadillac around to the terminal entrance. With a squeal of tyres the car drew up the curb and Stephanie climbed into the back while Devlin waited for the redcap and the driver to load her luggage. The back of the car was luxurious, a large leather bench seat, thick wool carpets, a television and a carphone. The windows were all blacked out. No one could see inside.

Stephanie made herself comfortable on the back seat. The redcap was tipped generously by Devlin who then settled down beside her as the car pulled away.

'Would you like a drink?' he said indicating the bar built into the partition behind the driver.

'No, I've had quite enough champagne on the flight.'

Devlin appeared nervous and uneasy, as though he wanted to say something but was not at all sure how to put it.

The car headed out of the terminal and on to the main freeway into New York. Stephanie stripped off her fur.

'Is anything wrong, Devlin?' Stephanie said sensing his mood. Sensing his mood was, after all, her specialty.

'No,' he said in a way that clearly meant yes.

'Devlin,' she said firmly.

'I've been thinking a lot about you. I've missed you.'

'I missed you too.' She meant it but knew it was not the response he wanted.

'You see . . . I . . . When we were talking on the phone. You made me so hard. You turn me on so much. I lay awake at nights thinking about the things we've done, you've done to me. Nobody's ever made me feel what you've made me feel.

'Good.'

'I couldn't wait for you to arrive.'

Stephanie felt a wave of affection for Devlin, real affection like she had never felt for anyone in her life. But a display of affection was not what Devlin wanted. She didn't have to be a mind-reader to know what he was trying to say to her, what he wanted right here and now in the back of the huge car.

'And this is how you greet me? Is that a proper greeting?' The softness had gone from her voice. 'You're supposed to be infatuated with me and you slouch on the seat next to me. Did I give you permission to sit there?'

Stephanie felt a thrill course through her as she assumed the mantel of command: it was a role she had come to love, a game she would never tire of playing. In fact it was more than a game now. It was a part of her. And, apparently, a part of Devlin too.

'No,'

'No what?' she snapped her voice like the crack of a whip.

'No, mistress.'

'Then get down on the floor where you belong.'

The chauffeur of the Cadillac was black, his hair shaved into the shortest of crew cuts, his chauffeur's cap too small for his square head and a bull-like neck. Stephanie saw his eyes in the rearview mirror and they were not looking at the traffic. The divider between the driver and the passenger was firmly closed: he could not hear what was happening but there was nothing to stop him seeing.

139

This did not appear to inhibit Devlin. He slid on to the floor of the car and sat at her feet. He looked up like an adoring dog waiting for his next command.

'Kiss my feet,' Stephanie said, crossing her legs and dangling one red leather clad foot in front of him. He kissed the front of her ankle, then the arch of her foot until his mouth met the leather of the shoe. 'Lick the shoe,' she ordered when he hesitated and he obeyed immediately. 'And the heel, suck on the heel.'

Devlin obeyed again. She could see his erection growing but, what was more, could feel her own excitement. She recrossed her legs so that Devlin was presented with the other foot. He licked enthusiastically, then sucked the long pointed heel into his mouth. He was looking up Stephanie's short skirt. He could see her creamy thighs above the beige stockings, and a tiny patch of her knickers, a triangle of silk bordered by her thick growth of pubic hair.

'Did I tell you to stop,' Stephanie barked, nudging his cheek with the red leather toe.

'Sorry, mistress.'

He retraced his route, licking every inch of leather, kissing every millimetre of nylon.

'Now, Devlin. I want you to take my stockings off.'

He started to get up. She pushed him back with her foot.

'Stay where you are. Do it from there.'

Eagerly he ran his hands up her long slender legs, his fingers rasping against the nylon until they reached the little nub of rubber that cinched the nylon into the metal loop of the suspender at the side of her thigh. He fumbled, not able to see what he was doing from where he was kneeling on the rich carpeting of the Cadillac.

'Don't be so clumsy,' Stephanie chided. In kneeling forward his cock was pressed against her calves. She could feel how hard he was.

Devlin could feel the flesh above the welt of the stocking. It felt so soft in contrast to the harshness of the nylon, so warm and inviting. Finally he managed to push the circle of rubber through the metal ring. He moved his hands on to the top of her thigh and found the other suspender. He fumbled again, his excitement making his fingers difficult to control.

Stephanie prodded his erection with the tip of her leather shoe.

He unclipped the second suspender but before he could begin to pull the stocking down Stephanie crossed her legs again.

'Now the other one,' she said.

He repeated the process while the tip of Stephanie's shoe tapped against his erection.

Stephanie watched as his fingers worked on the suspenders. Her skirt had ridden up on the leather seat and an expanse of thigh above the stockings was clearly visible. The chauffeur's eyes were glued to the rearview mirror. He would like to have adjusted it, she knew, tilting it down so he could see into her lap. But he dare not for fear the movement would attract attention.

As soon as Devlin had freed both suspenders on her other leg Stephanie put the sole of her foot on Devlin's chest and kicked him back. Off balance he sprawled out on the floor of the car.

The car was slowing to go across the Queensboro Bridge into the centre of Manhattan. Stephanie pulled off her shoes and slowly, very slowly rolled down her stockings. She had an audience. Two pairs of eyes peered into the rear-view mirror to try and catch every movement.

By the time they had crossed the bridge Stephanie was pulling the second stocking from the end of her toe. She threw it down on to Devlin's face, as she had the first one. It was still warm.

He was about to sit up.

'Stay where you are,' Stephanie snapped. She slid off the seat on to the floor, turned round, so that her bum was facing Devlin, then wriggled her skirt up until it was around her waist. She edged back along Devlin's body until she was kneeling over his face, the long slit of her sex covered by a slash of tight cream silk.

'Is that what you want?' she asked.

'Yes, oh yes!'

141

'Get on with it then.'

She lowered herself on to Devlin's mouth and immediately felt his hot breath panting against her labia. His tongue licked at the thong of the G-string.

Now the chauffeur could see nothing but her shoulders and the back of her neck. They were on the streets of Manhattan, the car crawling along in the traffic, stopping for lights and police cops with truncheons and whistles, the heat escaping from the subway ventilation shafts and vaporising in the cold morning air.

Devlin's cock stood up from his trousers like a tent pole stretching the material of his trousers like the big top of a circus.

'Come on,' Stephanie urged. 'Use your tongue, Devlin.'

She felt his tongue try to push aside the thong of the knickers but it was buried deep between her labia.

'You're useless,' she scolded using her hand to pull the crotch of the knickers to one side. Instantly his tongue probed between her labia and up to her clitoris.

Up to now it had been a performance, a role she had played. But as Devlin's expert tongue worked on her clit her excitement took over, a massive charge coursing through her body like an electric shock as she felt her own wetness against his mouth. She squirmed down on Devlin's face, feeling his chin against her pubic bone, his bulbous nose edging between the lips of her cunt.

The car was stationary at traffic lights. As New Yorkers walked by they stared straight into the limousine, trying to see beyond the black glass and their own reflection, to see who might be inside. Stephanie could see their faces, staring at her, old men, young men, middle-aged women, staring straight into her eyes – or so it seemed. She was coming. She couldn't stop herself. Maybe it was the experience with Oscar on the plane, maybe all the staring faces, or maybe just the exquisite way Devlin's mouth and tongue worked on her. Whatever it was she felt the waves of feeling beginning to flood her body, waves whipped up rapidly until their peaks and troughs merged into one long peak and she moaned as she came over Devlin's artful tongue.

She felt, at the same time, a huge gush of her juices deep inside her cunt, running down, the silky waters soaking Devlin's face.

'You can't even make me come,' she said contradicting every nerve in her body. She slumped back into the leather seat. Devlin's face was covered, from the bridge of his nose to the end of his chin, with her wetness. 'I hope you're going to do better than that when we get to the hotel.'

Stephanie saw the chauffeur's eyes in the rearview mirror. She pulled her skirt back down over her thighs. She pushed the button that wound the divider between driver and passengers down. Electric motors whirred.

'How long will it be?'

'Nearly there, miss,' he said, his voice hoarse. He cleared his throat. 'Five minutes.'

She wound the divider up again.

'Don't think I'm finished with you,' she said.

Devlin didn't attempt to get back on to the seat. He spent the rest of the journey on the floor while Stephanie gazed at the skyscrapers. New York had changed a lot since her last visit but then New York was always changing. Skyscrapers, once landmarks, were demolished and replaced by new ones – higher, more impressive – almost overnight.

The Cadillac pulled up outside the Pierre hotel and Devlin quickly scrambled out stuffing Stephanie's stockings into his pocket. Stephanie shuckled herself into the fur coat and stepped out of the car, her bare legs feeling the cold outside. Porters loaded her cases on to a trolley while Devlin lead the way into the hotel. Stephanie glimpsed the trees of Central Park at the far end of the street.

They went straight up in the lift to the top floor. Devlin lead the way to their suite. The windows provided a panoramic view of Central Park and the surrounding skyscrapers, though it was the almost Gothic splendour of the Plaza hotel to one side of the park that dominated the scene.

The L-shaped living room was furnished with two sofas in a delicate floral print with the shorter end of the 'L' containing a walnut antique dining table and ten, nineteenth-century dining chairs. A flower arrangement sat in the centre of the table. A sideboard displayed a full array of drinks and glasses with a fridge for wine and ice concealed behind one of its doors.

But Stephanie was in no mood for admiring the decor or the view.

'Do you want any breakfast?' Devlin asked.

'Where's the bathroom?' she said maintaining her imperious mood.

'Through here.'

Devlin opened the door into a palatial bedroom with an extra wide double bed. The room was decorated with the same lavish attention to detail as the living room; the pattern on the counterpane picked up in the flounced edges of the heavy curtains and their tie-backs, the predominant burgundy colour echoed exactly in the carpet. The walls were lined with cream silk. Another huge arrangement of flowers, seemingly also colour coordinated to match the room, were set on burgundy lacquered table, in a niche presumably designed for the purpose.

The bathroom beyond was black marble.

'Unzip me,' Stephanie said not looking at Devlin at all, pretending he did not exist, that he was an object of no importance.

He obeyed. She stepped out of the dress, then pulled off the wet panties. She unhooked the suspender belt. Leaving Devlin in the bedroom she ran a shower and climbed under it.

The bellboy arrived with the luggage, bringing it in from the bedroom door that lead directly to the corridor. He laid the cases out on folding luggage stands. Devlin tipped the boy.

'I've booked a table at the Four Seasons for tonight,' Devlin said as Stephanie came out of the bathroom, rubbing herself dry with a towel. Her naked body looked tanned in the harsh northern light of New York.

'So you can't even make me come,' she said ignoring his attempt at small talk. 'I gave you your chance, didn't I? Get your clothes off?'

144

Devlin pulled off his clothes as fast as he could. Stephanie felt a rush of excitement as she saw his erect cock. After her experiences on the plane and in the car what her body wanted now was to be fucked, being fucked by Devlin was not like being fucked by any other man.

'Open my cases. The keys are in my bag,' she ordered when Devlin was naked. While Devlin hurried to obey she finished drying her body. In the second case he opened he found what she wanted, the short riding crop with the braided leather grip.

She lay down on the bed. Devlin's erection was massive, gnarled and ugly.

'I'm going to give you a second chance. Get your head down here.' She had bent her knees and opened her legs wide apart. Her hairy sex seemed to wink at him as she touched it with the tip of the whip.

Devlin knelt up on the bed and immediately plunged his mouth down on to her sex, his body at right angles to hers, his arse in the air, round and vulnerable.

His tongue found her clitoris again, as it had in the car. The shower had dried her juices. Her labia were arid, uncooperative, intractable. He used his saliva to moisten the tender flesh stroking her clitoris from side to side. Almost instantly he felt her juices starting to flow, her labia soften, her whole sex melting over his mouth.

Raising the whip she slapped it down on his arse. She felt hot breath expel from his mouth in pain but he did not break his rhythm. She whipped him again and suddenly felt the change in her body, like a change of gear, the change from pleasant sensation to sexual need. She whipped him again, harder, then dropped the whip and arched up off the bed to hold his head down on to her cunt with her hands, pulling at his hair. Her dryness had turned to a copious flood.

'You're useless,' she said feeling the opposite. 'Use your finger.' She saw the pictures of their first night in her mind, his finger in her cunt, the photographs laid out on the polished yew chest of drawers. She remembered the pictures, she remembered the event. The two memories

145

were confused, fused. She didn't know which turned her on more.

Without taking his mouth away from her cunt she felt his huge finger nose between the lips of her cunt. In one smooth lunge his finger was inside her, as deep as a cock and as thick. Unlike a cock a finger could bend and flex and scratch against the very top of her womb and crook itself to explore every inch of the cavern of her cunt, all the time stretching it, challenging it, pulling at its elasticity, feelings only Devlin could give.

Stephanie felt herself coming. She picked up the whip and slashed it across Devlin's body. This time it missed the fleshy arse and landed on his back. Then the feelings he was creating in her body, in her sex, took over, wiped away everything but the feeling of orgasm as her body spasmed over his finger and mouth.

'You're useless,' she scowled, her eyes closed, the words turning another screw of tension in her body. She was not finished yet. 'Useless. I want more. Harder.'

He plunged his finger in and out of her, reaming it into her now soaking wet cunt.

'Make me come,' she screamed whipping the crop down again, this time hitting the meat of his arse.

He worked feverishly with his tongue as his finger pumped into her cunt. With all the wetness he could feel the little bud of her arse. It seemed to be open, inviting. He posed his finger over it, not knowing whether to risk probing deeper.

Stephanie felt what he was doing. She didn't know whether she'd be able to take his huge finger in her arse. They'd never tried. 'Do it,' she ordered.

He didn't need a second invitation. His finger probed up to his first knuckle. There was no resistance. He pushed further. He felt Stephanie's reaction, he felt her cunt contracting as she shuddered to another climax. It was like no other feeling she'd ever had. Two massive fingers, bigger than most cocks, stretching her delicate sex in every direction. Her nerves convulsed, her muscles locked.

'Deeper,' she moaned wanting more.

He pushed forward to the next knuckle. She felt herself on the brink again but this time Devlin took the initiative, driving his second finger right up inside her anus so it was alongside the first, separated only by the thin membranes of her body.

If she experienced a wave of pain at having this huge object thrust into her, it was a pain so closely allied to pleasure that it rocketed her orgasm so high she could not feel or see anything but a solid wall of dark ecstasy, a wall that surrounded her, encased her, taking over every sense in her body and subjecting it to seamless pleasure.

Devlin felt the tensions of her body relax. He pulled his fingers out gently. But the ripples of sensation that this caused made Stephanie quiver again. She felt little knots of feelings untie, echoes of the greater release she had just experienced. She lay for a long time in the furrow of pleasure she had ploughed.

But the game was not over.

'You're completely useless,' she lied. 'I might as well have had the chauffeur fuck me for all the use you are.'

Stephanie stood up and went to find her handbag.

'Well, what good are you to me? Perhaps you'd like to watch me fuck the chauffeur?'

'No, mistress.'

'I suppose you've used up all your energy wanking, haven't you? I found your wanking pit, Devlin.' She took the envelope from her bag and threw the photographs down on the bed. Pictures of her naked body stared up at her. 'Well don't tell me you didn't use these to wank with. All the body oil. A vibrator in your arse. Those little panties wrapped round your cock. I can just see it.'

For the first time since she had known him she saw Devlin blush, a deep crimson. He could not look her in the eyes.

'Well I want a demonstration. I want to see how you do it. Come on wank for me. There's the pictures. Or do you need the video too?'

'I haven't done it since I met you,' he said weakly.

'I bet you haven't. Come on, I told you what to do. Do it.'

Devlin's huge hand circled his erection. She picked up the whip from the bed and thwacked it across the top of his thigh.

'I want to see you spunk.'

'Please,' he said.

'Please what?'

He began wanking himself slowly, his giant fist moving up and down his equally large cock. Stephanie whipped his arse again. The sound of leather against flesh seemed to echo through the room. There was already a grid of red welts on his white flesh.

'Please what?' she repeated.

'I want to fuck you.'

Without letting him see her face Stephanie could not help smiling.

'After all you've done. You want to be allowed to fuck me?'

'Please.'

'You're going to wank and like it. After what I found at the house I might never allow you to fuck me again. You must like wanking so much. Going to all that trouble. Getting your wanking pit all fitted out. How many times a week was it? Once a day?'

Devlin knelt on the bed, his hand pounding at his erection. 'I don't know,' he lied.

Stephanie slashed the whip across his arse again. 'Keep going, I want to see spunk.'

She knelt on the bed in front of him, her arse facing his cock. Over her shoulder she said, 'Spunk, Devlin, all over my arse.'

But once again what she said bore no resemblance to what she meant. Planting herself on all fours she moved backwards until the cheeks of her arse grazed his cock. She wriggled it from side to side. He would be able to see the lips of her cunt, wet still from her orgasm. He would be able to feel its heat too.

She looked down between her legs, her thick pubic hair framing his cock behind her.

'Spunk, Devlin. You're useless.'

He could take it no longer, not half a second longer, as she knew he couldn't. In one fluid movement he grabbed Stephanie by the hips and literally pulled her back on to his cock. There was no resistance from the wet channel of her cunt. He was completely out of control. He didn't care what she did to him. He had to have her, had to fuck her. He plunged as deep as he could go feeling her cunt tight around his cock.

It would not last long. The images she had created, the game, the performance, the ache, the urge, the need she had stimulated, as only she had ever done, were the images and urges of his deepest sexual needs. She had tapped his psyche, drawn out the essence of his sexuality, laid him bare. He felt his spunk rising as he stroked in and out of her. He felt his cock start to spasm. He jammed himself into her one final time and then stopped moving. He waited, waited for the images – his laying on the floor of the Cadillac licking her feet – and the feelings – the welts across his arse hot and stinging – to drive the spunk deep into her pliant cunt. He had found his place.

His eyes lighted on the photographs strewn over the bed. There she was, bent over, facing the oil painting that had so long dominated his sex life, the crimson vulva at its centre still appearing to be alive, even in the tiny photograph. He could see it throbbing as it always had. How many times had he come looking at that picture, staring into the depths of that unique vision? As he did now, his orgasm raking through every nerve, flooding spunk out into the place he had found, the hot wet cunt contracting around him.

Devlin lay on the bed for a long time with Stephanie's head cradled on his shoulder. He did not close his eyes. She was the most remarkable woman he had ever met, of that he was quite sure.

NINE

The Cadillac headed down the Avenue of the Americas to Wall Street. As it ground to a halt in the endless traffic Stephanie watched the amazing diversity of the city buildings, as the huge modern skyscrapers gave way to the nineteenth-century brownstones and the small family-owned shops of Greenwich Village. As the car turned on to Broadway, the only road to run from one end of the island of Manhattan to the other, the scenery changed again, and they were suddenly in a charnel house of animal carcasses as articulated lorries unloaded beef and veal and lamb into the cavernous halls of the meat markets two blocks from Wall Street.

Devlin was preoccupied, pouring through the papers in his briefcase, his mood changed entirely from this morning. The millionaire businessman had replaced the grovelling slave.

'So what's the problem?' Stephanie asked.

Devlin set the papers aside. 'I wish I knew. Everything was going fine. Then he just started backtracking. As far as I'm concerned the deal was done.'

'What is it all about?'

'He owns a block of shares in a company I need. He's agreed to sell and accept options on the rest of the stock he owns over various time periods, until I finally take control. Now he's causing difficulties. He just keeps finding reasons not to sign on the dotted line.'

'Perhaps he's had a better offer.'

'I doubt it. The company is a perfect fit for my business. On its own it wouldn't be worth half the money.'

'Isn't there another company it would fit just as well?'

'Could be, I suppose.'

The Cadillac pulled up outside a sixty-storey office building in Pearl Street. Devlin kissed Stephanie on the cheek.

'See you back at the hotel. Have a good time this afternoon. And keep George with you. This is a rough city for someone who attracts as much attention as you do.'

'I'll be careful. See you later.'

They drove back into midtown. Stephanie had been to New York once before on an advertising conference but the trip had been rushed and she had seen little of the sights. Now she intended to put that right and asked George, the black bull-necked chauffeur, to take her to the Museum of Modern Art. There she spent two hours wondering through the masterpieces of twentieth-century art.

Strangely it was not one of the European artists that she found herself most drawn to, but an American, Andrew Wyeth, whose work fascinated her. The colour of the wheat fields, and the drama of the crippled Christina, somehow stranded in the middle of the open fields, gave the pictures a poignancy and energy Stephanie found difficult to tear herself away from.

With her mind full of colour and form and shape, she got back into the Cadillac. The speed of Concorde was doing strange things to her body clock. Though it was the middle of the afternoon her stomach told her, with loud rumples of complaint, that it was well passed the time it should have been fed. There was no way she was going to be able to manage to wait for dinner.

She wound the electric divider down.

'I need a snack, George,' she said.

'Yes miss. What you want? Pastrami on rye. Tuna fish sandwich?'

'Something like that.'

'Three blocks from here. Wolffe's deli. Best place in town and no hassles.'

'Take me there.'

He was right. The pastrami sandwich was filled with two

151

inches of delicious spiced meat and the coffee that came with it was hot and strong. Though Stephanie was modestly dressed in a black suit Devlin was right. She attracted a lot of attention from members of both sexes. Envious glances from the women, various degrees of looks – leering, smiling admiration, ogling stares – from the men. But there were several other single women sitting in the deli and Stephanie could see George, leaning against the car, watching her every second through the windows.

After her stomach had been calmed by the sandwich she had George take her to Bergdorf Goodman's. She browsed in the very English interior of the store and bought one or two items of lingerie. Across the road she went into Tiffany's and browsed there too, though she had no desire to buy any of the elaborate concoctions of silver, diamonds and gold that were displayed in the heavy glass cases that lined the aisles of the store's main hall.

She had George take her to Macy's – because she had loved the Ginger Rogers' film which featured the store – and was disappointed to find it had been modernised so totally as to be unrecognisable. She wondered through Bloomingdales, too, but bought little.

Back in the Cadillac she instructed George to go to the hotel. She wasn't in the mood for more shopping or sightseeing. She wanted to have plenty of time to get dressed up for tonight's dinner.

In the suite she unpacked some of the purchases she had made, then stood at the windows for a long time as the dusk turned to darkness and the first lights came on in the skyscrapers all around. Soon the city was transformed, a mystical transformation, from the grimy harsh reality of daylight to the almost magical light show of night, as gigantic towers lit up and long strings of street lamps snaked across the island, in dramatic contrast to the almost total darkness of Central Park like some vast black and bottomless lake.

Snapping herself out of the hypnotic state the city seemed to have imposed on her, Stephanie turned her attention to her outfit for dinner.

She wanted to wear something special. The dress she had in mind was special. Full length with full sleeves and a neckline up to her throat, the dress covered most of her body with the exception of her thigh on the left side as here the dress was split almost to the hip. The material of the dress clung to her body, following the line of her bust, the slimness of her waist and the flatness of her navel. At the back it moulded itself to her spine, before following the rise of her buttocks. But it was not only the cut of the material that was sensational but the material itself, a shiny black beaded with thousands upon thousands of tiny glass beads, that caught the light and made the whole dress shimmer as its owner moved.

After showering she chose a pair of sheer black tights – the slit in the dress was too high for stockings – and rolled them over her long legs before wriggling into the dress. There was no need for a bra, the dress supported her perfectly. Pulling on a pair of black suede high heels with a little motif in the same glass beads sown on the toe, she stood to admire herself in the mirror, legs apart, arms akimbo.

She held her hair up on her head deciding whether to wear it up or down. Deciding to wear it up, she pinned it to her head revealing her long neck before it disappeared into the high neckline.

'My God you look wonderful,' Devlin said letting himself into the bedroom from the corridor door just as she finished her hair. He was looking at the way the dress shaped itself to her arse. It made it look ripe, pert and inviting.

'How did it go?'

'Everything's agreed.' His tone was depressed.

'But?'

'What's that American word? Gridlock. It's gridlocked. He won't sign. I think I have to admit defeat. There's nothing I can do. You win some you lose some. Would you like a drink?'

'Well it is cocktail time. Since we're in New York I'll have a Manhattan.'

Devlin ordered the drinks from room service. 'I'm very glad you came over.'

'So am I.'

Devlin put his hands on her shoulders and looked at her face in the mirror. He looked deep into her brown eyes. They sparkled with intelligence and energy and pleasure.

'You are a most beautiful woman, Stephanie.'

'And you are an incredibly ugly man, Devlin.'

They both laughed. It was an old joke between them. Beauty and the beast.

Before either of them could say anything else the drinks arrived with the room service waiter.

They clinked their glasses and toasted New York.

George ran round to open the rear door of the Cadillac and eyed Stephanie's long leg as the skirt of the dress split open as she climbed out of the car and wrapped her fur around her against the cold of the New York night. The Cadillac was parked outside the glass doors of the Four Seasons restaurant on the corner of East 52nd Street.

Devlin led her through the doors, and a blast of warmth soon dispelled the chill as they walked up the wide modern staircase to the first floor restaurant where they were greeted by the maître d', and shown to a corner table in the long banquette that ran the whole length and breadth of the room.

As Stephanie's fur was removed and she walked across the restaurant a bevy of male eyes followed every detail of the rise and fall of her buttocks so perfectly outlined in the tight material.

It was not like any restaurant Stephanie had ever been in before. The main room was actually a gallery, a big rectangular floor area, but a gallery nevertheless, reached by the wide staircase they had just climbed, in a forty-foot tall room formed on two sides by enormous sheets of plate glass. A ten-foot glass sculpture made from moulded glass tubes was virtually the only ornament: the beauty and drama of the room needed no further decoration.

The food was delicious too. Devlin warned her that it was a restaurant renown for its desserts so Stephanie ate comparatively lightly, choosing the little neck clams and the

154

broiled monkfish. When the sweet trolley arrived she, thus, had room for a good portion of Chocolate Velvet which Devlin assured her was the restaurant's specialty.

It was only after the sweet trolley had been wheeled away that Stephanie noticed the young man waving to attract her attention on the other side of the room. It was Oscar. He was sitting with another, much older man. How long he had been there she didn't know but with a single crooked finger she beckoned him over.

'It's the boy I met on the plane,' she explained to Devlin as Oscar approached, his long legs affecting a loping gait.

'Hi!' he said with delight in his eyes.

'Oscar this is Devlin,' Stephanie said repeating the introduction in the reverse order.

'Very pleased to meet you, sir,' Oscar said, taking Devlin's proffered hand. Devlin's hand engulfed his, like an adult's hand with that of a tiny child. 'Are you enjoying the food? I'm out with my pa. He always likes to come here. Ma's on the West Coast so we're eating out.' As she spoke he hopped, uneasily, from one foot to another.

'Well it's nice to see you again,' Stephanie said, 'Oscar's at Oxford.'

'Rhodes scholar?' Devlin asked.

'Yes sir. Reading English. I better get back.' He wanted to remind Stephanie that he really wanted to see her again but daren't in front of the intimidating Devlin. He hoped the pleading look in his eyes were easily translated.

'My God,' Devlin said as he watched the boy join his father again.

'What?'

'That's him.'

'Who?'

'The boy's father. It's Henry Caplin.'

'Who's Henry Caplin?'

Oscar was pointing Stephanie out to his father. He too had recognised Devlin. They exchanged polite nods of the head.

'The man I've been trying to do this bloody deal with.'

'Really?'

155

'Yes.'

'Well invite them over for coffee. Perhaps I can get Oscar to work on his father for you.'

As Stephanie swooned over the delights of Chocolate Velvet the waiters added more chairs to the table and Oscar and his father walked over to join them. Oscar introduced his father to Stephanie. Henry Caplin was a tall man and looked strongly built. His immaculately groomed hair was totally white which made him look older than he actually was. His eyes were sharp and very blue and his complexion clear though there was a dark shadow around his jaw where he shaved what was clearly a heavy beard. He was an extremely attractive man.

Coffee was ordered and a bottle of Chateau Yquiem to go with a silver-tiered dish of petit fours.

'Oscar told me all about you,' Henry Caplin said.

'Not all I hope. We have to have some secrets, don't we, Oscar?'

Oscar blushed immediately. Stephanie was sure he had not told his father everything.

'I don't suppose you've had any further thoughts, Henry?' Devlin asked.

'Let's not get into that tonight.'

'It makes such good sense,' Devlin persisted.

'Come on,' Stephanie said, 'Let's forget about all that.' Caplin, she had realised, was not going to respond to the direct approach.

The wine arrived and Stephanie sipped the golden nectar from her glass. It smelt and tasted of the essence of the sweetest grape, a reminder of the richness of autumn.

'Wonderful,' she announced, eating a white chocolate truffle from the dish of petit fours. 'So shall we all go on somewhere? This is New York after all. Night life capital of the world. I'm certainly not in the mood for bed.' Mischievously she looked directly at Oscar as she said, 'Not yet anyway.'

Oscar blushed again.

'How hot do you like your night life?' Caplin asked.

The question was deliberately provocative. Stephanie

had no intention of backing away. 'Very,' she said looking at him directly with fierce uncontradictable eyes.

'I was going to take my son to the Shades of Hades.'

'Sounds interesting,' Stephanie said.

'There won't be any women there. It's mostly for men.'

'I like things that are mostly for men,' Stephanie consciously licked her lips with the tip of her tongue.

'You've no objection, Devlin?' Caplin asked.

'No. I don't think there's anything in Hades that would shock Stephanie.'

'You never know,' Caplin said.

'I do actually,' Devlin replied flatly.

'Have you ever been there, Devlin?' Stephanie asked.

'Once or twice.' He put his hand on Stephanie's knee exposed by the long split in her skirt. 'You'll enjoy it,' he whispered.

They finished the wine and drank coffee. Every time Stephanie looked at Henry Caplin, his eyes were on her. She could see them roaming over her body, staring at her bosom as if trying to imagine what lay under the glitter of the dress, not that his son was any less thorough in his attentions. Father and son appeared to be totally captivated by her.

Devlin paid the bill. Stephanie's fur was brought up from the cloakroom. The three men watched her, her perfect figure outlined by the clinging material of the dress, as she was helped into the coat by a waiter, each, no doubt, wishing they could palm their hand down over the curves of her apple-shaped arse.

They decided to all go in the Cadillac. Caplin's stretched Mercedes limousine was dismissed. Stephanie sat in the back seat between Devlin and Caplin with Oscar on the jump seat facing them, with his view of Stephanie's leg, more or less completely exposed by the dress, unimpeded.

Caplin gave George the address and the big car swung away from the curb.

It wasn't more than ten blocks down towards the East River. Smoothly the Cadillac rolled up outside an elderly row of buildings, their ground floors serving as shops, a

K-Mart, a Laundromat and a dry cleaners. There was also a very large and very busy hamburger joint and bar. The windows of the bar, garishly illuminated by Budweiser-neon advertising, were steamed up from the heat inside.

Caplin led the way. At first Stephanie thought they were going into the bar until she saw there was another door immediately adjacent to the bar entrance. Caplin punched a series of numbers into the computer pad that operated the lock and the battered blue door sprung open. They crowded into a small vestibule, hardly big enough to contain the four of them. The vestibule was badly lit and carpeted in a rich dark blue carpet. The walls, ceilings and doors were all also covered in the carpet. Nowhere was there any sign indicating the name of the club.

Taking a card from his wallet Caplin passed it through a card reader on the side of the inner door jamb. Once again, after a moment, the inner door sprung open. Caplin led the way down a corridor, in the same dark blue carpeting on all surfaces including the several doors on each side of the passage, and into a quite large and very normal looking bar. Though the bar was relatively busy there was plenty of room among the dark blue leather armchairs and semi-circular banquettes that ran alone one wall.

The four stood surveying the scene. As far as she could see Stephanie was the only woman.

'May I take your coat?' The man who had appeared behind her was tall and very blond. Like all the club employees he was dressed in tight leather trousers and a vest, like a running vest, but made in red leather. It displayed his bulging biceps and pectorals.

Stephanie slipped the coat from her shoulders and he took it away. She felt every pair of eyes in the room on her.

'When does the show start?' Caplin asked the man behind the bar.

'Fifteen minutes, Mr Caplin,' the barman replied.

'Just in time for a drink then.'

'It's all been arranged, sir,' the barman said. 'That table over there,' he continued, pointing to a semi-circular banquette in the middle of the wall.

158

'Champagne, I think. Dom Perignon.'

Stephanie saw Caplin pass a hundred-dollar bill over the counter which the barman palmed with alacrity.

'Thank you, sir,' the barman said. 'The drinks'll be right over.'

The numerous pairs of eyes watched Stephanie's progress across the room, following the swing of her hips and the tantalising way her nylon-clad leg was revealed by the dress as her left leg moved forward, only to be covered again, as the right was extended.

At the banquette Stephanie slid in first. Oscar and his father sat on her left and Devlin on her right. The barman brought over the champagne in a silver wine cooler full of ice and opened the bottle. He poured an inch into the glass he had placed in front of Caplin, who tasted it and nodded his approval.

Stephanie studied the rest of the large room. In fact there were two other women in the bar. She had not noticed them when she'd first come in but they sat with three men in an arrangement of leather armchairs in the centre of the bar. Curiously none of the five appeared to be drinking, there were no glasses on the coffee table in front of them. One of the women was a flaming redhead, the other, as far as Stephanie could see a brunette. As they sat with their back to her it was difficult to see any details of their appearance.

'What do you think?' Devlin asked Stephanie in a whisper.

'I don't know. What sort of place is this?'

'Very private. Very pricey. You have to be very wealthy to be a member. Discretion guaranteed.'

'Are you a member?'

'No. I've only been here as a guest. It isn't really for me.'

'Aren't we going to miss the show?' Stephanie asked Caplin. It had been about fifteen minutes since the barman had brought the champagne.

'No, don't worry. We won't miss a thing.' Caplin assured her.

She looked at Oscar. He appeared nervous and uncomfortable, as though he would rather not have been there at

159

all. His father, on the other hand, was expectant, his eyes sparkling with anticipation, his whole manner suggesting his excitement.

'You bitch!'

Everyone in the room looked round to see who had shouted so loudly. The man at the table with the two women had leapt to his feet and was standing in front of the redhead.

'You bitch!' he screamed again. 'You can't treat me like that.'

'Fuck off!' the redhead replied, not even looking at him.

The man was big and muscular. He stooped and pulled the woman to her feet in front of him.

'Don't tell me what to do in front of my friends.'

He slapped her across the face with the back of his hand. Immediately she slapped him back, first with the back of her hand and then with the palm, a double blow.

The other two men at the table both sprung to their feet.

'I told you to fuck off,' she said. 'And take your moronic friends with you.'

The redhead wore a full-length black velvet dress covering every inch of her body with the exception of one shoulder and one arm where it was cut away toga-fashion. Stephanie could just see the heels of her very high-heeled shoes.

'No one hits me, bitch,' the man shouted.

The leather-clad barman had come over.

'Cool it, gents. Just cool it,' he said.

'Tell him to fuck off then,' the redhead said.

'I think you should leave, lady,' the barman replied.

'No, she's going to stay,' the man who she had slapped said firmly. At that moment the two other men grabbed the redhead by the arms. She struggled furiously and managed to land a kick on the barman's shin. He howled with pain.

But she had not escaped the clutches of the men who held her so tightly.

'Let's see what you've got, you little prickteaser,' the slapped man said. He grabbed the neck of the black velvet dress and pulled. The whole front of the dress came away in the man's hand. Underneath the woman was wearing a black lacy bra, a thin black suspender belt holding up black stockings and a pair of matching lace panties. With his next swipe the man tore the bra away. The woman's tits were not big, but she had large erect nipples.

'Let's see the rest of her.' The man ripped the rest of the dress away. He hooked his hand into the waist of the panties and tried to rip them away too. But the material was too strong. Instead he tried to pull them down her legs but she was struggling and kicking her legs and he could make little progress. He reached into his pocket and took out the handle of a flick knife. In a second a wicked looking blade sprung into view, glistening in the light.

The redhead stopped struggling at once. 'No,' she breathed.

He pointed the knife at her belly.

For a second Stephanie felt her whole body tense, she was about to leap from her seat. Devlin held her back.

The man threaded the knife under the side of the panties and cut through the material. He repeated the process at the other side. The woman remained stock still staring at the blade of the knife. The man pulled the remnants of the panties out from between her legs, then folded the blade away and put the knife back into his pocket. The woman's pubic hair was thick and as red as the hair on her head.

'You're not man enough,' the redhead sneered. The man stripped off the jacket of his suit. He pulled off his shoes and unbuttoned his trousers pulling them off. He was not wearing socks or underpants. His cock was already erect. It shone under the lights as though it had been oiled. His muscular body was hairless and looked as though it had been oiled too. He had the physique of a body builder.

'You can't do that in here,' the barman said ineffectively.

'Fuck off, faggot,' the man said.

The redhead must have felt the tension in the arms of her captives lessen. Suddenly she wrested herself free. Naked, apart from the stockings and suspender belt she ran across the room. She ran straight to Caplin's table.

'Help me,' she said.

161

But the two men had run after her. As she got to the table they caught her by the arms again, but this time they pulled her forward, over the top of the table, sliding into the banquette next to Caplin on one side and Devlin on the other, each man holding her wrist in both hands, stretching her arm out across the table, her head a few inches from the silver wine cooler.

'Help me, please,' she pleaded looking straight into Caplin's eyes.

'Devlin . . .' Stephanie said wanting to do something.

It was only when she saw the faintest of smiles on Devlin's face that she realised what was going on. The velvet dress that ripped away so easily, the oiled body of the man, the compliance of everyone else in the room: this was the show.

'They're not going to help you, bitch,' the naked man said. 'They want to watch you taking it.'

He came up to the table. With the open palm of his hand he slapped her fleshy arse. The room echoed with the thwack of flesh on flesh.

'No!' the woman cried trying to struggle. Held as she was it was almost impossible for her to move.

'Yes,' the man said smacking her again.

Stephanie could see his erection bobbing in front of him. All his pubic hair had been shaved off. Even his balls were hairless. He advanced until his cock was poised at the lips of her cunt.

'Take it bitch.'

He rammed his cock into her. She screamed and fought the hands that held her.

'You bastard, you bastard!'

Stephanie could see everything so clearly, her tits squeezed flat by the table, the man's oiled cock pumping into her. That was why the barman had told Caplin it had all been arranged. That was why the woman had run to this table.

The man was fucking her hard. After no more than twelve or thirteen strokes he pulled out of her, took his cock in his hand, and wanked it twice. Then he held it tight and Stephanie saw spunk explode from its tip, out all over the woman's buttocks and back, even over the thin black lace of the suspender belt.

The two men released the woman's wrists and she slipped slowly off the table and down on to the floor.

'No one does that to my sister.' The voice rang out across the room. Stephanie had forgotten about the other woman, the brunette, who had been sitting at the table. Now she stood in the middle of the room. From somewhere a long bull-whip had appeared in her hand. She cracked it and the whip whistled through the air. With her other hand she pulled at the front of her crimson red dress. With the rent of parting Velcro the whole of the front of the dress came away in her hand, just as her 'sister's' black velvet dress had. Underneath the woman wore a costume of studded black leather. Fitted to her body like a glove, the garment was shaped like a leotard, cut high on the hip, its plunging neckline embossed with steel studs. Her thigh length boots left only a thin band of flesh visible between the top of the boot and the bottom of the leather costume, and were also black leather, their spiked high heels adding inches to the woman's already considerable height. But it was her body itself that was her most remarkable feature. Her arms and thighs were thick with muscle, deep, cultured muscle. Stephanie could see rippling muscle around her shoulders and pectorals too. This woman was a body builder of substantial strength.

If Stephanie had been fooled into thinking that the incident with the redhead was genuine – which she had – the management now dropped the attempt at pretence. A spotlight was snapped on to illuminate the Amazonian woman in her bizarre outfit and as she cracked the whip again music began to play, throbbing, sensual electronic chords.

The two men who had held the redhead over their table now also plucked away their suits, with the ease of Velcro fastening, and stood naked, their well-defined muscles oiled and smooth, their loins clad in leather G-strings. In a second they had caught the wrists of their erstwhile com-

163

panion, just as before they'd held the wrists of his victim. They started to drag him over to the Amazon.

'What are you doing,' he shouted struggling.

The whip cracked again.

'You're not using that thing on me. You hired me to fuck that girl. That was the end of the story lady. I did what you wanted. Now give me my money and let me go.'

'No one does that to my sister.'

'You hired me to do that,' he shouted. 'For Christ's sake I only did what you told me to do.'

Stephanie had not noticed the redhead disappear. She must have slipped away to change because now she appeared dressed, if dressed is the right word, in a series of black leather straps, cinched around her body, over her breasts and down between her legs. Coming up behind the captive she begun to pull a leather hood over his head. As soon as he realised what was going on he shook his head violently to push the hood away but inexorably the redhead pulled it down until it covered his eyes and mouth and chin. She strapped it in place. There were no holes in the hood apart from a small opening for his nostrils.

The two men dragged him over to the table where the whole scene had started. The Amazon had pulled a bar stool into the pool of light that now illuminated the area. The men pulled their captive off the stool, his face down; with practised ease the Amazon took four thick straps, binding his wrists to the front legs of the stool and his ankles to the back. Her hand stroked the long curve of his buttocks, bent over the stool.

'Your privilege, I think,' she said to the redhead.

'Yes.' The redhead took the whip. Stephanie could hear the man protesting but the words were muffled by the leather hood. The redhead raised the whip and slashed it across the white cheeks of his arse six times.

At each stroke of the whip the whole room whooped like a point had been scored at some sporting event. Everyone leant forward to watch.

Despite the room's air-conditioning, sweat was beaded on the redhead's brow, her body glistening with effort.

'And now . . .' the Amazon announced. There was no need to be more specific about what the 'and now' meant. While attention had been centred on the whip, the massive brunette had strapped on a huge black dildo. It protruded from her loins like a bizarre totem, the rim of its artificial glans, like some sleek aerodynamic fairing.

'Take the hood off.'

The redhead unstrapped the hood and pulled it off. The Amazon came round to face the man, the phallus in front of his face.

'Lick it,' she ordered.

'You're not using that thing on me.' His voice sounded hoarse. 'I only did what you told me,' he pleaded.

'Lick it,' she repeated.

He obeyed taking the dildo into his mouth.

Satisfied she pulled away and came round until she was behind him.

'No, no, no!' he screamed.

She parted the cheeks of his arse. Apart from the throbbing music there was complete silence in the room. The Amazon looked around the eager faces straining to see more.

'Yes?' she asked like the gladiator in the coliseum.

'Yes,' came a chorus of men's voices.

She reached forward and took the man's hips in her hands, her muscles bulging. She bucked her hips forward. At that second the lights went out, as a blood-curdling scream, an almost animal noise, echoed through the room.

It was no more than ten seconds before the lights came back on and the tableau in the centre of the room had disappeared, performers, armchairs, everything, presumably dropped into some stage trap in the floor.

'Well?' Caplin asked looking straight at Stephanie.

'It was all a performance?' Though she was quite sure the first part of the show had been a set up, she wasn't at all sure whether the man had been raped or not.

'Of course,' Caplin said. 'Every night there's something different but it's all a show.'

'I'm not so sure,' Stephanie said.

'It is.' Caplin assured her.

'I think he's right,' Devlin said.

Stephanie took a large swig of her champagne not at all sure that she had found what she'd seen exciting. Oscar certainly hadn't. He looked as white as a sheet and she could see his hand was trembling. His father on the other hand was clearly very excited by the whole thing.

'It's so clever, don't you think?' he said to Stephanie.

'It's original,' she said.

A moment later the trap in the floor, obviously operated by some sort of hydraulics, reappeared and on it the five performers. There was a smuttering of applause. Two leather-clad waiters toured the tables collecting slips of paper passed to them by the members.

The waiter arrived at their table.

'Will you be bidding tonight, Mr Caplin?' he asked.

'I was going to bid for the first victim. Present for my son,' he said, 'but we have guests.'

'Please,' Devlin said, 'don't let us spoil your plans.'

'Well, Oscar?'

'Can we just get out of here, dad?'

'It appears we're not interested.'

The waiters gave the slips of paper to the barman who sorted through them while the five performers waited. Then he handed them each one slip of paper and they quickly went over to whichever member had bid the most for their services. The Amazon strode over to her bidder, the whip still in her hand, her strong muscled body glistening in the light. Stephanie could see Caplin's eyes following her as she led the man out.

'Can we go, dad?'

'If that's what you want,' Caplin said, making the universal sign for the bill to the barman.

'Do you come here often?' she asked. Being American he would not understand the currency of the phrase; this was a long way from the Saturday night pally.

'Just to unwind. The Amazon has a very vivid imagination. You never quite know what she's going to do next.'

'I bet,' Stephanie said thinking that her imagination had been known to be vivid too.

Retrieving her fur from the cloakroom they passed down the long blue corridor and out through the two entrance doors to the street. It was cold. A police siren wailed in the background while the subway trains rumbled underfoot.

George waited, scurrying out of the Cadillac to open the rear door. The four climbed inside. He had been running the motor with the heater on so the car would be warm. Stephanie indicated for Oscar to sit on the rear seat next to her this time. Caplin sat beside her on the other side with Devlin in the jump seat.

'Back to our suite for a nightcap?' he suggested.

'Why not? The night is young,' Caplin agreed.

Stephanie put her hand on Oscar's thigh as a gesture of comfort, but the boy still looked pale and unhappy. On the other side of her, his father was in the opposite mood. Stephanie could feel his excitement radiating from his body as it pressed into her side. It was almost as though his body was vibrating.

'Did you have a good time, my dear?' he asked. She got the impression he was eager to feed off her reaction, that he would have been glad if she had been shocked.

'It was okay,' she said non-committally, not wanting to give him any vampirish delight.

TEN

In their suite at the Pierre hotel, Devlin poured brandy from a very special bottle of 1949 Armagnac he had found in a little shop on West 57th Street. They all swilled the liquid up the sides of the huge balloon glasses, its viscosity making it cling to the walls of the glass, before sipping it appreciatively. All that is, with the exception of Oscar, who gulped it down like a man who had been in a desert. At least it brought a little colour back into his cheeks.

Reluctantly Caplin was drawn into a business discussion. Over their second glass they sat at the dining table as Devlin pulled papers from his briefcase to illustrate a point he wanted to make. Stephanie remained on the sofa next to Oscar.

'You feeling better?' she said.

'I didn't mean to be a wimp,' he said dolefully.

'You weren't. You don't have to like that stuff.'

'My pa's really into it. But, I mean, they started to fuck that guy. Gruesome.'

'I'm sure there must be something we could do to take your mind off it.'

'How can people do things like that?'

'Can't we?'

'What?'

'Take your mind off it? Make you feel better.'

'I'll be all right.'

'Good. Come with me then.'

'Where?'

'To the bedroom.'

'Now?'

'They're going to be hours. We've got to do something to entertain ourselves, haven't we?'

She took Oscar's hand and lead him into the bedroom. She hadn't had time to analyses her own reaction to what she had seen at the Shades of Hades club. It had not excited her as much, say, as the image of Devlin sprawled on the floor of the Cadillac, but there was no denying that she had been excited by it, especially when she realised it was all a performance. But she felt, her initial fear and surprise had stopped her enjoying the spectacle as much as she might have done otherwise. Clearly this was the exact opposite reaction to most of the members of the club including Caplin.

'Close the door,' she said once they were in the bedroom. She stood by the bed.

'Shall I lock it?' He pressed the button in the centre of the door handle which deadlocked the catch, without waiting for her reply.

'You'll have to pull it off.'

'What?' he said puzzled.

'My dress. Pull it over my head.'

He hesitated, not quite knowing what she expected him to do. Then he went over to her, and took the sides of her dress in his hands. He gathered the material up until he held the hem around her thighs then pulled it up over her body. She bowed her head and slipped out of the dress, standing in front of him in her sheer tights and suede high heels.

'No bra marks, do you lie in the sun nude?' Oscar asked.

'Yes. Take my tights off now.'

He pulled at the waist of the tights with both hands. They rolled down her legs. He dropped on to his knees to ease them off her calves. She kicked her shoes off and he pulled the nylon from her feet and looking up into her thick thatch of pubic hair.

'God you're some beautiful woman.'

She put her hand out to touch his hair.

'Thank you.'

Oscar seemed instantly different, more confident and relaxed, no doubt because his father was no longer around.

She picked up one of the packages from Bergdorf Goldman that she had not yet unwrapped.

'I want to show you what I bought.' She walked into the bathroom.

'Can't I watch.'

'Ruins the element of surprise.' She left the bathroom door open so they could talk.

'Won't Devlin mind?'

'Mind what?'

'You. Me. In here.'

'He does what he's told.'

'What sort of relationship do you have?'

'Open.'

'You seem very close.'

'We are.'

'But he doesn't mind if you . . .'

'Oscar. He has certain needs. I cater them. What else I do is up to me, isn't it?'

'Sounds ideal.'

She had pulled on the cream silk and lace teddy she had bought. It was the softest silk she had ever felt. The delicate lace panels cupped her breasts, with V-shaped inserts of lace at the hips half revealing, half hiding the long sculpted contours of her flanks, and the curious depression at the top of each thigh where it joined the pelvic bone.

Stephanie pinned her hair up again. Pulling the dress over her head had made some strands fall loose.

'Well, is this more to your taste?' she asked stepping out of the bathroom and turning round so he could see every angle.

'It looks sensational. You look sensational.' He sat on the edge of the bed.

'And you look a new man.'

'I feel it.'

'You're so straight, aren't you?' She smiled to herself.

'Am I? In contrast to pa I guess I am.'

Stephanie came to stand right in front of him. She could

170

see his eyes on her body, on her breasts under the lace, on the dark shadow of her pubic hair. 'This silk is so soft. Feel.'

She picked his hand up and put it on her naval. He caressed the silk. It was slippery smooth.

'What if pa goes home?'

'They'll talk for hours.'

'Devlin might want to go to bed.'

'He'll have to sleep on the couch.'

Stephanie slid herself on to her knees, took his head in her hands and kissed him full on the mouth, probing her tongue deep between his lips, kissing him hard and not letting him up for air. She would have liked to have thrown the bedroom doors open and let the two older men watch, but after his reaction to the Shades of Hades club, she thought she'd better not suggest it.

Stephanie felt her sexual excitement mounting. It was like a ravenous hunger waiting to be fed. In the old days, that seemed so long ago but were no more than months ago, she would have suppressed her needs, waited until the man took the initiative, until the man decided the moment was right for him. All that had gone.

She slipped off Oscar's lap. 'Take your clothes off, Oscar.' There was no room for discussion in her tone.

Standing up he pulled off his jacket and shirt. Stephanie was impatient. She dropped to her knees, unbuttoned his trousers and pulled the zip of his fly down over the bulge already growing under it. As his trousers fell away she pulled his little black briefs down to his ankles. She instantly seized the shaft of his penis in one hand.

'I remember this,' she said before gobbling his cock into her mouth urgently. She was in no mood for subtlety. Holding his cock steady with her hand, she used her tongue to grease its length with her saliva, then pushed it deep until she could feel it right at the back of her throat. She pulled back, back until it was almost at her lips again, until she was sucking at its tip, her tongue probing its little orifice before she plunged forward, and her lips felt the brush of his pubic hair.

He was moaning. He put his hand on her head to stop her

but he could not resist the feelings she was creating in him. Instead of stopping her his hands encouraged, giving her the rhythm, the right degree of oscillation. In seconds he felt his spunk, prompted by her hands gently pulling at his balls, rising in his cock and knew it was too late to do anything to prevent himself from coming. He was out of control.

Stephanie knew it too. She pushed down on his cock until it was buried deep in her throat, then she sucked on the shaft with her lips, sucking the spunk out of him. She felt him tense, his whole body rigid, and then the spasms of his cock as it spat spunk out into her throat. She swallowed it enthusiastically.

'I'm sorry . . . I can't . . .'

'Don't apologise. It's what I wanted.'

'You're just so good.'

'Lie on the bed,' she said gently.

'But . . .'

She got up from her knees and put a finger to his lips, 'Sh . . .' she whispered.

While he lay on the huge double bed Stephanie unlocked the bedroom door and walked out into the living room. She poured more Armagnac into the two balloon glasses and carried them back into the bedroom. Devlin and Caplin sat at the table, a set of documents now spread out between them. Neither appeared to notice Stephanie.

'There,' she said handing Oscar a glass. 'Drink this. You're going to need it.'

She sipped the brandy then put the glass down on the bedside table.

'What are they doing?' Oscar looked anxious.

'Still talking. I told you.'

'Did you lock the door?'

'Yes, Oscar. I locked the door. You're safe.'

'I don't think I'll be able . . .' He was looking down at his flaccid penis.

'Sh,' she said again.

Stephanie reached down between her legs to unfasten the three press studs that held the crotch of the teddy in place. She pulled it up over her head and threw it aside. Naked, she slowly picked the pins out of her hair. When they were all gone she combed it out using her fingers for a brush.

She saw his eyes on her body.

'Do you like my body, Oscar?'

'It's amazing.'

'You have to do as I tell you Oscar. Will you?'

'Yes,' he said almost hypnotically.

She picked up the silk teddy from the floor and, kneeling beside him on the bed, trailed it across his navel. The silk was still warm. She trailed it over his cock and down his thighs, then threw it aside again.

Stephanie cupped her breasts in her hands and kneaded them hard before moving to touch just her nipples, holding them between the thumb and forefinger of each hand.

'You mustn't touch, Oscar. Just watch.'

She pinched each nipple in turn, feeling the sharp thrill their nerves sent through her body.

'I like being watched. Have you ever watched a woman masturbate, Oscar?' she asked wetting her dry lips with her tongue.

He shook his head.

'It'll be a new experience for you then.'

Her left hand had snaked down her side, smoothing and caressing her flesh as it went. Her fingertips combed through her pubic hair until she found the crease of her labia. She delved down to expose her clitoris then tapped it lightly making her finger like a little hammer.

'Oh, it feels so good.'

It did. She felt the circle begin, the inertia of the heavy flywheel that controlled her orgasm, slowly overcome. It begun to turn, turn for her. She knew her body so well now, she thought, better than she ever had before. She knew all its tricks, all its secrets; its means of delay or acceleration.

Oscar's cock began to swell.

She changed from the little tapping movements to a gentle side to side pressure. Taking her other hand away from her breast she passed it under her bottom and into the lips of her cunt, using it to penetrate while her other hand remorselessly wanked her clitoris.

'Can you see?' she asked unnecessarily, his eyes riveted to the movements between her legs.

'Yes,' he said hoarsely.

'I'm going to make myself come,' she said than moaned as her fingers and his eyes sent a new shock wave of pleasure through her body, cranking the flywheel faster.

His cock was fully erect again, hard and red.

She concentrated on herself, she took the rhythm that she knew would bring her off. She closed her eyes and felt her excitement, indulged the endless sexual images she could call up, tasted his spunk in her mouth and, as she felt the flywheel spinning out of control, needing no more impulsion as her body came off, her two hands knotting every nerve in her body, she saw the woman in the club stretched out on the table inches away from her, her eyes pleading to be saved.

But her orgasm was just the beginning.

'Now it's your turn, Oscar. Don't you want to fuck me?'

He needed no further bidding. Even before she could get off her knees he sprang on her like a tiger, his mouth searching for her as he pushed her back, her head almost off the foot of the bed. His cock penetrated her in one movement, as though a practised skill. He did not pause. As soon as it was in her he started pistoning into the silky wet cunt as it clung to his hard cock. He started fast and got faster. Faster and faster, ramming her like a steam-hammer pushing her up of the end of the bed until her head hung down, her long hair streaming on to the floor. Faster and faster.

She had created his need. He'd never seen a woman do what she had just done in front of his eyes. She was so wild, so free.

His hands were kneading her breasts, pinching her nipples as he'd watched her do moments before.

She thought he would come quickly but he didn't. Instead his urgency made her come. There was something about her head hanging down as it was, almost like coming upside down, maybe because of all the blood rushing to her brain. No, she knew what it was. For once she was not in control, off balance, she couldn't stop him, stop herself. At any moment she might fall off the bed completely. He would fall on top of her, they'd be uncoupled.

Her orgasm roared through her, at any moment expecting to be quelched as they fell over. But it wasn't. She managed the precarious position, even as she lost all control, her head almost touching the carpet, her long hair spread out like a waterfall, her breasts inverted, pointing to her neck, her back arch over the end of the bed.

Without coming out of her Oscar hauled her sideways back up on to the sheets, immediately resuming his almost maniac rhythm, plunging into her without the slightest pause.

She felt herself coming again, coming over his remorseless cock, loving his energy and his power. She felt her cunt contracting, her clitoris, pinched between their two bodies, throbbing, her previous orgasms lingering, echoing, reverberating with this one, her whole body sensitised, penetrated and fucked.

The feeling of her cunt contracting around his cock was the last straw for Oscar. As he pumped he felt his cock exploding, shooting spunk into her as he continued to ram forward.

He had no idea he had any spunk left. It appeared he had copious amounts. It was a long time before his motion subsided. He still stroked in and out, almost unconsciously, enjoying the little tremors of feeling still left in his body.

He rolled off her as soon as his flaccid cock slipped out of her. He looked down at it. His cock and his pubic hair was wet, soaking wet.

'My God . . .' was all he could say. Stephanie did not attempt to get up. Oscar propped himself on one elbow, kissed her cheek, then delicately parted the hair that had strayed over her face.

'Can I tell you something?' Oscar said seriously.

'Of course.'

'Pa was taking me out to get me laid tonight. That's why he took me to the Shades of Hades club. He was going to buy me one of the whores. Except, it wouldn't have worked. After what I saw I wouldn't have been able to do much. It would have been a disaster.'

'Why did he want you to get laid?'

'He said it was time.'

'Time?'

'I'm a virgin.' He corrected himself immediately, 'I was a virgin.'

'Oscar,' Stephanie said.

'Yes.'

'If you hadn't have told me I'd never have known.'

'Really?' He looked pleased.

'Really,' she said smiling into his earnest face. Then he smiled too.

Devlin had gone downstairs to breakfast with a New York banker to tell him the bad news, that despite the late night attempt to win Caplin round, he still refused to sign the deal. They had gone over several clauses and Devlin had increased his offer and there appeared now to be no areas of disagreement. But Caplin still refused to sign.

Not wanting more than black coffee and orange juice Stephanie took a long bath, soaking in the big tub, in her own concoction of the four types of bath oil provided, topped up by an ample sachet of bubble bath.

She had been laying enjoying the feeling for about fifteen minutes when the phone rang. She could reach the phone on the wall in the bathroom without getting out of the bath.

'Hello,' she said brushing the bubbles off her arm.

'Stephanie?' The voice belonged to Caplin.

'Hi,' she said cheerily.

'Is Devlin there?'

'No, sorry. He's having breakfast downstairs. Hold on and I'll have him paged.'

'No, no. It was you I wanted to speak to.'

'Oh?'

'I wondered . . .' he hesitated then decided to take the

bull by the horns. 'I wondered if you'd like to have lunch with me.'

She thought about it for a moment.

'Alone you mean,' she said innocently knowing perfectly well that's what he meant, 'without Devlin?'

'Yes, just the two of us.'

'Mr Caplin, what are you suggesting?' she said in mock horror.

'I haven't been able to stop thinking about you.'

'Really?'

'I find you such an interesting woman. I'm so attracted to you.'

'And what about Devlin?'

'You tell me?'

'Shall I tell Devlin we're having lunch together?'

'That's up to you.'

She paused, making him wait.

'Okay. Pick me up here at twelve thirty.'

'Twelve,' he said.

'Twelve thirty,' she insisted. 'We each lunch late in England.'

'Twelve thirty at the Pierre then. I look forward to it.'

'So do I,' she said hooking the phone back on to the wall.

She was dried and made-up by the time Devlin arrived back in the suite, and wrapped in one of the hotel bathrobes.

'Guess who's just called me,' she said.

'Caplin.'

'How did you guess?'

'I thought he was rather interested in you. He couldn't take his eyes off you most of the evening.'

'He's taking me out to lunch. Definitely doesn't want you to be there.'

'I wonder . . .' She saw Devlin's mind working.

'If I can I will,' she said knowing what he was thinking.

'Will what?' he said.

'Get him to sign the contract.'

'You think he might?'

'Depends what he wants from me, doesn't it?'

'And how badly.'

'Exactly.'

'I'd take a copy with you, just in case. All he's got to do is sign.'

'He was very turned on at the club, wasn't he?'

'Very. I had no idea he was into all that.'

'Well maybe I can find out exactly what he is into.' Changing the subject she said, 'I was thinking about that club.'

'What about it?'

'Was that all a performance? I mean the girl who was raped. And the guy. It seemed so real.'

'I know. It struck me the first time I went there too.'

'It was the same?'

'No. But you didn't know whether it was a performance or not. There was this woman, she pretended to be drunk. At least I assume she was pretending. She went round the table trying to get a man to fuck her. Finally one of the men agreed. She stripped all his clothes off and got him all hard. Then she started to strip. She had nice breasts, not big but quite shapely. Anyway this guy was chafing at the bit, all hot, couldn't wait, all his friends egging him on. He comes up behind her, starts to pull her knickers down and then jumps away like he's been bitten by a rattlesnake. The woman was a man, cock the size of a donkey.'

'God.'

'I never knew whether that was all a set up.'

Stephanie opened the wardrobe door and stared at the array of clothes.

'Well I'd better wear something slinky for Mr Caplin, I think. But not too obvious.'

She stripped off the towelling robe and walked across to the chest of drawers where she had put the vast selection of lingerie she had brought with her.

Devlin sat watching, sitting on the edge of the bed, as she slipped a black bra over her firm breasts, clipped a suspender belt around her slim waist and pulled a pair of French knickers, slit at the sides almost to the waist, up over her hips. She tucked the suspenders under the knickers.

'You do it,' she said, throwing a packet of gunmetal grey stockings on to the bed. 'And don't ladder them.'

Devlin carefully opened the cellophane packet as Stephanie sat on the bed beside him. He picked out the nylons and lay them on his lap. Taking one in his huge hands, he bunched the material to make a neat little pocket around the nylon reinforcement at the toe and held it out for her. She pointed her toe and then held her leg out straight so that Devlin could roll the stocking up over her calf and over the long muscles of her thigh, smoothing and stretching it as he went, watching as the tight grey material encased the leg. His banana-sized fingers worked with surprising dexterity. He repeated the process with the other leg. When the stockings were in place, Stephanie fastened the suspenders, after Devlin had tried and failed. That was one art Devlin had not yet mastered.

'So,' she stood up.

'So,' Devlin said, adopting the sort of sheepishness that overcame him even now, after all these months, when he wanted to introduce sex into the conversation.

Stephanie saw a bulge tenting his trousers. When she had first met him Devlin's ability to achieve an erection was limited and certainly never spontaneous. Discovering his sexual proclivities, she had changed all that, though only when they slipped into their respective roles, master and slave. This was a new development; though she had ordered him to put the stockings on it was hardly the full-scale performance. She thought it deserved a reward.

She climbed on to the bed on her knees and pushed him back until he was lying flat.

'Well,' she said circling the material of his trousers around his hard cock.

She unzipped his fly. His cock burst out like a dog jumping through a paper hoop. Without hesitation she plunged her mouth down on it. She felt the huge gnarled and veined shaft filling her, its tip, bulbous and hot, at the back of her throat. No woman would be able to take all of Devlin into her mouth. Her lips were pursed no more than halfway down the engorged flesh.

She eased her hand into his boxer shorts and found his balls, cupping them in her hand, playing with them, juggling them up and down. She heard Devlin moan. She sucked hard, using her tongue to tease the ridge of his glans before she started an insistent rhythm, moving her mouth up and down, back and forth, taking as much of him as she possibly could.

Devlin was bucking his hips off the bed, matching her rhythm. She was making him come. His mind was not full of images of anything but her – her body, wrapped in the sleek black lingerie, the arch of her breasts exaggerated by the bra, her thighs bisected by the grey welt of the stockings, the black suspender on the top of her thigh loose and slack, the one at the side stretched and taut, pulling the stockings into a high peak against the creamy tanned flesh. They were not playing games. This was real.

She felt his cock reacting, throbbing, pumping spunk ready to ejaculate. She altered her position, moving her leg over his head so she was kneeling above his face, directly above, not because she wanted him to reciprocate – she didn't – but because she wanted him to be able to see the crease of her labia, the long slit of her sex only slightly veiled by the loose folds of the black French knickers.

He stared up at her. Her cunt seemed to be alive, pulsing like an animal, a hungry furry animal. He could see the tight curves of her buttocks under the black silk. He could see the way the muscles of her thighs, the sinews and tendons, were stretched open. He felt himself coming.

Stephanie sucked his cock and squeezed his balls, her rhythm as regular as a metronome. She felt his spunk begin its journey, felt it in his hard shaft, felt his whole body tense as he reached out to stop her head pulling away again, wanting to come as deep in her throat as he could. His cock jerked and great gobs of white spunk splashed into her mouth, down her throat, as his eyes devoured the shape and lines and details of her cunt.

Stephanie rolled onto her back. Some spunk escaped from the side of her mouth, but most of it she swallowed. It tasted salty.

'Your turn,' he said running his hand up her thigh.

'No,' she said catching his hand by the wrist.

But it was too late. She was too aroused to put up genuine resistance. The tip of his huge finger had already grazed the soft flesh of her labia and her body had already responded, almost unconsciously, by pushing down on it. The loose crotch of the French knickers were no hindrance. In a second Devlin's finger was buried up to the knuckle in the silky walls of her sex and Stephanie was using it, riding it, fucking it. She pushed down hard, wanting to feel the finger at the neck of her womb. It filled her as only Devlin could.

She tasted his spunk in her mouth. She opened her eyes and looked at Devlin, most of this clothes still on, as he was bent over her, supported on one elbow, wanking her effortlessly with just one finger. There was something in that picture that made her come, suddenly, unexpectedly. Her body tensed and before she realised that was happening her eyes were closing so she could see, in the blackness behind them, the fireworks of her body as it sunk into a bed of perfect ecstasy.

It might have been hours before she opened her eyes again. She couldn't remember feeling his finger come out of her.

They lay together without moving. She would need to find another pair of black French knickers.

The black Mercedes limousine drew up outside the Pierre at exactly 12.30 p.m. One of the many uniformed commissionaires – mostly Negro – opened the rear door of the black-windowed car and Henry Caplin got out, a vicuña coat over his shoulders, his immaculately cut suit a grey Prince of Wales check, his white silk shirt and pink tie perfectly colour coordinated. His cuff-links were gold, his shoes handmade. His head of white hair was so carefully combed and brushed and parted that not a strand of hair was out of place. He looked precisely what he was: a man of wealth and substance.

Walking through the swing doors, held open for him by

yet another commissionaire, he strode up to Stephanie who was standing in the foyer.

'Hi,' he said, 'wonderful to see you.' He looked as though he meant it. 'You look marvellous.'

'Thank you,' she said kissing him perfunctorily on the cheek, and knowing it was true. The plain black dress she had chosen was a piece of expensive tailoring that emphasised the slimness of her waist and the strong curve of her bust. Its V-neck line was modest in comparison with other items in her wardrobe. It revealed little.

'I booked at the Algonquin. The English always eat there.'

'Do they? I've never been.'

'You'll like it. It's part of old New York. The Critics Circle, H. L. Mencken and Dorothy Parker. When New York had some style.'

'Doesn't it now?'

'Not really.' He indicated the car. 'Your carriage awaits.'

The interior of the Mercedes was not quite as luxurious as the Cadillac – no television, no bar – but it was just as comfortable and spacious. Stephanie settled into the leather seat with Caplin beside her, as the car pulled out into the seemingly endless stream of honking, noisy, irritable, New York traffic.

'Stephanie,' Caplin said, 'first I want to thank you.'

'For what?'

'For Oscar. For what you did for Oscar.'

'He told you,' she was astonished.

'No, of course not.'

'How do you know what I did then?'

'It did not take much imagination my dear. I know I was involved with Devlin. But you left the bedroom door open when you came to get the brandies. You were hardly dressed to play a game of scrabble.

'No, I suppose not,' she laughed.

'And even if I hadn't seen you, well Oscar's a different person. He suddenly seems to have grown up.'

'You were taking him to the Shades of Hades to have him,' she searched for the right word, 'initiated.'

'Have to confess I was. It was a mistake. I just thought it

might be fun. Obviously he didn't agree. He's such a serious boy. He's a Rhodes scholar you know. Doing unbelievably well. But he doesn't seem to have much fun.'

That was a picture of Oscar Stephanie did not recognise but she thought it best not to say so.

The car had crawled down 5th Avenue, the twenty blocks to the Algonquin. The chauffeur opened the rear passenger door.

Caplin led the way into the tiny Blue Bar by the front entrance. They sat on the leather-covered banquette.

'Best martinis in town,' Caplin said.

'I'd love one.'

The martinis arrived in bell-shaped cocktail glasses. Caplin was right. The martini was very cold and lethal. Stephanie felt the liquor warming her stomach.

In the Oak Room they eat oysters and grilled Maine lobster and Crystal champagne.

Caplin was attentive and charming. He was undoubtedly an extremely attractive man. Though the meal he made no attempt to proposition her. By the time coffee arrived she had decided – it seemed to be her role nowadays – she had to take the initiative.

'So why where you so anxious to see me on my own, Caplin?' she asked her voice clear and businesslike.

'I thought that would be obvious.'

'So did I. But apparently not.'

'Oh yes,' he hesitated. 'Yes. I suppose you're right. To tell you the truth I'm not sure where to begin. Especially with what happened to Oscar.'

'What's Oscar got to do with it?'

'Nothing. I just wouldn't want you to think . . .'

'What?'

'Father and son. That there was any . . .'

'Conspiracy?'

'Connection.'

'I don't. You're a very attractive man. I find you attractive. I find your reticence a little annoying but perhaps I can understand it in view of the fact that last night I was fucking your son.'

183

Judging by the 'well really' muttered by the middle-aged woman at the next table, she had clearly heard all or part of the conversation. Stephanie caught her eye and smiled angelically. The woman looked away in disgust.

'You're very direct.'

'I suppose so.'

'And what about Devlin?'

'What about Devlin? What do you want to know?'

'Your relationship?'

'Do you care?'

Caplin hesitated for a moment clearly thinking about the question. 'To be absolutely honest, no I don't.'

'Well then.'

'I suppose I'm not used to this.'

'This what?'

'Modern women. I'm used to doing all the leading.'

'Caplin, either you want to fuck me or you don't. If that's what this lunch is all about it's perfectly all right with me. I don't need the small talk. I don't even need the lunch come to that. You could just as well have had me in the back of your limousine. You only had to ask. If that scares you or puts you off then I'll leave now.'

'It doesn't. I find it very stimulating.'

'Good. Then we seem to have arrived on mutual ground. So what are we going to do about it?'

'What do you think we should do?' Before she could answer he laughed heartily. 'I'm doing it again aren't I? I should be telling you.'

'No. I'll tell you. Go out to the desk and see if there's a room available in the hotel.'

'Now?'

'Yes, now.' She said letting her annoyance into her voice. 'Go up to the room. Order another bottle of champagne from room service, phone me here with the room number, then take all your clothes off and wait. Does that sound interesting?' She touched his hand on the table.

'Very.'

He got up to go. The maître d' arrived in alarm that something might be wrong.

184

'Is everything all right, Mr Caplin?'

'Everything is fine, Albert. Look after the lady for me will you. See she has everything she needs.'

Albert's palm was gifted with a set of hundred dollar notes.

'Certainly, Mr Caplin.'

As Caplin walked through to the lobby Albert swarmed over to Stephanie and asked if there was anything she wanted. She ordered another coffee which came almost at once. She looked across at the two women on the next table, dry, wizened women, their faces lined with wrinkles, and caked with too much make-up. The one who had overheard Stephanie's conversation glanced at her again, her eyes examining her as though she were some exotic but dangerous specimen in a private zoo.

Albert, the maître d' approached with a cordless phone in his hand. Stephanie was slightly disappointed. She had expected him to bring a phone to the table and plug it in: that's what they'd always done in the Humphrey Bogart films.

'Telephone call, madam,' he said handing her the phone.

'Thank you.'

She took the phone. 'Caplin,' she said.

'Room 510,' he said.

'Got it.'

Leaving the telephone on the table, she walked out of the restaurant and into the oak-panelled lounge littered with heavy and ancient armchairs, no two the same, and carpeted in what had once been a rich patterned red Wilton, but was now faded and worn, almost threadbare. Stephanie waited for the equally ancient lift. It arrived with a clanging and grinding of metal. The liftboy – in fact a man of sixty-five plus – opened the metal gates.

'Floor please,' he said automatically.

'Five.'

'English?'

'Yes.'

'We get a lot of English here.'

Using the wheel-like handle he stopped the lift at the fifth floor, gauging the height and speed of the lift perfectly, as he stopped it level with the floor. It was his own private game. He had been playing it for thirty years.

Stephanie followed the arrows to Room 510. It was in the corner where the corridor turned at right angles. The door was ajar. Closing it firmly behind her she found herself in a small sitting room with a television and two small sofas. Beyond was a double door into the bedroom. One of the doors was ajar too.

She pushed the door open. Caplin was lying on the bed naked, though covered, to the waist at least, by a sheet. He had a glass of champagne in his hand.

'Very good,' Stephanie said going over to the dressing table where the bottle sat in a wine cooler and pouring herself a glass.

'Just as you ordered,' Caplin said enjoying the word 'ordered'. She sat on the bed and sipped the wine running her other hand down Caplin's throat into the thick hair of his chest, most of which was as white as the hair on his head. His body was firm and muscled. His arms looked strong.

He reached forward and pulled down the long zip at the back of her dress. She put her glass down on the bedside table. He did the same.

'You're a very beautiful woman.'

'You're a very attractive man.' Stephanie stood up and pulled the dress from each shoulder in turn. She held it at her bust for a moment, looking into Caplin's eyes, before letting it fall to the floor. She stepped out of it, picked it up and threw it on to the chair where Caplin had folded his suit.

Stephanie could see herself in the long mirror at the side of the bed; the bra pushing her breasts up into a plump arch above its black silk and lace, the suspender belt hidden under the waistband of the French knickers but with its suspenders emerging like long alien fingers pointing down to her feet.

She was just about to reach behind her back to unclasp the bra when Caplin caught her hand.

'No,' he said pulling her back on to the bed. 'No.'

He pushed her down on to the sheets and covered her mouth with his, kissing her hard, his tongue hot between her lips, exploring her mouth, her hands running all over his body, feeling, touching, caressing. He squeezed at her breasts under the bra, smoothed at the silk of the knickers, felt the contrast between flesh and nylon in the middle of her thighs, ran his hand down under the nylon stocking, feeling the rasp of nylon on the back of his hand, then going up again to press the black silk into the curve of her pubic bone.

He broke the kiss and used his mouth to nibble and kiss her ear. At the same time he pulled her across the bed so she was squarely in the middle. His mouth moved to her neck while his hand lay flat on her navel, lifting the waistband of the knickers and venturing down until his fingertips felt the fringes of her black pubic hair.

Stephanie felt his erect cock at the side of her thigh. She tried to reach it with her hand but he pulled her wrist away and slammed it down on the bed just above her head.

'No,' he said again firmly.

His hand was delving into the forest of hair, searching it, combing it for his objective. His mouth worked down her neck, kissing, licking, nibbling, stopping short of biting but only just.

The tip of his finger found her clitoris. It was wet. Stephanie was wet, her cunt awash with passion. It did not surprise her. He was so strong, so hard, so forceful. He was exactly what she wanted.

The finger moved in little circles. She could hear the silk russle as his hand moved. The presence of his hand had pulled the crotch of the knickers, trapped at the back between the sheets and her arse, into the slit of her labia. She could feel the material rubbing against her nether lips as his hand moved. He was making the little circles right on the knot of her clitoris. He was making her come with his touch. For the second time that day she came suddenly, almost instantly. None of her usual slow build-up. One minute she was able to feel and think and enjoy what he was doing to her: the next her whole body seemed to collapse

187

inward, every feeling concentrated on the tiniest movements on her clitoris, delicious, sensational movements, and she could do nothing but fall into a pit of black, bottomless feeling.

He felt her come. He felt her whole body quiver, every nerve responding without reference to mind. He didn't stop. For a second her body arched in involuntary protest but the protest was short-lived. Her body subsided, the feelings he was generating too strong to make her want to stop him.

It was as though he had entered her orgasm, as though he were right inside it, standing in the middle of the ripples of feeling spreading out from her like a stone thrown into a pond. His finger was like a stone, hard, impenetrable, unstoppable. She felt her orgasm erupting again, again flooding over his finger, again provoked by his seemingly perfect knowledge of the rhythms of her body. She wouldn't have believed it possible to come so quickly again but her body knew differently. Again it locked around her, taking its pleasure, plunging her into a maelstrom of sensation.

This time his finger left her. He was pulling at the waistband of her knickers, pulling them off. Stephanie, befuddled by her feelings, took a moment to realise what was required of her. Then, feeling him trying to tug the material from under her buttocks, she lifted her hips off the bed. Caplin pulled the knickers away. As he unhooked them from around her ankles, he bent forward to kiss the arch of her foot. He pulled her high heels off one by one, then kissed each foot in turn, working up from the ankle to the knee, up as far as the clip of the suspender in the middle of her thigh before going back to the foot on the other leg and starting again. When he reached the thigh the second time he continued up until his mouth was on the little dimple of flesh just under the crease where thigh met pelvis.

She knew what he was going to do next. She wanted it. Her cunt cried out for it as though it had had no completion. She opened her legs wide.

His mouth fell on her labia, his tongue darting out, pressing into her cunt, licking the wet flesh between her cunt's lips. His mouth felt so hot, burning hot. He seemed to be lapping up the juices from her body like a cat lapping cream.

She felt herself coming again, uncontrollably as his tongue probed her sex. Each orgasm seemed to have made her hotter, more sensitive, more turned on. Each seemed to take her higher. This time she felt her climax roar through her body, shaking her every nerve, like a low-flying jet plane. Her body quivered in its wake her cunt contracting involuntarily. Suddenly his mouth was gone and in a split second was replaced by his cock, driven into her up to the hilt, right up her soaking, aching cunt. But it did not move. He did not stroke it in and out of her. He kept it pressed deep inside, rigid and unmoving in her melting flesh. The feelings in her body were so intense she could not tell, or even think about whether the orgasm that raked through her body now was yet another climax or merely the same one, driven higher and deeper by his cock. All Stephanie could do was feel. She knew she was literally screaming with pleasure. She knew she had wrapped herself around Caplin's muscular body. She knew she was trembling hopelessly. But that was all she could cope with consciously. The rest of the feelings that tore through her body were beyond objective thought.

As he felt her body slowly relax, her trembling subside like the calming of a sea, he relaxed too, allowing his cock to pull back a little. He looked down into her eyes. He saw her struggling to focus.

Then, almost imperceptibly at first, he began to move his cock inside her, a gentle movement, hardly more than a half an inch to begin with. Stephanie moaned. After the climatic sensations it was soothing.

She slipped her hands down to his buttocks and clasped him in her hands. She wanted him to come now. She pushed him forward so his cock went deeper. He responded, increasing the length of his stroke, and moving faster too. Using her hands she encouraged, persuaded, urged. She pushed her body up, angling herself so he could feel how hungry she was for him.

'Give it to me, please,' she whispered in his ear.

He was plunging into her now, full strokes of his hard cock. He didn't care about her now, only himself, his body driving him, freed of constraints, allowed to take its pleasure. He had found his rhythm. The rhythm that would bring him off. The melting, pliant woman underneath him made him, by contrast feel so hard, so masculine, so sexy. He looked down, down to where their bodies were joined. He could see his cock sliding in and out of her, from the dark growth of her pubic hair at the base of her iron flat navel, and, on her thigh, the welt of the stocking top dividing her leg in two, making the soft creamy flesh above the nylon seem that much more vulnerable and exposed.

He felt his cock moving inexorably to climax. His mind was so full of pictures – how she had slipped her dress off, the look in her eyes, so knowing – and his body so full of feeling that he knew he was past the point of no return.

Sensing his condition Stephanie snaked her left hand under his thigh to find his balls. At the same time she sent her right hand to grope between their bodies for his nipple. She cupped his balls in her hand and, at the same time, pinched his nipple. He moaned. That was it, he plunged in one more time like a man possessed then stopped, completely, stopped with his cock in her to the hilt, his pubic bone crushed against her clitoris, the head of his cock at the neck of her womb, his whole body poised on the edge of a monumental precipice. He felt his cock spasm and, a millisecond later, a rush of relief as it jetted spunk out into her waiting cunt, and his body convulsed with pleasure. It seemed to go on forever, wave after wave of spunk, each producing a shock of sensation. Finally his cock was empty. His body shook involuntarily, like a dog out of water, shaking itself to extract the last drop of spunk. It did this twice, each time a surprise to him, each time provoking little aftershocks, echoes of the orgasm that had gone before.

Slowly their bodies relaxed. His cock shrunk and was

expelled by the pressure of her cunt. It slipped out, wet and flaccid. Only then did he roll off her to lie by her side.

He began to laugh.

'What is it?' she said.

'Didn't even take your bra off,' he said. 'Must really have been in a hurry.'

'It didn't matter.'

'You'll telling me.'

They didn't say anything else for awhile. They lay wrapped in their feelings, Caplin tracing his finger – the tip of a regularly manicured finger – in little circles on the top of Stephanie's arm.

Stephanie reached behind her back and unclipped her bra. She pulled it away from her breasts and rested back on the bed. Her nipples were hard and erect.

Caplin immediately cupped a hand over the firm flesh. 'Hm . . . nice,' he said.

'Tell me something. At the Shades of Hades . . .'

'Yes?'

'You were very turned on, weren't you?'

'I guess so.'

'What by?' Stephanie asked. She thought she knew the answer.

'You want to know the truth?' he said looking into her eyes. Perhaps he was trying to decide whether he could trust her with the truth.

'If you want to tell me.'

'I've always had a . . . what would you call it, a fantasy I suppose,' he hesitated again.

'Go on.'

'I've never told anyone this before.'

'You don't have to tell me. I am just curious.'

'I've always had a fantasy about being, what's the right word . . . dominated. The woman in all that leather gear, the way she was using that guy. I supposed it struck a chord is all.'

'You've never done anything about it?'

'The truth again?'

She nodded.

'I've been to the club a few times. I've been on the point of bidding for the woman, the Amazon. But I've always chickened out. I did go to a prostitute once.' He looked at her earnestly. He wasn't all at sure why he was telling her all this. 'I've never told anyone this either.'

'And?'

He got off the bed and poured himself a glass of champagne. His cock was still wet and the hair around his balls was plastered down with her juices. He offered a drink to Stephanie by signing with the bottle but she refused.

'Why are you so interested?' he asked sitting on the bed again.

'It fascinates me,' she said. It was perfectly true.

'There was an ad in the paper. It just happened to catch my eye – "Miss Strictland. By Appointment Only." – I made an appointment.'

'What happened?' Stephanie said genuinely interested.

'It wasn't very satisfactory.'

'Tell me more.'

'It was sordid. Oh it was a very swanky apartment. And she was very expensive and I suppose she was good at what she did.'

'What did she do?'

'She beat me. Abused me. Made me lick her shoes. Stuff like that.'

'Did you come?'

'Yes. But I hated it. It wasn't what I'd imagined. It wasn't real. She was just doing it for the money. That wasn't my fantasy. I'd always wanted someone who was real.'

'Real?'

'A woman who was really into it, really wanted to dominate men, not just because it paid well.'

'Like me,' Stephanie said quietly.

'I never went back.' He was caught up in his own thoughts. Then he seemed to realise what she had said. 'Like you? What do you mean?'

'What I said,' she hardened the tone of her voice.

'I don't understand.'

'Are you particularly dim? What you said you wanted is a

woman who enjoys being in control, is excited by it?'

'Yes.'

'Who is not pretending?'

'Exactly.'

'Sex is a strange animal, isn't it? Like a chameleon. So many different colours, colours to blend into the surroundings. But they also change colours to match their mood, did you know that?'

'No.'

'Oh yes they do. So many different moods. So many different ways to get pleasure.'

'I suppose so.'

'*My* pleasure.' Her voice was edged with steel now. She felt a frisson of excitement shudder through her body. It was an excitement that she had only experienced since she had met Devlin. But then Devlin had introduced her to so much that was new. 'Put your glass down.'

Caplin looked puzzled. Stephanie stood up. Putting each foot in turn on the edge of the bed she stretched and smoothed the stockings over her legs, fastening them again in the suspenders. She took her time. Caplin's eyes never left her hands. When this task was completed, she stroked the thick thatch of her pubic hair, stroking it like it was an animal needing attention.

'Do as I say,' she barked.

Caplin obeyed immediately this time, though, he did not take his eyes from her body. Stephanie smiled. Caplin was about to have his dreams come true.

'Why aren't you erect? That's not much good to me is it? It's pathetic. You stare at me and can't manage an erection? Turn on your stomach, lie flat. Now.'

He hesitated. She saw his cock beginning to unfurl.

'Do it,' she snapped.

He obeyed burying his head in the pillow. His mind was racing. Her voice was so hard, so full of authority, exactly as he'd always imagined.

In the belt loops of his trousers she found a thin leather belt. She stripped it out of the trousers and wound the buckle end around her hand. Without pause she raised her arm and thwacked the end of the belt across his bare buttocks.

'This is what I like,' she said, delivering a second blow. 'Now do you understand?'

She reigned blows down on to his arse. Five, six. He didn't utter so much as a whimper. The sound of leather on flesh filled the room.

'Oh my God,' he said when she stopped after the eighth blow. 'What are you doing to me?'

'Giving you the beating you deserve. Stand up.'

He obeyed as though his life depended on it. As he got off the bed his penis sprung out from his groin, a totem to his needs. Regardless of the fact that he had only just come it was throbbing with excitement.

'Bend over the bed,' she ordered.

Again he obeyed at once. He'd always dreamt of obeying. He stuck his arse in the air; it was already crisscrossed with red welts and radiating heat.

'Now Caplin, you little worm, you're going to come for me. Exactly when I tell you. I'm going to count to ten. At ten you will come. Understood?'

'Yes.'

'Yes what?' she slashed the belt down for his insolence.

'Yes, mistress.'

'Start then.'

He circled his cock and started to wank. The belt fell again on his buttocks, the stroke vibrating through his body, through all the feeling centred on his cock.

'One,' Stephanie entoned.

He knew he'd never last till ten. His pleasure was too sharp. Stephanie had reached inside him, was manipulating the most sensitive nerve of all, the nerve over which he had absolutely no control – his mind.

'Two.' Another stroke.

His mind was full of fantasy. He'd heard that voice, hard and demanding, for years, heard it in his head, while he'd masturbated. He felt the whip falling, seen a woman standing above him. Now it was all real. He looked back at Stephanie, her long hair flowing, her naked breasts

194

trembling with her effort, her long stocking clad legs, and the slash of her sex wet and exposed. But most of all, as she reached the count of five and his cock exploded in his hand pumping spunk all over his fist and the rumpled sheets of the bed, he knew what had brought him off, knew what he would always remember about that first time. It was the look in Stephanie's dark brown eyes, the look of excitement, of sheer pleasure, sparkling in those knowing eyes.

Stephanie sat on the terrace outside her bedroom wearing a satin dressing gown she had bought at Bergdorf Goodman's. For the hundredth, or was it the thousandth, time she admired the view. Lake Trasimeno was perfectly calm. The sun was altogether lower in the sky now, and its midsummer heat had gone. But it was still a pleasant temperature and Stephanie sipped blood red orange juice and nibbled at a brioche while she waited for the powerboat to arrive.

She didn't have to wait for long. A long white wake soon bisected the calm waters, sending out a delta of ripples for hundreds of yards as the boat headed for the island and the castle.

Stephanie went into the bedroom and changed into a flame red Lycra catsuit. The shiny material clung to every contour of her body, so tight it even delineated the crease of her sex and the precipitous cleft of her arse. It flattened her breasts slightly but their roundness and firmness was still apparent. So were her hardened nipples. She found Ferré high heels in an almost matching red.

By the time she got down to the jetty the powerboat was near enough for her to see the two people seating on the padded seats in the transom, as she had arranged.

As the boat approached she could see that Venetia was smiling. She was always struck by her beauty. She could never suppress a pang of lust whenever she saw that long fair hair, her high cheek bones, green emerald eyes and that long lithe body that had given her so much pleasure in the past. As they had not indulged in London it had been some time since Stephanie had experienced Venetia's exquisite sexually specific expertise.

The boat glided into the rubber tyres suspended alongside the jetty. The boatman tied the lines fore and aft. He had been the boatman at the castle for years; the appearance of the passenger sitting next to Venetia came as no surprise to him. On Stephanie's explicit instructions the man was naked but for the hard leather covered metal pouch chained over his genitals by Venetia aboard the Learjet, and a leather harness strapped across his chest, which, at the back, held his arms bound and immovable.

Over his head a rubber mask had been pulled, one of those depicting various famous faces, politicians or film stars. This mask was, incongruously, a vivid representation of Marilyn Monroe. Under the mask he was gagged.

As soon as the boat was secure Venetia pulled the man to his feet by a chain attached to the leather harness just below his throat. She manoeuvred him on to the jetty.

The man's ice blue eyes saw Stephanie through the mask. It was only a week since he had last seen her.

'Welcome to the castle, Caplin,' Stephanie said. 'I'm sure you won't be disappointed.'

She had described what she was going to subject him to. She had told him in great detail in the suite of the Algonquin hotel. When she had then produced Devlin's contract, his objections to signing it had miraculously disappeared. To make sure there were no mistakes they had called in a room service waiter to witness his signature. He signed both copies. He would have done anything after what he had just experienced, anything to ensure that Stephanie remained part of his life. He had never met a woman like her: the woman of his dreams.

'This way.' Stephanie took the leash from Venetia and lead him up the narrow stone steps. Through the mask he could see the way the shiny red Lycra moulded itself to her buttocks as she walked ahead of him. At the top of her thighs, just under her sex, there was a clear channel where her flesh curved inwards. The Lycra made it seem more obvious, more inviting. Immediately he felt his cock stirring, and a cold shock, as the unyielding metal reminded him there was no room in his bondage for unwarranted pleasure.

They led him into the castle and down into the cellars, through into a tiny cell. If the pouch chained around him had allowed it, he would have been fully erect by the time he was installed in his new accommodation.

'Well, Caplin,' Stephanie said pulling off the rubber mask then smoothing his white hair back into at least a rough order, 'I have some surprises for you. Some you'll like. Some you won't. Some you will no doubt find unpleasant.' She rubbed herself against his body, knowing what the feel of the slippery Lycra would do to him. 'New York is your city. Over here, at the castle, this is my place, my domain.' She took his cheeks in her hand and squeezed, and added, 'Stephanie's domain.'

NEW BOOKS

Coming up from Nexus and Black Lace

Fallen Angels by Kendal Grahame
July 1994   Price: £4.99   ISBN: 0 352 32934 3
A mysterious stranger sets two young ladies the ultimate lascivious challenge: to engage in as many sexual acts with as many people as possible. Rich rewards await them if they succeed – but the task proves to be its own reward!

The Teaching of Faith by Elizabeth Bruce
July 1994   Price: £4.99   ISBN: 0 352 32936 X
Until she met Alex, Faith had never experienced the full range of pleasures that sex can bring. But after her initiation into his exclusive set of libertines, a whole new realm of prurient possibilities is opened up for her.

The Training Grounds by Sarah Veitch
August 1994   Price: £4.99   ISBN: 0 352 32940 8
Charlotte was expecting to spend her time on the island relaxing and enjoying the sun. But now, having been handed over to the Master, she has discovered the island to be a vast correction centre. She'll soon have a healthy glow anyway ...

Memoirs of a Cornish Governess by Yolanda Celbridge
August 1994   Price: £4.99   ISBN: 0 352 32941 6
As Governess to a Lord and Lady, Miss Constance's chief task is to educate their son Freddie. But word soon gets about of her unusual techniques, and before long, most of the village is popping in for some good old-fashioned correction.

The Gift of Shame by Sarah Hope-Walker
July 1994   Price: £4.99   ISBN: 0 352 32935 1
Helen had always thought that her fantasies would remain just
that – wild and deviant whimsies with no place in everyday
life. But Jeffrey soon changes that, helping her overcome her
reservations to enjoy their decadent games to the full.

Summer of Enlightenment by Cheryl Mildenhall
July 1994   Price: £4.99   ISBN: 0 352 32937 8
Karin's love life takes a turn for the better when she is introduced to the charming Nicolai. She is drawn to him in spite of
his womanising – and the fact that he is married to her friend.
As their flirting escalates, further temptations place themselves
in her path.

Juliet Rising by Cleo Cordell
August 1994   Price: £4.99   ISBN: 0 352 32938 6
At Madame Nicol's strict academy for young ladies, 18th-
century values are by turns enforced with severity and
flagrantly scorned. Juliet joins in her lessons enthusiastically;
but whether she has learnt them well enough to resist the
charms of the devious Reynard is another question.

A Bouquet of Black Orchids by Roxanne Carr
August 1994   Price: £4.99   ISBN: 0 352 32939 4
The luxurious Black Orchid Club once more provides the
setting for a modern tale of decadence. Maggie's lustful adven-
tures at the exclusive health spa take an intriguing turn when
a charismatic man makes her a tempting offer.

NEXUS BACKLIST

Where a month is marked on the right, this book will not be
published until that month in 1994. All books are priced £4.99
unless another price is given.

CONTEMPORARY EROTICA

CONTOURS OF DARKNESS	Marco Vassi		
THE DEVIL'S ADVOCATE	Anonymous		
THE DOMINO TATTOO	Cyrian Amberlake	£4.50	
THE DOMINO ENIGMA	Cyrian Amberlake		
THE DOMINO QUEEN	Cyrian Amberlake		
ELAINE	Stephen Ferris		
EMMA'S SECRET WORLD	Hilary James		
EMMA ENSLAVED	Hilary James		
FALLEN ANGELS	Kendal Grahame		
THE FANTASIES OF JOSEPHINE SCOTT	Josephine Scott		
THE GENTLE DEGENERATES	Marco Vassi		
HEART OF DESIRE	Maria del Rey		
HELEN – A MODERN ODALISQUE	Larry Stern		
HIS MISTRESS'S VOICE	G. C. Scott		Nov
THE HOUSE OF MALDONA	Yolanda Celbridge		Dec
THE INSTITUTE	Maria del Rey		
SISTERHOOD OF THE INSTITUTE	Maria del Rey		Sep
JENNIFER'S INSTRUCTION	Cyrian Amberlake		
MELINDA AND THE MASTER	Susanna Hughes		
MELINDA AND ESMERALDA	Susanna Hughes		
MELINDA AND THE COUNTESS	Susanna Hughes		Dec
MIND BLOWER	Marco Vassi		

- -

Please send me the books I have ticked above.

Name   . . . .

Address   . . . .

                   . . . .

                   . . . . Post code   . . . .

Send to: **Cash Sales, Nexus Books, 332 Ladbroke Grove, London W10 5AH**

Please enclose a cheque or postal order, made payable to **Nexus Books**, to the value of the books you have ordered plus postage and packing costs as follows:

UK and BFPO – £1.00 for the first book, 50p for the second book, and 30p for each subsequent book to a maximum of £3.00;

Overseas (including Republic of Ireland) – £2.00 for the first book, £1.00 for the second book, and 50p for each subsequent book.

If you would prefer to pay by VISA or ACCESS/MASTERCARD, please write your card number here:

Please allow up to 28 days for delivery

— — — —   — — — —   — — — —   — — — —

Signature: _____